DEVOTED

SOUL SEER CHRONICLES, BOOK 6

S.J. CAIRNS

Black Thumb
Publishing

Cover design by Getcovers
Logo created by S.J. Cairns
Logo image by CNuisin depositphotos.com ID 265803116
Tree vector by Nikhomtreevector depositphotos.com ID 391682124

ISBN 978-1-7782611-5-2 (Ebook)
ISBN 978-1-7782611-6-9 (Paperback)
ISBN 978-1-7782611-7-6 (Hardcover)

Black Thumb Publishing
Ontario, Canada
www.sjcairns.com

✽ Created with Vellum

ACKNOWLEDGMENTS

Self-publishing has been a learning curve for me. A fun yet intimidating one. Without Vania Rheault's assistance, it likely would not have occurred at all. Thank you for your honest and kindness-wrapped opinions and encouragement as well as your patience with late night questions and manuscript changes. Your presence along my publishing journey is invaluable.

I also can't forget my writing group – The Quillies. You people rock socks.

To my brothers, Jon and Tyler:
Because...Well, because you're my younger brothers and can't tell me
what to do.

1

THE EMBODIMENT OF MISTAKES

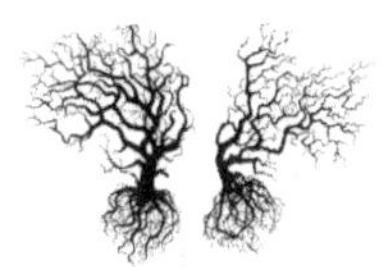

Donovan

The oppression of the cinderblock walls, the cold cement floors numbing my bare feet, and the faint thrum of Sophie's anxiety across the connection all fell away when the door of the cell my father stashed me in opened. No slow creak like a haunted house in a D-class horror movie, yet no complicated mechanisms either. Magically locked.

Tobias filled the opening and took a couple of steps in and to the side with confidence I wouldn't try to attack or bolt past him. His pulled-back dark hair and full beard were tamed as always, manicured so no one questioned how unhinged he was and what lengths he would go to control everyone he crossed, Magics and Blind alike.

"Never grasped the concept of obedience, did we?" The smug smile on Tobias's face had me grinding my teeth. Whether he was listening to my thoughts or not, he proved he hadn't changed a bit.

I didn't answer him. Which was fine by Tobias since he preferred me quiet unless spitting his self-serving rhetoric. Instead, he walked into the small cell, the door closing behind him on its own, yet at his will. Step by step, he took a casual stroll around me as if tiptoeing through the freakin' tulips. I refused to cower under his intimidation tactics. He refrained from sharing his opinions of me. They were tired and meant to break me down, and failing to hit the mark, though I doubted he could keep his mouth shut for long.

The asshole loved to talk.

Tobias concluded his walkabout and stopped in front of me. I met his glare, chin level, displaying the disobedience resulting in my punishment time and time again for simply daring to meet him eye-to-eye. None of his subordinates would dare challenge him with such transparent antagonism, tactics I could manage without the ability to use my power in this cement box. He raised me as the future leader of an entire coven of Tainted Magics, he would have to suffer the result of his life lessons.

Having not considered Tobias my true father or Master since well before puberty, I refused to cower beneath the severity of the bastard's oppression. The air around my father was starved for the release of tension, as if he were aching to put me down like a petulant servant.

Interesting. Something in his stare surveyed me with an overcompensation he lacked when I was a kid. His broad shoulders were relaxed yet held an underlying stiffness or hint of something he tried to hide and lost the fight.

It took me a moment to realize that hint of something was failure.

Tobias failed to shape me into the Magic he bred. Unaccustomed to the concept of disappointment, his over-posturing was his current downfall. Influential people didn't need to flex their muscles. Others saw it, felt it, experienced its step above the rest without the transparent display. For the others in Tobias's flock, they never saw him as anything less than their Master who would teach them the ways of the world and lead them to greatness, as long as they retained an air of servitude and didn't surpass the Master in ability or political standing in the coven. When dealing with me, his flaws were highlighted like a strip club's neon sign in the dead of the night, and I was walking around as the embodiment of every one of his mistakes.

Realizing this made it impossible for me not to crack a smile.

Tobias's already dark features somehow blackened as he glanced down at my dimples before taking in a controlled breath. "Sophie is not mine to contend with. Proximity requires her presence within my Compound for a time. Once her use has expired, she will be at the mercy of others."

I struggled to retain my smile, even knowing whose mercy Sophie would suffer beneath once Tobias was done using her.

My father took a half-step forward to invade my personal space. I held onto my smile and remained, what I hoped passed for, unimpressed.

Tobias's smug grin widened. "The Conception Rituals begin this night."

What? Wait…The Conception Rituals? No. He couldn't.

Was this a ploy to screw with my head? Was his desperation so thick?

Whatever the prick thought of me, whatever his mission was now, how could putting me through all that again accomplish it?

Of course. It wasn't about his mission or his end goal. The sick fuck wanted me damaged beyond any hope of repair. Too damaged to live the way I always wanted outside of his compound and all the plans he drew up before I was a person he could try and control. He couldn't get to me like he used to before my voice dropped. This way, he could level my new life in a way he never could before.

"I see you remember your first sojourn with the Conception Rituals." Tobias showcased renewed arrogance with zero attempts to hide his enthusiasm as he looked on at what was probably my subdued horror. "You will serve your purpose as you were created to do so at birth, Donovan. You may have been living lavishly in the ignorance of the Blind and in a false state of power at the head of the pathetic Sect you acquired and yet need assistance to shepherd. But hear me…" he continued slowly, "son…you *will* take your last shuddered breaths inside my walls, yet *not* until your use has run its course to my utmost satisfaction." With a smirk I ignored every time I looked in the mirror, Tobias straightened his posture, savouring his win, before turning on his heel and disappearing through the heavy metal door.

I didn't even see if he did anything to make it open. I was too dumbfounded to focus.

Heat swept over my back to my shoulders and then from my chest. Instinct sparked a drive to charge for the exit before I was locked in. I don't think I moved, yet everything in me flexed to bolt for freedom. Escaping worked before. I could kill the guard stationed outside the door—I just had to wait for an opportune moment. When food was brought in, maybe? Or when they took me to prepare for the rituals? Cutting it close meant a higher chance of death. Mine and Sophie's. Tobias would likely have more than one guard on me. I could still take them out if I knew exactly where Sophie was. And she would also be heavily guarded.

Fuck! I scraped my hands over my face. How could this be happening? Shit. I need to think. There's a way to escape this intact. Both of us.

I need...What do I need? I need a plan.

It took a few rounds of humiliation and torture of the Conception Rituals before I made my last escape in a long list of attempts. Abandoning Sophie here wasn't an option, and we couldn't use our powers inside of the cells. Our connection was still there, even if only in part. Nothing could truly separate us, but we couldn't communicate through it. Not well enough to coordinate the finer details needed to escape this place alive.

Indecision froze me to my spot. What am I doing? How could I stand here and do nothing? Tobias can't subject me to this again. I can't let him.

Concern sparked in the connection. Enough for me to dig my fingers into the spot.

Sophie. She knew something was wrong. No matter her imagination, she would never guess how sideways things were about to go if my father played out his plans the way he bragged about. No matter how I lived my life, the people I used, the shit I stole, or the lies I told without so much as a guilty flinch, Sophie didn't deserve the brutality of the consequences for being shackled to me.

Would my father warn her of the Conception Rituals as he did me? What if he didn't tell her? She wouldn't understand what was happening. She wouldn't know I would rather die than drag her through the ruthlessness of what was to come.

The only thing on my side, the thing that would equally haul her through the depravity of the ritual, would be that I could use our connection to evoke a sense of disgust. She could read this from me. As confusing as it would be, she would know to question what she sensed. She had to know.

The faces of those from the first round of the archaic ritual my father put me through were still etched into my brain, flipping by like a macabre picture book in a haze when I closed my eyes or tried to sleep. No amount of whisky I drank drowned them for good. It helped me pass the fuck out, but the faces remained, as did other faces of the ones I chose in bar bathroom stalls and endless apartments. Nothing erased them.

Fuck. Oh my god. This can't be happening. It can't be. Not again.

I wanted to tear my skin off.

Fox's tattoo ink concoction was genius, yet how could we know perverse visions sent by my father would activate the newly tatted protection sigil and put us in a more dangerous position instead of safety? And to different locations. Aunt Lacey's home was my safety net in some real dark times. She never shut me out no matter the condition I showed up in when I dragged my ass across her threshold. So, of course the sigil would send me there. Plus, it was now my home.

Wherever Sophie ended up, she wasn't with me at my house. Which would've been confusing, but we would've worked through it and returned to Olive's in one piece. Annoyed, not trapped in my father's fucking cells.

Where was safety to Sophie? After this place, it wouldn't be anywhere near me again, regardless of how my father's plans concluded.

Did Tobias know about Fox's tattoo concoction? Shit. The Apporter did. Smartest assumption is that the asshole told my father everything. Which meant he not only knew everything about the Mother Coven's plans to reopen the Creation, but he also knew anything crucial he witnessed while towing Ranlyn and the Elders all over the world to meet with contacts in secret locations now compromised by the intel leak.

He also knew about Sophie's contacts, too.

Olive and the estate attic, Sophie's parents, her siblings, all of the Ballard flock...every one of them was in danger if Tobias wanted them to be. No way they knew how deep the shit ran. Hell, some of them were Seedlings, Blind, or practically Blind.

If Olson returned to the attic without us and with some half-way believable story about not being able to find us, they would have no reason to be suspicious or know where to start looking for us. The spells safeguarding my father's compound would block the craftiest of location spells. Would it confuse Kim's guiding light gift, too?

Ouch! What the fuck?

I didn't realize I was biting my nails until a rip of skin shot a zing of pain through my hand. Blood welled, shining in the oppressive ceiling light. The taste of iron washed over my molars, a short distraction from the precise trauma awaiting me and Sophie.

What if this is more than we can handle? I've been through imprisonment and torture. Sophie doesn't know what's awaiting her in the aftermath.

My father's bloodline needed fresh DNA to ensure its continued strength and freedom from genetic abnormalities. Ancient excuse to justify engineering Tainted spawn. Now the family who screwed with my head and kept me alive enough to shadow me in responsibility would have a turn at damaging the woman I loved in a way I could never forgive or be forgiven for.

Maybe I should end us right now before the ritual gets that far? Sophie wouldn't want me to hit the reset button, but she didn't know what was coming and I saw the tidal wave gathering strength behind us. I could make our death quick. Relatively painless. We would come back as different people, yet still connected to each other. Chances were Vincent would find us again and fill in some of what we missed. My father might have been killed or died by then. Those in the Creation might be dead, too. Sophie definitely wouldn't like that or leaving her family to fend for themselves against Evaristus. The Elders might move forward with all of their plans, but who knows what the state of Magics would be by the time we came back.

I exhaled a heavy breath, the what ifs and possible outcomes if I made a move one way or the other exhausting me.

I used to think I trashed everything I came into contact with, wrapped them in my inner evil and squeezed every morsel of goodness they possessed through mere contact no matter how shallow or deep it ran. Aunt Lacey and Fox helped me fight those thoughts everyday. They shouldn't have bothered. I was right all along.

2

————

BEHIND THE SCENES

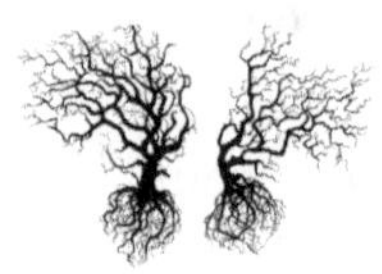

Kim

Vincent kept calling for immediate and aggressive action, Ranlyn kept insisting on patience and waiting for intelligence, and Veata sat back in a vintage upholstered chair in the Ballard attic while I watched them squabble over how best to handle the Sophie and Donovan disappearing act.

The Ballard Coven and my Sect waited around for the bigwigs to figure out their next move. The Apporter was supposed to retrieve them. He was gone or cut off or something—presumed a traitor. Vincent kept checking his phone, pacing, making a show at busying himself all the while he was twitchy as if he were counting down every half-second as his patience grew thinner and thinner.

He said he might know someone across enemy lines who would've heard about their kidnapping. He didn't say who and I knew better than to expect a direct answer and saved my breath.

I didn't know the guy as well as Sophie did. Nonetheless, I figured if he wasn't an Elder with Elder responsibilities and expectations, he would have taken off from here searching for Sophie himself the second we realized they weren't returning on their own. Maybe he knew where she might be and was trying to contact someone on his payroll or in his metaphorical black book who could do the dirty work for them?

Sometimes leadership was shackling.

If that's the case, I sort of got how he felt. Coven meetings weren't as fun while worrying about if I was running them properly. No way I was giving them up. I was a sucker if I ever thought they were easy. Aunt Lacey had a habit of making everything look easy. Though, I guess most things were easy for her.

Vincent was glued to his phone a few more times yet paced far more. I couldn't hear him talking to anyone, even when he passed by. Even with the attic flush with voices, I should still have heard something from him. It took me a few minutes to realize he must have been using some kind of privacy spell. A good move on his part.

Or maybe he was a shady bastard and had something to do with Sophie and Donovan not returning yet. I tried not to think like that, but I couldn't help it. He seemed to care a whole lot about Sophie, but I could never tell with that guy. He held on to his secrets to the point of danger to others more than for himself. And more than once.

I could believe Vincent would axe Donovan from the picture if he could do it without killing Sophie. When it came to her, he would continue to stalk her through lifetimes. Probably secretly in love with her.

I shook my hands and took a step off the conspiracy theory carousel. We needed to get Sophie back.

Vincent stopped pacing, took his phone back out of his pocket, checked the screen for the hundredth time, and then crossed the crowd with purpose, focused on the attic exit hatch. He was quick, moving through the big group without stopping. I caught up to him before he got all the way outside.

I assumed he arrived with the Apporter and the other Elders until I saw his big, white SUV parked in Olive's driveway.

"Find a radder party to hit up, Vincent?"

He didn't stop or answer me as I kept following him across the snow-covered driveway to his vehicle.

"I get you care about her." He spun at me with subdued rage in his green eyes so quickly I yelped. "Damn! Them. I meant them." And then mumbled, "Of course."

He continued on towards his SUV.

I raced to grab the passenger side door handle, finding it locked. He started the vehicle as I spouted off a quick unlocking spell, squealing in success when it popped. If it was locked by Vincent's spell and not a manufacturer's default special, no way I could have bypassed it. He was way too strong for me.

I thanked my lucky stars and jumped into the passenger's seat.

"Nice try, Vincey-boy. Where're we headed?"

Instead of answering, kicking me to the pavement, or using his soul ripping powers on me, Vincent shifted the vehicle into gear and took off on the estate's snowy, treelined driveway.

I tightened my belt as the monster of an SUV bounced over potholes and snowdrifts. Subdued madness was in Vincent's stone features, enough to make me rethink tagging along. Especially when my internal organs vibrated like a shaken martini as we vaulted onto the main drag from the estate's road through the cemetery.

I didn't want to risk getting the boot now that I got this far, so I kept all my questions to myself and clutched my stomach. If I puked, it was his fault, and I didn't feel a tad bad about replacing his new car smell.

Driving long enough for me to lose track of my surroundings, it occurred to me that Sophie and Donovan might be held up in a room together somewhere. Maybe Donovan killed Olson so he couldn't stop them from gettin' busy. Though if they were and put us through all of this because of some bizarre emotional sex loop, I was going to beat Sophie with a hairbrush and fix a testosterone blocking spell on Donovan. A loop strong enough to stick them in a trance and nearly get down and dirty on a beach in front of hundreds of onlookers was one thing. Taking out the one cock-blocking you for your own good was a strict no-no in my books.

The silence in the SUV was killing me. How could Vincent not be bursting with information? He didn't even bother to let the other Elders know he was taking off. If this was bad, wouldn't he be pissed or worried? How could he stay so quiet?

The guy didn't even have the radio on.

The child in me buzzed with repressed hyperactivity, tapping the windowsill, fiddling with my hair far too much, and rubbing the seatbelt between my fingers to the point of a friction burn. I wanted answers. I wanted to be wherever we were going already. Was Sophie and Donovan there? If so, why would he let me stowaway and not tell anyone else?

Shit. Was Vincent hoping I couldn't contain myself and follow him? Did I set myself up to be another hostage alongside Sophie and Donovan?

Vincent grabbed his phone. He moved so fast I thought he heard my thoughts and was going to attack me.

I flinched. Hard.

He hit a button without looking, and said, "No," before hanging up.

No what? Was "no" a good thing or a bad thing? Was it about Sophie and Donovan? About me? Was he telling someone he wasn't alone?

We started to slow down. I stopped myself from sitting forward in my seat to check where we were, peering through my passenger window without moving my head instead. Empty farmland stretched for kilometres next to us and through the snow-speckled windshield. A rundown farmhouse stood dark and dilapidated, prime spot for a horror movie set. Rats definitely took the stage in there.

Blech.

Was this it? Would he bring me this far to kill me? Was Sophie and Donovan in there? The windows were black, no light shining within. If they were inside, they weren't meeting us outside and

Vincent didn't try to conceal us pulling up. Unless there was some kind of boundary spell to hide us when we reached a certain point.

Damn. With Magics it's possible something similar was going down.

"Who are we waking up?" The words spilled from my mouth before I could cap them. Of all the things I could ask, that was what escaped?

"No one."

I was surprised he answered me. Even though his answer didn't tell me anything.

Vincent got out into the now blowing snow, heading for the farmhouse before I could process his tone as informative or threatening.

"Okay, girl," I talked to myself. "You've been through worse. And he could've killed you already. If you're going to do it, do it now. Sophie could be waiting."

A frigid wind blasted me in the face when I opened the SUV's door. I followed Vincent because I didn't know what else to do. I came this far. May as well keep going.

Again, he didn't stop me from going after him, and I was loud enough for him to hear me. Maybe I was stupid for taking the risk, but I wasn't waiting around in the SUV. He wasn't talking much, and I couldn't expect him to fill me in. I wanted details, so it meant getting them firsthand.

Wind whipped snow in our faces from snowbanks deep enough to swallow my Eddie Bauer winter boots and soak me from ankle to calf. I buried my face into my coat collar, the green wool doing nothing to save my eyelashes from freezing. I took off from the attic too quickly to grab my scarf and regretted it.

Instead of heading up the farmhouse stairs to a fire-heated parlour as I prayed to Hecate for, Vincent led me around the side of the broken-down building.

Close up, wood shingles hung on for dear life. The eaves were equally useless, spilling over with icicles, and blacked-out windows weren't covered by drapes as I thought. Gross wood paneling plastered the boxy place. Nothing less than a bulldozer could make it look any better.

Vincent knelt in the snow, using his bare hands to rummage around for something. Before I could mother him about frostbite or decide if he was less of a threat to me without fingers, he lifted a square slab of wood that opened up to a large hole in the ground. A cellar? Falling snow from the top of the door rained down into pitch black, the dank smell hitting me harder and distracting me from thinking of what was down there.

Vincent kept moving the same as he did since we left the estate— without concern for me—not skipping a step as he descended into the darkness or looking back to see if I was following. He was smart enough to know I would, even though an island-sized chunk of me was knocking myself upside the head forcing me to realize the danger I was putting myself in. Reminding myself people outside of other Magics cared about me and wouldn't fully understand what had happened to me or why I disappeared was a task I thought about a lot. No amount of worrying tripped me up when it came down to it.

Now, I understood why Frog said I was inconsiderate of his feelings when it came to the magic side of my life. Look at me right now. When was the last time I called him to let him know I was safe? He has no clue the kind of danger I'm dealing with. Caring about him doesn't stop me from doing anything that might take me away from him on a permanent basis. Maybe he had a point?

I grabbed the wooden hatch from Vincent to stop it from falling as the heavy wood wouldn't remain upright on its own. Slick cement steps disappeared into a place beyond the clouded moonlight's reach, Vincent's loafers slapping against the ground getting farther from me as I closed the door behind me and cut off all source of safety and light.

Did Vincent use a spell to access or reveal the cellar door? I didn't hear anything because of the wind, meaning I could split if things got crazy...theoretically. Who knew what wards someone put on this place? No matter how weak or strong they were, if Vincent didn't want me to leave, he could easily ensure I didn't.

Not everything was beyond my control. I took a moment to think of Vincent before the silvery guiding light of mine showed me he was about fifteen feet in front of me, getting farther and farther away by the second. I tried to use it to look for Sophie, Donovan, and even the Apporter with no luck, so they weren't waiting for us like I hoped.

I knew without seeing that this wasn't a box-like cellar where people would have stored canned goods or seasonal equipment. We were in a thin tunnel, the smell of earthy dankness surrounding us.

Power irritated my skin, my own power, threatening to get wild as I was thinking too fast and panting in icy air to near panic. If this wasn't a scenario devised to kill me—and I was beginning to assume it wasn't since Vincent could have killed me a thousand times by now— then I couldn't screw up whatever this was. If shit did hit the fan, I was unprepared. How could I have left myself unprotected? I always squirreled away a safeguard or two to protect myself with, from herbs to a pocketknife. Now, I didn't even have my purse. I was going to start keeping emergency backups in my bra.

I squeezed my chilled hands into fists, forcing my shoulders away from my ears to find courage to keep following Vincent, my guiding light still showing him getting farther and farther away from me.

A crisp noise made me squeak and flinch so hard I almost peed my D&G jeans.

So much for courage.

Vincent's snap set off an industrial string of lights. They blinked and hummed until they found a way to stay on, running along the walls on either side of an endless tunnel in front of us.

At one point the walls may have been covered in concrete. Now, they were crumbling cement so old it couldn't keep the snow from seeping in anymore. Wood bracing kept the place from collapsing. The ground was frozen dirt and didn't stop us from hearing the thuds of our footsteps.

A dripping sheen of half-frozen algae and mold coated the ceiling and the walls. Calcium build-up settled in furry white spots, reminding me of the hairy back of the Pompeii Worm we put into Donovan's head to connect with Caine in the Creation.

Ugh. Poor Caine.

Nope. None of that right now, girl. Once we figured out this Sophie and Donovan debacle, then we could refocus on rescuing Caine and the survivors from the Creation and pray this didn't drag on so long that the survivors weren't amongst the living anymore once we popped Diluculo open.

A few quick steps caught me up to Vincent in his fancy shoes. I crouched an inch or two away from the gross ceiling and tucked my arms in from the walls, so I didn't stain my Burberry or catch it on a nail in the claustrophobic tunnel. Vincent didn't duck. Even without his relenting confidence, it was clear he was no stranger to this tunnel. Would have been nice for him to share information on any potential dangers, like a flesh-eating disease if I tripped and grazed the fuzzy stuff.

Pounding on the dirt floor somewhere in front of us joined the sound of our footsteps. Big ones. Vincent maintained his pace as the boots-wearer came closer. Must have been a contact of Vincent's. Not comforting considering how old Vincent was. It could be anyone and I couldn't see around him in the cramped space to see who.

Vincent's head jolted with a curt nod as he reached in front of him. He stopped as if to shake someone's hand. I stretched to my tiptoes to see over his shoulder. All I saw was long, dirty-blond hair.

"Hand it over, Lewy." A flinch railed through me at the deep voice belonging to the blond, the accent nothing I could identify, nor did I know what he was talking about. "Who's this?" The question and a scuff on the frozen floor preceded a head peering around Vincent, showcasing ice water blues, and an air of straight-up Viking warrior. I was willing to bet my fell-off-the-truck Birkin Bag he was another immortal.

Vincent moved aside a few inches and glared at me over his shoulder before facing front as if I was inconveniencing him for distracting his contact. Too bad. If he didn't want me ogling Mr. Tall and Hunky, he should have shoved me out of his SUV before leaving the estate.

Not that I wanted Mr. Tall and Hunky to know any of that. I pressed my lips shut in a rare moment of passivity, stopping myself from saying something moronic.

"Kim. Sophie's other Sect Leader and best friend." Vincent's deadpan showcased his blatant annoyance. "And I owe nothing. Do you have—?"

"Oh no, Lewy." The Viking gave me a sly smile and shifted back to Vincent. "Bets I win are repaid in full."

Looking at the Viking's meaty hand now palm-up between the men, an instantaneous visual sprang to mind of the kind of heat those hands could create, without the need to remove the long leather coat hanging from the Viking's shoulders like a rock-ridged waterfall. It was as if he went Neanderthal style, gutted a sheep, flipped it inside out, and shrugged it on. Except this sheep had an off-centre open zipper and exposed seams telling me he bought it off the rack, hoping to appear more backwoods than he was.

A quick fantasy of how the coat could be put to better use tingled in my thighs.

The Viking's ice-blue eyes cut in my direction, his white teeth visible between full lips. "Creative."

"Out of my head, Viking." The heat in his eyes would have brought forth another fantasy of its own if I wasn't too busy dying of humiliation.

He chuckled. "Call me Hall. And I thought you were in mine, no?"

"*Pfft.*" I crossed my arms and prayed my cheeks weren't as bright as my hair.

Perfect. My thoughts were open to him. Time for another dose of mind-shielding herbs and work on guarding them more effectively. And while Hall may be the epitome of any sex god I could envision, and one who may have thrown out a salacious invitation to call my bluff, I reminded myself I wasn't single, and we were here for a reason.

Vincent didn't appreciate Hall's resonate laughter at whatever he now read from me. He redirected, pressing on about their bet while I replaced the shiver the Viking's laugh caused with a tantalizing scenario of Frog.

"The Apporter, Lewy." The Viking rolled his thick shoulders, uncomfortable in the tight space. "How do you think your lovers fell into the hands of the enemy?"

I pushed in closer, knocking Vincent aside a step. "What? Who has them?"

"You are certain it was Olson?" Vincent's voice was so frail it transformed the Viking's arrogance into bleak seriousness.

The Viking nodded. "Told you he was slimier than the snail that pushed him out."

Both men quieted, their expressions shifting in small ways as I looked back and forth between them.

"Are you two seriously chatting telepathically right now? I have a right to know what's going on."

Vincent stood in an unfocused stare looking as if he was playing through some personal Hell at whatever Hall told him.

Hall side-eyed Vincent before looking my way. "Recondite Magics are necessary on both sides. My turf was the oleaginous Father of the Sanctified—"

"Not in the cells? You are certain?" Vincent interrupted, receiving a nod in verification.

"Where's your turf?" I looked from one to the other again as they continued without saying anything useful to me, as if speaking in code. "What cells?" I wanted to scream as the Viking shook his head at Vincent. Neither answered me. "Spell it out or a boot-to-dick therapy session is about to start." No doubt Mr. Viking hid a concealed target I couldn't miss.

Hall chuckled. "Not to mention as thick as a tree truck and could beat you down before your boot left the floor, kitten."

"Har har. The placenta hasn't dried behind my ears, but my friends are missing. You know where they are, which is damn shady, and you're talkin' about oily fathers? How about some terminology I can follow without Googling it?"

Vincent was deep in thought again, remaining in a trance-like stare until Hall answered me for him. "Your friends are prisoners in Tobias Sorrel's compound."

"Tobias Sorrel? Donovan's father?" This I understood, making the cells Vincent mentioned something to do with the Sovereignty. Tobias was the lesser of two evils, I think, though I was clueless what either place meant for Sophie and Donovan. Cells sounded like they were in prison.

"Prison, yes." Hall answered my inner thoughts. "Tobias runs the joint like a father supporting his household. An oddity and a ploy as he is a king presiding over his kingdom. Most cannot tell selective breeding and heinous practices of torment created his family when his members are unwilling to fulfill their familial duties. The Blind see a private commune and nothing more."

"Are they together?" Whatever Sophie and Donovan faced, together was better. Or maybe I didn't want to think of Sophie alone.

Hall shook his head. "Separated upon arrival. Your lovers are in long-term holding. Comparably comfy cells with basic amenities magically bound to prevent escape. Donovan is a habitual flight risk, but not without his bride, so she's closely observed."

His bride? Odd way of describing Sophie considering they weren't married. Well, not in this lifetime. Sophie may keep secrets, but that wasn't one of them. However, Tobias was right, Donovan possessed the survival instincts of a cockroach; a committed one who would never abandon Sophie.

Vincent nodded, working out something he wasn't verbalizing.

I squared my shoulders at the Viking. "Vincent trusts you. Why should I? How do you know any of this?"

He tongued his back teeth and popped his eyebrows as if surprised at my audacity. "As explained, little Seedling, Recondite

Magics are necessary. I happen to be one." He squinted at Vincent and then focused on me when it was clear I was clueless about what a Recondite Magic was. "Think undercover mercenary working in dark realms to educate the good guys about the goings on behind the scenes. Olson has the same job, yet for the other side."

Of course the Apporter was a mole. Did everyone know? "So, you've been, what? Hired to infiltrate the Sorrel Compound?"

"Yes."

A straight answer. Though he did lie for a living, so what did I know? I was a member of the Mother Coven for years and never heard of the Sovereignty or Recondite Magics, nor understood the need for them until now. So much of this world was still a mystery to me. Aunt Lacey must have thought I couldn't handle knowing the gruesome bits. Why did she shelter all of us from what was happening in the Magic world outside of the Sect?

Hall turned to Vincent. "Olson's desperate, or confident, since he ended his assignment after the decades of undercover detail he put in with the Mother Coven. I'd put another grand down staking the time-frame to save your lovers is limited."

I couldn't help but scoff at Vincent. "For reals? You bet a grand on Olson having a clean soul? You don't have to see the creepy fuck's soul glow to know what he's about. Even Sophie said he was Tainted worse than Joelly who nuzzled up to Loring like a loyal purse dog."

Hall gave a smug, low-chested laugh.

"Without the talents of a Soul Seer to confirm otherwise, no reasonable doubt existed." Vincent ignored Hall's continued laughing. "Any rumblings on this timeline?"

"Many. Too many. One thing you can count on is Tobias holding off until he gets what he wants from your lovers, certain to afford you a morsel of time since the man loves his rituals. However, they've got the discus. It'll burn a hole in Tobias' pocket before too long. Others have already lobbied for him to reopen the Creation to free those inside. That kind of leverage affords him extra time and negotiating prowess."

"Have you actually seen the discus?" We held the only thing that could reopen the Creation until Hinapouri and Miklos stole it. The ex-Elders weren't Tainted, so it didn't make sense why they would steal it and give it to Tobias. Sure, the prophecy said reopening the Creation would divide the Mother Coven and cause a civil war. Unrest brewed before they stole the discus. All stealing it did was alienate them from their people. Why join the enemy when they could have destroyed or hid the discus instead?

Hall gave me that look of surprise at my question. "No."

"Interesting." I settled on my boot heel. "Especially since Tobias told Sophie and Donovan he didn't have it. He seems more of a gloater than a liar."

Hall shrugged his large shoulders. "His word is only biblical to his flock."

"Or he's bluffing."

"Doesn't matter. Tobias isn't keeping the girl long."

"Sophie." Vincent corrected before I could. "Why separate them?"

"Rumour has it someone else covets her more."

"Chase?"

Hall tilted his head at Vincent as if this was the obvious answer.

It took me a moment to remember Vincent's brother, and current head of the Sovereignty, went by Chase.

Vincent once told Sophie she was being used against him as a pawn because they knew each other over so many lifetimes. Something to do with Vincent's wife who he says was killed because he refused to join the family business. My knowledge of the Sovereignty couldn't fill a vial of liquid eyeliner, but Sophie being with them was worse than with Tobias. Sophie and Donovan couldn't defend themselves if stuck in that detached zombie mode state when a long distance separated them. Maybe that would work in their favour—numb and clueless? Though, the way Sophie described the obsessive thoughts of being without each other, probably not. The Sovereignty or the Sorrels obviously knew about it, or they would have imprisoned her away from him to take advantage.

"I'll contact you with developments." Hall stuffed his meaty hands into his jacket pockets as he drifted a step backward. "I have Conception Rituals to witness."

"Is Donovan the donor?" Vincent's tone was damn near strangled.

Hall's big shoulders lifted and paused before falling. "Whoever else, my old friend?"

I swallowed hard. Whatever the Conception Rituals were, it wasn't good. Judging by the name, I had an idea of the end goal. Since Vincent asked if Donovan was the donor and not Sophie, did it mean she wasn't involved?

"As always, I'll do what I can, Lewy." Hall drifted a few more steps back before smirking. "And next we meet I will be a grand richer."

Hall winked my way before turning his back to us. "*Nice to meet you, kitten.*"

I didn't answer his telepathic farewell, though I forced myself to ignore the gravel in his voice and focused on Vincent who pushed passed me in a rush on his way back down the tunnel where we entered.

Once up through the trap door, exposed to the blizzard, and inside the SUV, I closed my door to the near white-out conditions outside.

A shiver railed through my whole body and shook my voice. "Please tell me the Conception Rituals aren't what they sound like?"

Vincent met my stare for the first time since we left the attic and refrained from answering. He couldn't tell me what I wanted to hear.

3

CONSENT NEED NOT APPLY

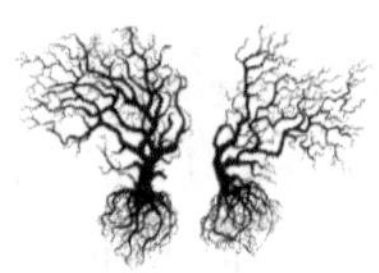

Donovan

Throbbing behind my eyes gave me the spins and my eyelids weren't even open. Did Sophie have a migraine? How can a Magic with healing abilities suffer so many headaches?

I blinked. Bright, hazy light above seared into my brain. My eyes watered. I went to swipe a tear from my cheek and my shoulder ached and wouldn't move.

Ugh. Goddammit! Was my arm asleep?

I tried to reach for it with my other hand and couldn't move it either. I blinked a couple of more times and shifted to look up, but still couldn't see through the blurry fog. The feeling of thick leather straps squeezed my wrists, trapping them high above my head, providing not even an inch of give as I twisted my arms and body on top of what felt like a wooden platform.

No. No, no, no, no. Please, no.

Terrifying clarity was a sucker punch to the liver. No way my father would give me up to anyone else, which meant I was still in the compound, however, not in a cell. When did they remove me from it?

They must have knocked me out with a spell. I don't remember smelling gas or tasting anything suspicious in the food or water.

The haze of sightless panic continued for far too long. Did the piece of shit blind me, too? I tried calling for my father and choked on my words. I couldn't speak let alone scream. Not that anyone cared if I was still inside the compound. My doting father made me blind and mute. Probably thought it weakened me.

If you can read my mind, come at me, asshole!

My vision cleared as if in answer to my challenge. As did my hearing I hadn't noticed was shut down as much as the rest of my senses.

A horde of people were around me. Witnesses. Gathered at all sides, clamoring bystanders filled every corner of the large theater-like room. Rows of them stared at me and whispered to each other, registering that I was able to see them now. Being strapped down in front of my father's flock was one thing. Knowing without looking down that I was buck naked was another.

The Conception Rituals had begun.

I wrenched on my hands and feet and spun in place to see my restraints better. Leather for sure, etched with symbols meant to keep me in place.

I wasn't going anywhere.

A suffocating heat blanketed my body and broke out of my pores, baking me against the platform under my ass; magic or panic driven I couldn't tell. The wood beneath me was wide enough for the offerings given to Priapus or whatever other god Tobias tapped to bless the ritual. A burning in my nostrils and scratching the back of my throat was from some spicy incense and something sweet as honey.

An oily, herbal mixture covered me from head to toe, leaving dark spots and sprigs of whatever they slathered me in. Someone stripped me and rubbed their hands all over me when I was unconscious. Not even a face to add to my future night terrors of who did it.

Shuffling from the witnesses grew as other Magics placed things around the room. I didn't look at what. I couldn't concentrate enough to see anything but people staring at me. Smug, cold, intrigued, judgemental faces. Fear from a kid no older than five, yet no one else paid attention to him. No Magic was too young to start desensitizing them to the art of public humiliation under bright, overhead lighting. I was an obscene museum display. Nothing more than an anatomically correct sex educational awareness doll where consent need not apply.

Jesus fuck, why put me through this again? Tobias milked me like a breeding bull years ago. What? Did he not secure any next generation bastards from me?

I gagged at the thought of children of mine watching in the crowd, living Tobias's repulsive plan to force an heir and watching a version of how they were conceived. Vomit rushed up my throat and burned in my nostrils as my stomach muscles screamed from involuntary spasms. I let the half-digested mushroom soup and baloney sandwiches I ate from my last meal splash all over their carefully chosen flowers, crystals, and other ritual bullshit they tucked around me to pretty up my rape scene and delude themselves into justifying it's for the betterment of the flock.

Where the fuck were the Elders? Or Vincent's fancy Tactical Team? I've sacrificed enough to expect the Mother Coven to swoop in and save my ass when it could do worse damage than at a potential execution. Memories die in death. This bullshit would be remembered every time I didn't want to remember anything at all. Spoiling everything I thought I finally built in my life. Especially with Sophie.

She was there along our connection, trying to calm me while amped and worried herself. I couldn't be comforted. She didn't know what was coming or how much she would wish she didn't bother trying to help me, remotely from her cell or otherwise.

My insides squirmed with the memories of the first round of Conception Rituals when I barely had pubes to impress the crowd. Thinking I was impervious to the damage this mind-fuck would cause this time around would have been a bravado beyond my greatest acting skills, even if just to soothe Sophie.

I couldn't even stop the trembling.

My father's booming voice rose above the crowd, quieting them. I strained to look around to find him, seeing him near my feet, dressed in a dark, heavy robe. He could have been reciting an Ozzy song, it didn't matter, his words were lost to me when I saw the line of women and girls file in behind him in white robes as if any of them were virginal. Maybe a few were.

Bile shot up through my teeth again and added to my mess, causing a few of the onlookers to gasp and turn away in disgust. Regurgitated prison food grossed them out, but not their coveted rape ritual?

How could I have ever been one of them? It didn't matter I was the child of their Master, was supposed to be their future Master, my seed was all the flock needed. The rest of me was expendable, my sanity never considered.

I coughed and wheezed, screaming internal apologies to Sophie for being unable to keep my shit together, hoping she could hear me, knowing Tobias would never allow it. If she was still in her cell, her powers were still as shut down as mine were.

The thought of her alone, undergoing what was about to happen, even if only through my emotions, sawed my heart in two.

I closed my eyes, envisioning her face. Not in our past lives where love spilled from her, but now, with her dark eyes full of guarded baggage and skepticism, except in pockets of honesty where she let me in. Those times were more precious than anything else she could have trusted me with.

I jumped when something brushed my thigh. A hand. My first ritual partner.

Squeezing my lids tight like a kid afraid of a closet monster, I refused to have the face of the body climbing on top of me burned into my memory. I carried a herd of nameless faces from the last round of Conception Rituals and spent the better part of the next decade trying to replace them with other nameless faces in back alleys and bar bathrooms. Ones I chose, but each and every one as unimportant. This time, I wouldn't survive with an updated catalogue to add to the originals.

Foreign hands braced weight on my thighs, saddling up on me higher. The tips of the female's nails dug in as she shifted before grabbing my limp dick. I wanted to scurry away, buck her off, dump her into the pile of vomit at my side, anything. I couldn't. I was frozen, freaking out too much in my fear and helplessness.

I buried my face into the side of my arm—the only thing I could do, yet it hid me from absolutely nothing. If only I could curl up and disappear.

Don't feel. I can't feel anything. Don't feel anything. Please! Turn it off!

Detachment, an inch of room, a tiny fucking fraction of space from feeling every finger wrapped around me might have...I couldn't control the shiver of disgust that rocked my whole body.

Fuck, it's all over me!

Panic kept me connected to the horror. Repulsion left me a useless lump of meat, and wait...I wasn't getting visions. How? Tobias. My asshole father ensured I couldn't escape what was right in front of me by hiding away in a psychometric memory, not this time. Anything I did funnel through the coven breeding line would have been of the nameless body overtaking mine, but it would still be better than the stadium of reality surrounding me.

How did he do it? Fox figured it out. Did Tobias get a hold of the concoction? Could the prick Apporter have stolen it?

Restored effort from the female on top of me created a bodily reaction I recoiled from, dropping me in a familiar pool of shame. No matter how much I told myself the brain didn't need to enjoy the ride for the body to, half-mast was still twice as much as I wanted to contribute and one hundred percent enough to make me feel like a wretched piece of shit.

Awkward shuffling from the crowd in anticipation of what may happen next since their donor was not as compliant as they were used to or at least promised. As a man, I should be grateful to fuck every viable vagina in the flock, right? I never understood the mentality.

Still refusing to focus my eyes on the owner of the first empty womb as I focused on my revulsion to keep myself as flaccid as possible, the sounds of a rising chanting began filling the room, meant to rally my libido, and one I still heard in my dreams on particularly nasty nights.

A bright flash hit me causing me to gasp.

I blinked. Was that a vision? Too quick to catch. Was it my power? No way Tobias would let me have a condom tip of power I could potentially use against him or spoil his plans.

Sensations within me awoke in a rush. Silky skin was smooth beneath my fingers. The blush of rosy cheeks encouraging. Warm breath washed over my neck. Long, dark hair brushed my chest. A languid, lusty smile.

That smile.

I dove in to crush my lips to Sophie's, every moment of attention gifted was more than I could justify stealing, yet failing to find a way to deny myself of what she offered and resulted in a heavy exhale and involuntary shutter.

The perfection above me wavered, blinked from existence, returned, and then was lost again to an unknown face looking down at me. One with thinner lips and sharper jaw than Sophie.

Wait...No. A vision? Tobias forced a vision on me of Sophie to impose my cooperation.

I scrambled to escape, to get out of her, twisting in my restraints, without creating an inch of distance from the first of my father's flock to do their coven duty now taking advantage of the ploy's success. If anything, my wriggling around was helping her cause instead of hindering it.

A cringe of pleasure shot through me. Sophie threw her head back in familiar bliss as she rode on top of me. I writhed as I twitched and pulsed inside of her, grabbing onto her hips to drive in deeper.

Sophie disappeared, replaced with the mousey-haired stranger. Fuck. Another vision.

Tobias had a well of memories of me with Sophie to siphon from to ensure he got what he wanted from me. From this life and any others I caught a glimpse of. He didn't have anything to work with the last Conception Rituals—I was a virgin. Now, Tobias could pick and choose as he pleased. He held all the control, all of the power, and all of me to ruin. He was winning.

I tried to look away, the pulses running through me against my will, forcing my eyes to roll. Tobias stood watching by the row of women awaiting their turn. The smirk on his face familiar and rage-inducing.

"Donovan," Sophie spoke in a desperate whisper, my name on her lips pulling me back to her.

No! It's not her!

I ground my molars together and fought against Tobias's visions as they overtook my senses, chiseling away at my efforts.

Sophie's moans egged me on, she needed me to keep up the pace.

She disappeared. Her face became someone else's.

Disappointment and revulsion crashed through me as I realized I was still in the compound and what I was doing and not doing to whom.

Betrayal piggy-backed my freak out. No, not my betrayal... Sophie's.

Did she know what was happening? Was she somewhere in the compound feeling everything I felt? Something told me she was. How? Tobias cut me off from her while in the cells. Can we feel everything the other does because I'm no longer in my cell? Did Tobias rig this up to ensure she felt everything but couldn't do anything about it?

If I ever wished I could break the connection, now was the time. She wouldn't know how powerless I was to stop this. How much I—

"Donovan." The ache in Sophie's voice was bursting with

urgency, a plea not to stop what I was doing for her as she grabbed my shoulder and ground her hips on me. She was close and so was I.

The grip of her nails in the flesh of my ribs pushed me over the edge, no complaints from either of us as I was overwhelmed, near collapse, and trying to keep a handle on riding it out for as long as I could manage. The cries of her orgasm above the grunts in my throat told me she wasn't short-changed.

Overcome with the need to hold her, I reached up to pull her close and couldn't move my arms. I went to look up at what stopped me. The brightness of the room blinded me. I blinked. Sophie didn't look right. Her hair hid her face, hair that wasn't the right colour. She reached for someone who held open a hand for her to grab. Before I could see who, Sophie tucked her hair behind her ear and climbed off me.

Fuck. Not Sophie.

Confusion broke down, replaced with disbelief as how the vision could be so strong to make me lose all sense of the present.

I struggled against my restraints until I thought my wrists would break. Wetness spilled over my thigh.

No, don't look.

Wherever Sophie really was, it felt like she was squatting inside me, her shock overwhelming her. I couldn't wrap her up in comforting apologies, couldn't explain or plead for forgiveness for the horrors my family has inflicted on her. She didn't deserve this.

I gagged with nothing left in my gut. The crowd glowered at me as if I was the monster. Sophie would, too, and they would all be right.

4

SECRET PLAYTHINGS

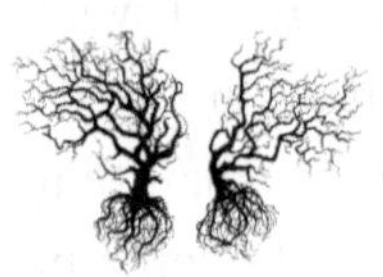

Kim

Standing inside the Ballard attic before my Sect and the Ballard Coven, as well as the Mother Coven Elders, Vincent relayed what we learned of the Apporter's position as a Recondite Magic for the Tainted and Sophie and Donovan's imprisonment by Donovan's father, including how the Sovereignty played into the plot to get their hands on Sophie once Tobias was done with them.

The Coveners were restless and wanted to know what the rescue plan involved and if this was yet another battle to look forward to or fear.

Too bad no one was on the same page on how to free Sophie and Donovan.

Most were pissed Vincent and I didn't tell them we were leaving to meet someone or where we were going in case we too never came back. And even more angry when Vincent refused to tell them the name of his contact inside the Sorrel Compound. He didn't apologize and I maintained I was an uninvited tagalong and nothing more.

Why? I wasn't fully sure and hated to think that if Olson could be a treasonous asshole after gaining the Elders' trust after so many years, then literally anyone could.

How did Aunt Lacey not know? Or did she know and choose not to confront him because she could use him as much as he used them?

Questions like that are going to keep me up at night.

Plus, the Viking was undercover still. Ratting him out wouldn't help bring Sophie and Donovan back. If for some reason it would, damn right I'd be singing his name at the top of my lungs.

Without confirmation Tobias actually possessed the discus, we were still stuck waiting to break into the Creation without control over the timeline, except for whenever Tobias was done with his sex ritual, which had to be finished soon. I mean, how long could Donovan last? He may be a stud, but he didn't have super sperm.

Thankfully, Vincent kept quiet about his backup plan for when he planned to breakdown the Sovereignty's current jailing system. The Apporter knew it was in another Creation like Diluculo, a pocket within the veil, however, not where or how it was accessed. Call Vincent paranoid, but his shadiness worked to his advantage this time. He knew Hall didn't trust Olson, maybe he trusted Hall just enough for it to make a difference.

The grossness of Donovan's father's version of a puppy mill was deleted from the official update. For most, it was rumor fuel and nothing else. Knowing Sophie as I did, she would hate people knowing and would rather the chance to tell them herself, if at all. Donovan may or may not since he didn't care what people thought about him, but it was still his tea to spill.

When we finished with promises of continued updates as they were discovered, Vincent and I motioned for Fox—who returned once hearing of Donovan's kidnapping—Olive, Ranlyn, and Veata to step in close for a side conversation. The others may not have needed to know, but this bunch was let in on the Conception Rituals.

"He'll survive it." Fox piped up after some quiet awkwardness with drawling reassurance as his fingers stroked his beard. "He has before."

This was news to everyone present judging by their expressions, including mine.

"But Donovan hasn't been in his father's coven since he was, what? A teen?" I probably should have remembered this.

Fox exhaled and shook his head. "Younger than you're thinking. Though he escaped a few different times and was dragged back."

"So, you're telling us that those sick fucks force teens or whatever to have sex with someone and people sit around and let it happen?"

"Not one person." Veata jumped in. "The Conception Rituals are not a one-on-one wrestling match with a one hundred percent expected audience rating. All those with birthing ability, be them thirteen, thirty, or sixty participate with adoration for their Master for being given the opportunity to carry and spit out the next king of their damaged flock. And no other coven dare step in unless they expect all other covens to trample on the rituals they deem inappropriate. And given the differences in morality and general regard for the human condition, the fighting would never cease."

I don't think I had ever heard Veata speak so many words at once.

Ranlyn was thumbing his bottom lip in thought. "Surely Tobias procured an heir during the first rituals."

Fox laughed in a short burst. "You'd think. Maybe he did. Maybe he created twenty and is disappointed in each one. And maybe this is just a way to fuck over the only son he can't control. Tobias is not the kind of man who likes to be told no, and Donovan has been screaming it at the top of his lungs since he learned he could."

I couldn't stop myself from asking. "What about Sophie? Would she be made to participate? 'Cuz no way in hell would she want to get knocked-up during some fucked up evil sex ritual. Plus, it would mean Tobias would be stealing the baby and Sophie sure as hell wouldn't let that happen."

"Oh, dear." Olive rubbed her forehead as if she was light-headed. "Maybe they'll want to breed a Soul Seer. If so, they'll keep Sophie alive longer to carry the child. Maybe even until the child displays the gift or not before trying again." This was a bonus in Olive's eyes.

I agreed with her horrific silver lining.

No one knew the answer or if Sophie wasn't a part of the ritual what it would mean for her connection with Donovan. Though, if she felt Donovan at all, then she felt what he was doing.

"My brother will remove Sophie from the Sorrel cells as soon as he can." Vincent fixed his glasses. "Which my contact believes is rather soon. Acquiring a prisoner with-child would not suit Chase's needs, nor be worth retaining his association with Tobias. If Tobias's plans involve Sophie in a direct matter as with Donovan, he would not inform Chase."

Fox cleared his throat. "Pregnant or used, it means we have time for a rescue mission instead of body retrieval."

Vincent nodded. "I have the right people for the job, including my inside contact to bolster our odds of losing few and gaining Sophie and Donovan as intact as possible."

"Who?" Ranlyn insisted on knowing.

Vincent hesitated. "I—"

"Am about to lose a fight, Vincent." Veata shifted and huffed. "You've kept your playthings a secret long enough."

Ranlyn glared at Veata without saying anything. I stopped myself from laughing. Of course Veata already knew what Vincent was about to say.

Vincent apparently agreed it was time. "The Tactical Team tracking the demon Gualichu is mine. Not simply a Sect headed by me, but an elite grouping handpicked for their abilities and employed for certain sensitive objectives. A project brought together in a time of one of the first failed attempts against my family and evolved into a guard of sorts for when the occasion called for Magics requiring protection or extraction. Flexible, dependent on client needs."

"You mean Anne-Marie and Lincoln? Those people? Don't we already know about them?" I met them at Ranlyn's and knew they were pivotal in closing the Creations.

"Among others, yes. They are known, yet the full scope of their employment was not."

Okay. A bit confusing. I shouldn't have been surprised Vincent was keeping details from his co-Elders.

"For hire?" Ranlyn's question was not what I expected.

Vincent tilted his head. "Differs from client to client and calculated by objective, scale of operation, risk assessment, exposure ratio... Variables are numerous."

Olive closed her sweater tighter around her. "I would hope they wouldn't expect a dime to retrieve Sophie and Donovan. If they did, of course it would be paid."

Vincent shook his head. "Their only requirement is my instruction."

Olive gave a quick nod as if she would have been insulted to hear anything different.

"What of the bottom dwellers?" Veata leaned into her cane, looking up at Vincent with her unseeing eyes.

The rest seemed to know who the hell she was talking about, except Olive. At least I wasn't the only one.

"What of them?" Vincent's tone was clipped.

Veata's wandering eyes narrowed. "Will they have a hand in this snake pit or are they sticking to their burrows like the bald poltroons their ancestors bred them to be?"

Vincent turned to his co-Elder. "Judgement from the likes of you is most hypocritical, is it not?"

When the comment hit, Veata grimaced at the low blow. "Some conceal their blunders in the infinite expanse of time, others within the fabric of the weakest minds." There was no guessing at which the Elder labelled herself and which was meant for Vincent. "Never before have you shied from the servitude of those you sought to exploit. Now when the moment arises, your defects shine brighter than your triumphs. You will lead those Seedlings you have stalked through time to death quicker than the hand of evil itself." Veata pivoted on her heel and walked off, done with the conversation I was totally lost in.

"Okay." I broke the tension of Veata leaving. "Whoever is involved in this crime-solving band of ninjas you've got up your sleeve, how fast can they pull their super suits on?"

Vincent looked down at me as if only because he felt obligated. "I will inform you when possible."

Not much of an answer. He walked away with his phone already coming up to his ear. I heard the name Rodney before he was either too far or, again, a spell covering his every word, leaving me in wonder of who the hell Rodney was.

5

REFUSED TO FALL

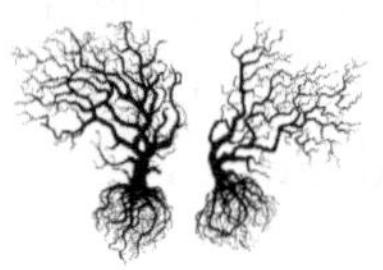

Caine

Time inside the Creation was slow torture. Seconds were tracked with precision. Other times they passed in a whirl of hours I couldn't count on my fingers and toes if I tried. Fear for what hid around the corner was a constant. As soon as we settled into a spot and set up camp, we were running for our lives until time jolted to a halt and we were setting up camp somewhere else, usually with fewer people.

Always with fewer people.

It didn't help Ness was hot and cold with me. Considering all the shit we were in it should have been furthest from my mind, but I couldn't help it. A distraction from the hell we faced every day was still a distraction and one I would welcome over abandoning, burying, or burning more bodies.

Instead of sleeping as I should have been after a day and half of no sleep, thoughts of Ness fluttered through my head. Her stubborn strength was part of her appeal. Not many women carried the strength she did. Blood-born power and innate instincts combined to survive and keep her brother breathing another day. If Felix wasn't here, would she fight so hard to live? Would I if Jet wasn't in here somewhere in enemy hands? I wasn't sure of either answer.

Giving up would be easier. Much easier. I am so tired of nothing changing for the good. Always something new and never a positive.

Picturing Ness as a Puppet or in a pile of the rotting dead helped focus me when rescuing Jet seemed hopeless.

Too preoccupied to sleep, and not wanting to picture Ness or anyone else dead in my dreams, I gave up and checked in with those on watch. Familiar snores came from Felix's tent. He was supposed to have switched with Ness hours ago, it being his turn to keep the illusion up around the camp, protecting us. She must have felt bad for the kid and was giving him extra rest. Sweet and sisterly, though it meant she wouldn't be rested enough tomorrow when it came to her shift again, and exhaustion equalled slow reflexes and greater odds of death for everyone.

I called Felix's name instead of shaking him, careful not to scare the shit out of the kid in the full dark. His eyes popped open, bloodshot, and confused until I explained how long he had been asleep. He apologized and grumbled something about Ness as we made our way to the watch spot set up for the Illusionists, stopping a few moments so Felix could piss against a tree.

Ness cocked her head to the side, her arms crossed when we approached her. "You're supposed to be sleeping."

"So are you." I nodded at Felix to get to work, and he took up his sister's post.

Ness stopped Felix before he could rouse his power. "You tire faster than I do. I'm not going to sleep anyway."

"I got this." Felix straightened, his power coming alive to meet his sister's without surpassing it, replicating the exact same image of the forest trees all around us to confuse any devotees passing by.

Without a job to do, Ness was left with no choice but to let it go. She spun on her Converse heel and stomped back towards camp.

"Wanna slow your roll?" When things were quiet, I walked the forest. She thought I was crazy, but it got me acquainted with where we were and gave me time to get my head together when I was pretty sure I was losing my mind.

She stopped and turned, her annoyance bleeding away in a heavy exhale through full lips. "I'm gonna try and sleep. So should you. You sleep less than anyone." Sometimes she was awkward and standoffish. Guess today was one of those days.

"I'm not alone."

It was enough to trip her up as it didn't quite fit with the conversation. I don't even know why I blurted it at all. I could have a million times since we've been in here, now seemed as good a time as any.

Instead of asking what I meant, she settled into resting her hands on her round hips, waiting for me to spell it out, she curious, yet braced as if ready to be annoyed if whatever I said didn't meet her expectations.

"In my head. I'm not alone." I stepped towards her, seeing her tense in case I got inside her personal bubble, a large one to keep most people away.

To break the tension, I started to retrace the path Felix and I took. She kept pace, looking around like the trees might come alive or as if she hoped they might in order to save her from the conversation. A prickle of power meant she cloaked us, guarding my privacy or doing her job, I wasn't sure.

Gareth was in the wings of my brain, his presence watchful as always, surprising me by shutting up and not taking over while I explained to Ness how I wasn't only a vessel to Gareth's power, the son of my now-deceased Coven Leader, Aunt Lacey, but how Gareth's spirit was within me as well and how he sometimes ran the show.

A few beats of silence passed as light filtered through the tree-tops, showcasing small hints of her expressions. "Kind of obvious."

"Obvious I'm a vessel for a suicidal ancient Magic related to my dead Coven Leader?" Gareth and his wife, Nya, may have ended their lives many years ago, but now he was all about living and reconnecting with the present, mostly in search of his wife.

She rolled her eyes—I heard her tone without her having to say a word—and shifted her dark-brown hair behind her ears, still uncomfortable with the growing length. Her almond-shaped eyes scanned everything and everywhere but at me. "Obvious that you're not normal. Some of us are Blind. Not morons. They all thought you were, like, schizophrenic or something. I didn't tell them about your second set of powers."

"Okay." We continued walking. "Why not tell the others?"

She shrugged. "'Cuz who cares what they think as long as those powers keep saving their useless asses?"

Harsh, though she was right. Their opinions didn't change anything. Neither did hers, but I cared about it more than theirs.

"Would you have pushed yourself to bring Gareth and his powers out if I hadn't encouraged you to?"

I stopped. "This isn't your fault."

She turned to me, arms still crossed.

Her expression was tense enough to make me back off. "Ness, I wouldn't change this."

"Mhmm."

"Look, I'd be dead without Gareth. As weird as it is having another person take up space in my body, I needed to do this."

"Sure. Gareth saved my life. He's badass. On point with an escape plan or hail Mary when we need it. But where does that leave you?"

I didn't have a good answer and the time for me to find one passed. She raised her once perfect brows, certain she made her point.

Ness walked on. "Sophie'll barely recognise you."

She said the name like a sucker-punch, and it landed so hard I was thankful she was in front of me, unable to see my face.

"I'm sorry I didn't tell you about her."

"Why?" Ness didn't stop. "You told me plenty about her."

I caught up to her with a couple of big steps. "Not the important stuff."

"Look. Who you're fucking or not fucking isn't any of my business. Let's—"

"It's not like that."

Ness's humourless laugh was unsettling. "That's what you said to that Donovan guy about me."

When Donovan's spirit or essence crossed the veil into the Creation to talk with us, I didn't trust it was him right away. Once he started talking, he was who he always was and didn't pretend to be anyone else. Even if he knew I preferred he not mention Sophie, he would have. Especially knowing she was watching through the magic of remote viewing and seeing everything he did.

"As if you would've wanted me to say differently?" I knew she didn't.

Ness didn't respond, though her lips pursed in the moonlight enough to know she knew I was right, but that I was missing the point.

"Seriously, Ness. What Sophie and I had was intense. With Donovan involved, it wasn't possible anymore and the fight became more than either of us were willing to put up with."

She scrunched up her face. "She was with both of you?"

"Not in the way it sounds. No soap opera style affair or anything. To Sophie's credit, though it broke me at the time, as soon as things progressed with Donovan, even if she didn't choose for it to, she and I were over."

Ness shook her head. "Why are you defending a skank?"

Unable to refrain from laughing at her bluntness, it took a second for me to compose myself while Ness stood dead serious waiting for me to respond.

"Sophie saved my life. That drew us together, but it wasn't enough. Gareth and Nya were part of us and how we found each other. Sophie and Donovan found each other centuries ago in other lives over and over. It's a whole thing."

Not that I wanted to retell how my father tried to kill me, but I settled for him sticking me in a sleeping curse and what it took for Sophie to save me. It felt good to tell her everything, even if the content made me sweat. She probably didn't want to know all this and didn't ask for specifics. She didn't stop me either once I got into the meat of it. Didn't say a word and was quiet when I finished.

"Too much to absorb?" Reading her thoughts would have been rude. She was trusting me to tell her the truth, or at least willing to listen. Now, I would see if she could take it.

"Not too much, though I don't believe after all that happened that you feel nothing for her. Not buying it. I mean, how can I? Girl saves guy's life, introduces him to a world he never knew existed when he should've been dead, and just so happens to share some creepy couple's suicidal essences inside of them. I somewhat understand the past-life thing with that other dude, but still. No one backs down so easy."

I sat on a fallen tree while Ness stood staring down at me. "Before we fought Evar, I told Sophie whenever she wanted, that if things didn't work with Donovan or if we could find a way around their connection, that I would be willing to try again. It wasn't right for me to say that to her, and she called me out on the spot. She was right to. Plus, you haven't seen her with Donovan. The way they interact, the things they have in common...Even without the connection, she wouldn't be looking my way for long."

"Soooo, this is you giving up?"

"Like I told Sophie, I'm not one to fight a sinking ship."

"Doesn't answer my question. You can't be over someone just because they don't want you."

"Hmm, yes I can."

"No. You either want them or you don't. It has nothing to do with Sophie being a fickle little twat."

"Ness—"

"Basing your feelings on hers is bull. The least you could do is own up to your shit."

"Fine." I stood and wiped my ass of tree debris. "Then how do you feel about me?"

Her right brow popped up.

"Since, according to your theory, it doesn't matter how I feel about you, it shouldn't sway your decision, right? So, how is it?"

She narrowed her eyes at me. "Right now, I think you're a dickhead."

"What?"

"You heard me. You're acting like a mangy dick. You spilled about five different reasons why Sophie was Miss Amazingness and how she left you for another guy and smashed your heart before spitting on the pieces, but that you'd wait for her if she lowered herself enough to take you back, and you want to know how I feel? Why? So we can return to the real world and I can watch you fawn over what you really want? Not a damn chance in hell is that ever going to happen. Not ever."

"I never said any of that." Gareth stirred from his invisible position, not liking the way Ness was speaking about Sophie—and consequently Nya—making me struggle to keep him at bay.

"It's my interpretation, which means I can't be wrong. I have a brain, and I can read the underlying meaning behind all your bullshit and attempts to justify it as a good enough reason to get with me."

"You can't be serious."

"I'm serious about not re-enacting some cheesy chick-flick where the guy and girl miraculously survive some tragedy and fall into happily-ever-after with their genitals stuck together. It didn't work for you and Miss Perfect, did it? Nope. It failed miserably, and it won't work for us."

Ness stormed off.

What the fuck just happened? So much for thinking the truth would guide things in a happy direction, though Gareth's passive relief was annoying. It's not what I wanted, and it should have pissed me off. In some respects, it did. Ness wasn't Sophie nor was she someone like my ditsy ex, Tracey.

Excluding the fact that Ness was deliciously beautiful in ways Sophie couldn't match, she was also willfully strong to the point of bullheadedness, dangerously witty, and sassy as hell. The fact that she refused to fall for me and risk being my backup choice illustrated why I didn't want to let her get away.

No one plans to get their heart stomped on when they could see it happening before it began. Ness had no reason to think otherwise, even if it wasn't how it would be.

Not yet anyway.

We needed to survive this place before I could prove her wrong about everything she filleted me for. I wasn't about to let her think her speech drove me to give up so easily. She would expect that, too.

Fine. I'd back off and focus on what we needed to do. The rest could wait. We were too busy with potential death and internal takeover to let petty shit distract us, but not saying anything when we could die any day felt like a wasted opportunity.

I followed her brooding shadow, realizing without her around, I was exposed to patrolling enemies. I didn't dare follow her into her lean-to. She was exhausted with her extra time on watch and with me in general. We needed our rest and space.

A crooked arm under my head was a piss-poor pillow and did nothing for my aching back after months of laying on the ground, yet still more comfortable than the conversation with Ness. The only thing comparable was my empty stomach as I stared up at a layer of stars in a clear night peeking through the holes in my makeshift home. They weren't real stars. The balls of blinking lights were a glimmer of Evaristus's memories of the real thing, faded and uninspiring; it didn't matter. It was something to stare at and better than acid rain or oppressive fog he found fit to keep the sense of oppression on us like a sweater of thorn bushes.

Shutting down meant shutting Gareth down, too. His emotions were warring with mine and I was done letting them get in the way. I wanted to feel nothing for a bit. Alcohol wasn't an option, nor was mindless TV, so the blanket of false stars would have to do.

6

ENDOWMENT

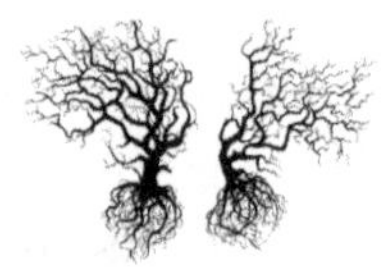

Sophie

Could I track the passing time by how many second-hand orgasms Donovan dragged me through? Multiples were one thing, a goal with an ideal partner to get sweaty with, but I didn't beg for these, and they wouldn't fucking stop. He wouldn't stop. When was enough, enough? At what point would his dick wave the white, encrusted flag?

When it seemed it was over, I pressed my back against the cinderblock wall, the cold floor cooling my temple while the rest of me shook with exhaustion, fought to dissociate, and create any amount of distance from Donovan and our connection.

Our emotional connection remained as it had for lifetimes, but our powers didn't work here. The concoction from Fox's tattoos snapped away when we were hit with visions back in the attic, and he was standing with Olson before he swept us away and I woke up in this box.

Was Donovan in on it with Olson? Could he have betrayed the Mother Coven without me knowing? Betrayed everything Aunt

Lacey fought to build? Maybe he did and, once he was free of me, he was celebrating by getting his rocks off without me cock-blocking him or breaking his cover.

If I could have cut him off completely, I would have. I didn't know how or why the connection worked normally sometimes and not others or why it seemed he controlled it when I couldn't.

The memory of how it started was a nagging insistence I couldn't keep from thinking of. I woke up on the floor, confused. Did I fall asleep? A sore and bloody lump on my head stung when I touched it. Shit. Did I faint? No healing ability meant a goose egg and a banging headache, one that didn't mean shit soon after. Not eating would end with me with a headache regardless. No way in hell did I trust the food when I was clueless about where I was and who was responsible for cooking it. Hunger pains were the least of my worries.

All thoughts of how I ended up on the floor disappeared as I felt hands on me. They ran down my sides, gripping, and pressure weighed on my thighs as if someone was sitting on me. Clearly no one was on me. Not me. On Donovan.

A tsunami of full-body disgust washed over me and I pushed the memories away with the thoughts of wanting to tear my skin off and suffocate Donovan with my bloody husk. I didn't want to think of everything I could feel for the duration it lasted.

Hours. Had to be hours.

Slimy piece of shit.

This place blocked the physical connection, but somehow it came back. Still no powers, and emotions took a back seat as time went on as if Donovan didn't want pesky things like a conscience messing with his blood flow. A marathon jerk-off session was too much to hope for. Nah, my supposed soulmate wasn't alone. I felt the hands of the others, their bodily pressure on mine, their physical reactions to what was being done to them.

Dozing breaks between orgasms happened as if the bastard was rejuvenating his fluids before stepping up to another challenge and taking me down with him into dreamworld only to replace the people

I couldn't see with faces I could. Ones I didn't want to see—Donovan's and Brock's, plus others I had never met. Everyone I saw came at me with unapologetic coercion, trying to convince me to enjoy the opportunity that was given to me, to understand that they were endowing me with a gift, not harming me. No matter what I said, they didn't hear me, didn't care how I felt, didn't stop to listen to my pleas, and resumed telling me this was a good thing as they continued to force themselves on me until my body gave in.

Waking up in a thrashing panic slammed me into the floor, praying to any higher power who might listen to wave their magic wand and send me back to my shitty apartment on my faded couch and chilling with Bosco in a safe space outside of this hamster cage I was trapped in. But no, my luck hadn't changed while I was being taken advantage of. Every sweat droplet was filled with resentment and invasive mistrust. I didn't possess the energy to stop myself from trembling, to quit the dry heaves, or to hold back the tears from my swollen eyes.

A scratchy loofah in a scalding shower couldn't scrub away the marathon sex I didn't technically have, so I didn't move, doing everything I could to ignore the mash of Donovan's emotions that hit me when I woke up. Morning—or whatever time it was—must have brought him the realities of what he did, and he couldn't dissociate from them anymore. I refused to hide my feelings as they were the only weapon I could fight with, yet I didn't engage him. I couldn't follow his emotional breakdown, no thank you. I had my own shit to process. He spiralled into anger, then gripping despair full of snot and tears, and then roaring in rageful outbursts I couldn't hear or physically feel yet sensed; another way of him forcing me to feel what he wanted whether I wanted it or not.

Instead of coddling his agony, I ignored him, and let his self-hatred chew him into chunks. Why he bothered to feel it at all didn't make sense when I know he enjoyed eking out every last thrust and ounce of impulse he could into whatever target he tossed his junk at. The punishment of letting him endure berating himself felt righteous, it being the sole amount of control I possessed inside these walls.

I couldn't stop him from doing what he wanted or feeling what he wanted, but I sure as hell didn't have to give him any attention, good or bad, so I didn't.

My weapon of silence and shunning lasted for as long as I could handle it. After all the time I spent dealing with what he did to me and what he made me feel while he was busy fulfilling needs I was apparently not satisfying for him, I was primed to let him hate himself forever. That was the plan, one I committed to, but I was in pain and beat up, and he wore me down.

Tears of frustration were the response he was looking for. He won those when I gave in and acknowledged him with a fraction of recognition. Not because I regretted punishing him by ignoring him and letting him punish himself, but because I was stuffed full of his rollercoaster of destruction and guilt, and I couldn't ride it with him any longer.

Donovan deserved every millisecond of pain he caused, and to bear my pain included. However, I couldn't be a part of it anymore. Couldn't be concerned for what may come if I ever got out of here alive. The thought of that was piggybacked with a sampling of shame for being stupid enough to believe Donovan was someone he wasn't. That he could be different than how most others saw him.

More shameful because I knew better. I fucking knew it. Every red flag whacked me in the face, and I batted them away as if they were a bothersome fruit fly and invited the piss-ant into every aspect of my life instead of shoving him into a bug zapper.

The connection we forged as young lovers all those years ago was everlasting, and yet it didn't mean I needed to love him now. I refused to believe that a former me fell for a former conniving asshole like him, so he must have been different back then, or I was a sucker for centuries. We could carry on as covenmates and comrades in the fight to reopen the Creation and whatever else came our way because I wasn't giving him the satisfaction of ruining what I built. Though, if he was on Olson's side, then he discovered ways to hide his Tainted soul from me and bamboozled a lot of players in this long-winded war. I mean, Olson did, why couldn't Donovan? He *was* the spawn of a Tainted Coven Master after all.

Besides, I could find someone to lick my wounds with and force Donovan to go through what I did all day and night. Not that I would have the stamina, though there's probably a spell for that. Maybe that's how he managed it. Kim probably knew one or possessed an herb that could manage it. Caine might be game. Ugh, who needed the complications. A few nameless anyones with the right timing was sufficient, though the thought of any sex, even consensual, made me nauseous.

I diverted dwelling on thoughts of Donovan, sifting through my memory for anything that occurred before Kim invited me to Aunt Lacey's that first night for a fake tea leaf reading party. I lived a life before all of this. A boring and sad life, yet some parts of it were worth getting back to instead of wasting away in this cement box.

Was this similar to a normal jail? A human, non-Magic jail?

With all the customers at The Lush who spoke of being locked up, I could only listen to their attempts to seem dangerous with an ear for their tip money. Brock was sent to juvie before I met him. His day-camp recalls of manipulating weak-minded guards into extra toilet paper or snacks as his consequence for being a small-time thief were nothing akin to adult incarceration. And if Vincent's description of the Sovereignty cells was anything close to accurate, then time inside these walls had yet to begin.

I didn't know how long ago the Apporter brought me here, wherever this was. All it brought me was a floor to pace, a disgusting toilet, and a bed to stare at with hate of how Donovan was using his.

None of this resembled a life I imagined worth living.

A loud clank sprang me to my feet. Pain bloomed through all my muscles, too tight and overused, yet I readied to face my captor for the first time.

Unless it was Donovan. I braced to attack him if it was, even if it meant pushing him out of the room and locking myself inside in order to stay away from him.

Vincent's brother, Chase, the head of the Sovereignty, entered clad in an expensive, tailored suit and looking like a butler while holding a tray of food I would never eat.

The door shut behind him before I could think of making a run for it.

A humourless laugh poured from me before I could stop it. "So, these are the fear-provoking Sovereignty cells where Magics disappear and never age to be tortured until forever? Is a visit from the Sovereignty's CEO, delivering what I'm sure is a totally trustworthy meal, a regular thing or am I super special?"

Smiling, Chase set the tray of food on the piece of metal sticking from the wall—I assumed it was supposed to be a desk—with an air of superiority as if he was doing maid's work. He took his time, slid his hands into his pockets, and peered around as if taking his first tour of the cell.

"This place, Firefly, is much cozier than my cells. Your current accommodation is care of the Sorrels. Your counterpart is in an identical pen awaiting the next stage of the process."

Wait. Donovan was in a cell? Clearly it didn't matter since he wasn't in his alone. Was Chase fucking with my head?

"Oh, yeah? Interesting." I didn't let my confusion colour my deadpanned tone. "Fifty-fifty chance of getting it right. Guess the Sorrels beat you to me." Makes sense that Donovan would bring me here. It would be near impossible for the Elders to retrieve me without a fight. However, if that was the case, he wouldn't also be a prisoner, would he?

Chase grinned at my petty dig.

"And my purpose in this lovely establishment, Mr. Vincent's Dimmer Brother?"

Chase shrugged. "It is what I want it to be."

Geez. He may as well piss on the wall. I got it. He wanted me to know Tobias would do his bidding.

"And what do you want it to be? Or is this a game? Charades? I didn't grow up in a game-night household, so keep it simple or grab a deck of cards."

He ignored my sass. "At the moment? Leverage."

I made a throaty noise. "Weak."

He laughed. "You think so?" He laughed harder. "How'd you enjoy your stay last night?" I steeled but didn't dare blink at his smarmy expression goading me. "You'll be here for as long as it works for us. You will continue here, alive, fed, and in relative health until it's time to transfer you. Though likely not until after the Creation is re-opened. Sorry you'll miss all the fuss."

His definition of "us" was unclear. "And why would the Sovereignty, the ultimate governing ruler of all us lowly Magic peasants, want Diluculo cracked open? You bury the secret of our power as if it's your prized bone like the rest of us. You forget your favourite watch in there while blowing Loring? Or is Evaristus more your taste? He should be. He is top dog, after all. Go for broke or all you end up with is bruised knees and a sore jaw instead of a penthouse and an expense account."

Chase narrowed his stare without losing that smarmy smile. "The Puppeteer will strike fear where it has lain dormant for a long time. The last war was monumental, historic. Many slaughtered, many triumphed in the face of untold odds and left idolized yet gained no one in a greater position than the Sovereignty. Evaristus will restore this image in the eyes of many who have lost faith, leaving my brother's alternative to our practices useless and illegal."

I stayed quiet as Chase paced a few steps in silence.

"You think I'm ignorant to my brother's substitute to the Sovereignty's rule? You think your precious Mother Coven is without its infiltrators?" He gave a smug grin unlike anything Vincent was capable of, making me wonder how the man in front of me could possibly be related.

Chase moved to leave, setting off a reflex in me to speak quickly, not yet wanting to be alone, even if my company was despicable. I also needed to suss out as much information from him as I could in case this was his one and only visit.

"Question, oh supreme ruler: If Vincent took the ultimate deal on the proverbial table, would you really take him back as one with your family in the Sovereignty?"

He turned and squared his shoulders to me. "Why wouldn't I?"

"Because you're a conniving donkey who enjoys Vincent's pain." Of course, he didn't deny the existence of the deal stating Vincent's wife's soul would be released and allowed to recycle if Vincent joined the company. I still didn't know how they imprisoned a soul to begin with.

"It's true, I enjoy seeing Vincent squirm. I never wanted his name tied to the business as our father insists, but I do thrive on the despondency in which my threat has caused my brother. I would welcome him in to watch him up close and personal as he lived every day within the walls he fought to break down for centuries. Christmas every day of the week." He laughed and kicked my cell door with expensive loafers, the only thing the two brothers had in common. Maybe it was an immortal rich guy thing.

The door opened, one hell of a guard sporting delicious lips and a long animal-skin coat filling the frame.

Without my power, who did they think I was going to kill? Certainly no one constituting the brick wall of a breath-taking Caveman watching over me. Before the door closed, he gave me a hard stare with dangerous blue eyes so light they sparkled. If I knew he was out there while Donovan was getting his rocks off with the menagerie delivered to his cell door instead of the suspicious food tray I got, I would have invited him in.

7

ISSUE WITH THE WORD

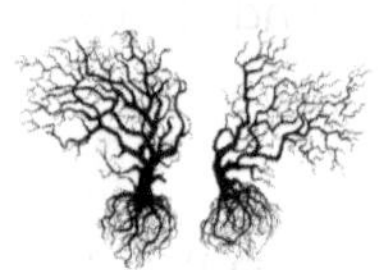

Kim

A coded text to Vincent brought us back to the stanky tunnel again, or so Vincent said when I bugged him about it. Unlike an old school spell, a techy enhancement from another contact of his created the private channel so he could communicate within new-age parameters of privacy. As an immortal, I imagined he had a contact in his back pocket for everything. This particular technological fanciness made anyone peeking over your shoulder or checking your phone history think you were meeting for a saucy liaison in a seedier place than the long, mildew-dripping tunnel in the middle of nowhere.

The system worked for Vincent and Hall for countless years, evolving with the times' gadgetry. The Viking was good at what he did, and Vincent was a shady secret keeper, this place another in his infinite box of treasures. While aware he could do a lot of damage with all the knowledge in his immortal brain, I was impressed, and took mental notes whenever I could.

No other way to learn but from the best. Or maybe the oldest?

Number one lesson? Meet as many Magics as you can and keep them in mind when things got hairy. They could either be directly useful depending on skill and knowledge or be familiar with others who were. Not every Magic was connected, but no point in ruining my chances of getting things done the way I needed because I was too good to network.

Ranlyn stopped us before we headed to the estate, insisting he ride along.

"No. Kim's presence has already been beyond the agreeable conditions of meeting my contact, yet established and uncontested. More leaks in protocol are an unnecessary risk. The Coven needs your stabilizing presence, one I am incapable of providing at this time."

While true, Vincent has appeared inches from losing it since Sophie and Donovan disappeared, I got the feeling he was more interested in keeping Ranlyn from knowing anything about Hall. To retain the Viking's cover? Didn't seem likely. Maybe he didn't like sharing his toys.

Ranlyn crossed his arms and narrowed a glare I didn't want to be the target of. "Your argument is that Kim is less of a security risk than I am and that the Coveners need a sympathetic ear. That's what you're trying to sell me? Do you think I am any less impacted by Olson's betrayal and Sophie and Donovan's capture?"

Vincent squared his shoulders to Ranlyn with an exaggerated calm I found more fearsome than if he was screaming at Ranlyn. "The meetings are spelled and leaves an imprint on those who attend so as others without invitation cannot discern the location from the weakest of minds. My contact did not balk at Kim's presence. The flock needs you and they need me to fix this. Stay. We are leaving."

Before Ranlyn could argue another angle, Vincent was walking away. I felt like I should be apologizing to Ranlyn for him being left behind or maybe because he was my Elder and I was joining another, newer Elder who enjoyed doing whatever the hell he wanted. I didn't always agree with Vincent's tactics, but I didn't want to miss learning more about getting Sophie and Donovan back.

On the way to the tunnel meeting spot, I kept thinking of the spell Vincent mentioned. If I could study and utilize the spell on a smaller scale, it would be wonderfully handy at any future Coven meetings. Less risk bringing in potential new Coveners as well, and not to mention another trick for my grimoire. If only I could collect them all like Pokémon cards.

The damp pressed in through my coat and chilled every inch of exposed skin as Vincent and I trudged our way through the tunnel. Hall's heavy boots were recognizable, but the unmistakable sound of a softer heel was not.

"Got my money, Lewy?" The echo of the Viking's deep voice resonated through the walls.

"No." Vincent was wound too tight for the running gag. When he leaned to look around Hall, I saw as he did. "Why are you here?"

Rosemary's dimples caved with her faux smile as she leaned around Hall to glare at Vincent. I never expected to meet up with Donovan's mother and, clearly, neither did Vincent.

Hall groaned. "Doesn't listen to the word no. Why is she here?" The leer he gave me didn't imply he was dissatisfied at seeing me again.

"Kim also has issues with the word."

I gave Vincent a back-handed slap to the shoulder. He wasn't exactly wrong, but he never told me I couldn't come. Instead, he pretty well insisted I come to ensure Ranlyn stayed far away.

Hall laughed in a low rumble. "In times past, aggression towards your Coven Elder held consequences involving limb removal."

"Aww, that's nice. And shows your age, old man."

Hall smiled as if I somehow encouraged him.

I internalized a snarl and reminded myself I wasn't single, even if I hadn't seen Frog much lately. "Can we move on to the part where you tell us what the fuck is going on with Sophie and Donovan that's so important we had to come back to this dank-ass place? They're a tad more important then you two thinking you're cutesy trying to leave the ladies in the car."

Of course, being pissed off didn't stop images of Hall from flitting through my head, since he was probably more useful naked than talking.

"Nudity *is* preferred but this location would compromise performance." His smirk and wink said he wasn't deterred if I was game.

Rosemary huffed. "You two can pant like tantric monkeys all night if you want. Save the veiled posturing for after we rescue my son."

Hall raised a brow at Rosemary's suggestion in my direction.

I ignored him, again, cursing my wide-open thoughts and reminding myself I needed another dose of telepathy blockers to hide them. Or maybe it was just this place.

Rosemary focused on Vincent. "The charge on Diluculo is tomorrow."

I gasped. "Why?"

"The Solstice."

"Shit." I completely forgot about Winter Solstice. How was it already the twentieth? No one talked about a celebration with all the craziness but choosing the date couldn't have been a coincidence. For comedic relief, bastardization of the holiday, or for the pure pleasure of morphing the day of festivity into a bloody mess, we were certain it was all a part of Tobias's plan, if he really secured the discus.

"And your intelligence derives from which source?" Vincent's suspicion was valid. Anything coming from Rosemary's Tainted mouth was worth questioning.

"Her information is accurate." Hall adopted a business-like demeanor. "I'm stationed in the ranks of the Compound Sentinels. A meeting was held dividing our ranks, some to guard Tobias on the battlefield, others to remain in the compound and watch the prisoners in the event their people made opportunistic use of the Master's absence. I worked myself into station outside Sophie's room and will be among those left protecting the compound. A rescue effort is expected but this would be prime in getting your lovers out alive. No matter who they leave behind during the battle, it's less than the flock's presence as a whole."

Rosemary pushed Hall aside and into the wall in the small space to close in on Vincent. Hall groaned and swiped at his coat of wall grossness. "The truce I formed with your Mother Coven is null and void. You will have no help from my Coven, nor will you be safe from them on the field outside the Creation."

Of course. "*Pfft*. After all the groveling you did for us to accept the truce in the first place, you're pulling out of your own deal?"

She ignored me and addressed Vincent. "The purpose of me revoking other commitments to be here is to inform you of a new deal, one brokered with Tobias to keep my son alive within the Sorrel Compound. In exchange for Donovan's continued breathing, and no assurances beyond that including the condition in which he may be in, Tobias insisted I drop the spell keeping my subordinates beneath my thumb. Since the allegiance spell's original purpose was to keep Donovan alive, I saw no defeat in its removal."

A hollow laugh escaped me. "Guess Sophie was right about the truce's only purpose was to save your son and not to keep peace with the Mother Coven. Too bad it took him enduring the Conception Rituals, and whatever else his fucked-up father did to him, for your motherly instincts to kick in."

G-forces hit my lungs with lightning strikes. The tunnel lights blurred. My spine screamed. Shell-shocked and confused, I strained to focus on the twinkling spots until the tunnel ceiling and string of lights came back into view. Heaviness on my chest made me cough and choke on stale, moldy air. I tried to cover my mouth and couldn't move my arms.

Violent yelling bounced off the tunnel walls. Someone attacked. How did they find us? Or did the ceiling collapse?

A growl and then movement on top of me shifted enough to allow me an extra deep breath that tasted like leather.

The yelling quieted, the groaning over me grew, and a shadow moved inches above me to block some of the tunnel's lights.

Hall's face appeared next to mine, his long hair tickling my cheek, a tendril or two resting across my throat. He was laying on top of me, shaking his head.

He lifted himself onto his elbows, bracing his own weight.

"Why are you on top of me?" He may have raised his body up an inch or two, but the rest of his bulky limbs were crushing me.

"Rosemary shut you down, kitten." Hall's voice croaked before he peered over his shoulder. "She scamper off?"

Vincent appeared, standing over Hall's shoulder, green eyes narrowed down at me. "Have you and Sophie taken classes on the perfection of antagonization?"

Rosemary attacked me? "Not our fault you're all so easy to rile."

It hadn't occurred to me that egging on a Magic such as Donovan's dimpled womb owner would end in my ass flattened. It wasn't my style to worry about the thought-to-mouth process. You would think Rosemary could handle a superficial dig more gracefully.

I tried to stand. Hall wouldn't budge. Instead, he looked down at me and smoothed some of my hair of my forehead, then laughed with the smell of something earthy on his breath. Beets?

Slapping his sharp jaw between my impatient palms, bypassing the fact I somehow found muscle there too, I focused on his ice-blue eyes. "Get the fuck off me, Viking."

A slow, stretching grin creased his cheeks before he swooped up to his feet in one fluid movement, bringing me to mine in the same motion. The blood drained from my head and the room pitched to the side. Hall twitched to catch me, but the wall did first. I pushed him and the wall away, the slimy brick enough to gather my head.

Vincent and Hall went back to talking, Vincent nodding as he looked too distracted to pay full attention while Hall suggested Vincent's Tactical Team be reallocated to the field outside Diluculo.

"No." Vincent blinked, refocusing on the conversation. "Their skills would be better utilized in the compound. The Mother Coven can portal through, near the Creation to converge on the enemy, as could the people of—"

Vincent's lips kept moving but I couldn't hear a word. It was as if he was censored like a snitch ratting out a friend on a reality cop show. Why couldn't I hear him?

Hall's brows raised. "Nora agreed to fight?"

Vincent shook his head. "Rodney."

"Wait...Who's Nora and Rodney? What just happened?" I needed an index to follow them.

Neither answered.

"A true Seedling, I see." A frown flickered on Hall's lips.

"Oh, whatever. Get on with it. I'll know eventually."

Hall straightened his coat. It was matted in places from the wet ground and walls. "A speedy reopening of Diluculo works in your lovers' favour."

"No kidding."

"Not only for the obviousness of getting out from under Tobias and Chase." Hall hesitated and turned to Vincent. "The Conception Rituals have been repeated."

Vincent's eyes widened. "A second time?"

Hall nodded. "I was present for most of the first round before taking up post outside the Soul Seer's door. The ritual affected her greatly on both occasions. The cells are magically sealed and yet, she still senses him emotionally through their connection. Not even Tobias expected this. During the rituals, the spell to keep a Magic from accessing their powers was tweaked. A slight variation to include their physical connection while still dulling their power."

"So, you're saying, what exactly?" I wasn't sure I wanted to know.

Hall let out a heavy exhale. "The Soul Seer endured the rituals as well, in full, and without knowledge of the particulars of what it consisted of. She's entertained but one visitor between the rituals and they did not inform her of the context of what she experienced."

Oh my god! I couldn't imagine what that did to Sophie. I tried to picture it and wanted to believe that Hall was exaggerating.

"What visitor?" Vincent asked.

Hall pegged Vincent with a side-eyed glare. "Your brother."

Vincent's whole body tensed, yet he didn't say anything as Hall continued.

"Briefly, though it was clear Sophie wasn't told of what was happening with her mate or why. She presumes disloyalty."

"How do you know what Sophie thinks? You said only Chase visited her." I could only imagine what was going through Sophie's mind.

Shifting his stance and crossing his arms, Hall glared down at me. "I know because I heard her cries grow angry with the betrayal. I witnessed her through the wall, as the cell she is held in dampens her magic, yet allows us to see and hear everything inside, as well as use Magic against her if needed. The horror of what she thought Donovan was doing made her physically ill. She refuses food and drink and only moves from a spot on the floor, one she chose instead of enduring the bed and her poisonous thoughts of what Donovan does in his, to use the washroom when required. That type of despair only comes from broken hearts."

Vincent braced his hands on his hips as if he needed a place to sit down. "She has consumed nothing since her capture?"

Hall shook his head.

Vincent removed his glasses and rubbed his eye before putting them back on. "She may lack the energy to escape."

Maybe she was scared the food was drugged. I have seen the girl eat, and portion control was not in her vocabulary. Damn her and her awesome metabolism. She must be starving.

"This is her way." Hall rolled his shoulders. "After being forced to endure all she has, I won't force her to do anything else, including eat. Donovan is worse. You can imagine what he has been subjected to. I could hardly watch him struggle. To be a part of it..." He shook his head. "Donovan is caught in a tumult of shame and self-deprecation. Disgusted to his very core for putting Sophie through it with him, knowing what it would do to her." He cleared his throat. "So much so, he was unable to perform during the ritual. Tobias used rooted visions to make him believe he was with Sophie."

I heard my gasp before realizing I made it.

"The cells that trap them, where he was put back once the rituals ended, are the only reason the Soul Seer is not subjected to his physical fury as he destroys his room, trashes his body fighting the cement walls, or rubs his skin in his shower to the point of bleeding without the relief of washing what was done to him away. He also calls to her."

"That's normal, no?" I assumed he knew Sophie couldn't hear him, but he would still try.

"Normal, yet useless. Due to the dissociative state she reverted to in order to save herself from enduring the memory of the rituals, he can't feel her anymore."

Vincent's loafer scuffed in the dirt. "He cannot feel her, emotionally you mean? Not at all?"

"No. Nothing."

I put my hand up. "Wait a sec. I understand Sophie's hurt. To go through that not once but twice and to think he enjoyed it...? Shit. She's gotta be losing it. A case of wine and a few girl-talk sessions might help, but this kind of thing can't reverse their connection, right? Once free of the cells and hearing Donovan wasn't dicking his whole father's coven for funsies, Sophie will come around. The rest would leave a traumatic mark, of course. I mean, it can't remove their Soul Magic, though, can it?"

"Soul Magic!" The Viking's bellow rattled in my bones. He stepped close and pointed in Vincent's face. "You know—"

"I know!"

"What?" I looked between the men, surprised at the fury coming off of both of them. "Someone say something."

Vincent fixed his glasses with a slow, controlled push of his fingers. "Can you honestly say you have seen—"

"Yes. I can!" Hall's voice ricocheted off the tight walls as Vincent stood unflinching.

"Then prevent it." Vincent matched the Viking's intensity without raising his voice as I stood confused as hell. "Gaining entry to the compound cannot be done from my side. You have access."

The men stared each other down. Having another telepathic conversation?

A growl broke free from between Hall's clenched jaw. "It's not easy infiltrating a Tainted syndicate and remaining within it for years just to breach my role to save a couple stupid enough to use Soul Magic in the first place."

"Stop griping. Lines will be drawn next nightfall. Sides chosen. Use your honed skills of lies and deceit for something besides padding your pockets and warming your bed."

Hall's face twisted at Vincent's attempt to manipulate him. "Tomorrow I'll work on releasing your lovers when Tobias leaves for the field. Have your team ready."

I stepped closer. "I'm going with you."

He chuckled. "Not a place for pretty faces, kitten."

"Fuck you." I earned a Viking-sized brow. "You don't even know Sophie or Donovan. I can do this better than running around a field dodging Magics who outweigh me by years of honed abilities. Even if you can distract the other guards while I free Sophie and Donovan, it'll be easier than you doing it alone. Plus, I have power to guide me to them. I won't need you for that."

He squinted. "Do you now?"

"Yeah, I do."

After clutching silence, Hall relented. "I'd hate to see a fascinating tyrant of a redhead perish for the fool's errand of saving her imbecilic friends, but your life is yours to forfeit as you please. If you know others who can be of use, recruit them." He dipped his head closer to mine. "Choose wisely, for you send them to their potential death."

Hall stormed off down the tunnel. Watching as he left without a backwards glance, I lingered until his big shoulders disappeared into the darkness and his footfalls dissipated before following

Vincent through the dank tunnel into the whipping snow and into the SUV.

In Vincent's focused quiet, without the radio to distract me, I recounted how lucky I was that Rosemary didn't end me. Maybe luckier than my Burberry smeared with mold from the ground and gross tunnel walls. Either Vincent did his Soul Extractor thing and partially removed her soul as Hall shielded me, or Rosemary threw the hit and took off before Vincent gained a chance to make her rethink her strategy. Both Magics saw the attack coming and I was too much of a Seedling to detect the rush of power until it sent me crashing in panicked flurry, trapped under limb-numbing heaviness.

When I said I was more useful in a small-scale operation, I meant it, and I wasn't about to allow my pride to kill me or anyone else. While others in my Sect would be in the field, they would have many in the Mother Coven on their side. They needed me to save two integral Sect members. We were all taking a chance with our lives. I didn't expect them to concentrate their efforts on two people when they had their own reasons to face their enemies in the field.

Unable to handle so much quiet, I asked Vincent about Soul Magic and why it pissed Hall off so much. Too distracted by his own thoughts to hear me, I repeated myself to gain his attention.

Vincent's tongue ran over his bottom lip as he negotiated a left turn through heavy traffic. "Soul Magic...." He paused for a long moment and exhaled. "Soul Magic should never be used." Another pause. "I warned Sophie against such a spell, but it was too late. The connection between them was solidified before the lifetime of our first acquaintance. Of all the years they have showcased as main characters in my life, and others where they were merely passing through, I possess no inkling of how long Sophie and Donovan have been finding each other through time or precisely when they pledged to live and die next to each other."

Damn. Vincent was old and somehow their souls were older. I wondered if Sophie and Donovan found each other their first go around or if they lived any lives without being joined at the hip.

"I still don't get why it's a big deal. So, they loved each other enough to work a spell to keep the love rolling. Most would call it romantic and bank a bajillion dollars on the movie rights."

"A variable *Romeo and Juliet* classic without focusing on the blatant tragedy of the tale."

"Okay. But more specifically...?"

He stalled again, shoulder checking too slow as if he needed an extra sliver of time to think. "Soul Magic is too much to ask of two souls." He stopped at a red light, now the only one on the road, yet unwilling to chance a cop wasn't hiding somewhere like I would have. "When we recycle—"

"You mean 'us' since you definitely haven't."

His jaw clenched at the reminder, focusing on the dash. "When souls return, their lives consist of new experiences, new people crossing paths, new destinies to fulfill, with little or no memory of the previous life's wisdom to draw from. Soul Magic intervenes where new life continues. The two paths collide, causing rifts in the consequent lives of others because the old could not adjust to the truth of their existence being perpetual yet ever-changing."

"Collide how? Wait, was Sophie supposed to be with Caine in this life, but the connection with Donovan got in the way of it?"

He shook his head. "The Soul Magic itself would have re-written that conclusion before any of them were recycled. However, I believe in most cases we are not destined for anyone at the recycling stage. That if we find someone it is because our paths and consequent decisions brought us together."

"And since Sophie and Donovan prearranged that plan, then no matter what, their paths are forced to collide."

Vincent nodded and fell silent before driving on when the light changed.

"In a weird way, though I'd hate to admit it to the asshole, Donovan and Sophie are perfect for each other. Factoring in the balance of their experiences before meeting in this life, once you got to know them, they work out far better than I thought they would. Somehow."

"Soul Magic does not fabricate compatibility. Sophie and Donovan achieve that on their own."

"Soooo, they are supposed to be together?"

This time, his head shake of annoyance needled me.

"What do you expect? You talk in circles like a sheisty car salesman and I'm getting rolling eyes? Spell it in airplane smoke if you want. Why is Soul Magic such a bad thing?"

"It is dangerous." Vincent's voice met mine, far too loud. "The sacrifice comes when the connected souls turn against the magic."

"Against it?"

"Yes, against it." His tone normalized. "In cases where Soul Magic turns ugly, if the lovers fall out of love or are jilted and sever their companionship, Soul Magic converts the souls into husks of hatred and jagged resentment." His words slowed, as did his speed. "Worse than any evil." Listening to the ache in his voice was heartbreaking. "As you heard, Donovan can no longer feel Sophie through their connection. She believes the Conception Rituals were an arbitrary dalliance where Donovan chose another to seek carnal comfort at the expense of Sophie's feelings. Soul Magic tainted by such infidelity destroys and sickens the souls until all motivations consist of torturing the other. Instead of the magic cradling such transcendent love, it will drive hatred, leaving them forever seeking wholeness while never being able to repair the tear created as the souls rip apart. This not only changes the connection by destroying it but alters the people who created the Soul Magic as they stole fate's designs to recreate their own.

"With that said, some ascertain Soul Magic is only gifted to those deemed deserving by those on the other side, suggesting the fates are aware of the soul union and have prepared allotments for it."

I turned sideways in my seat. "There's no way to know that."

"No documented proof exists to corroborate the authenticity of such a claim, no. Life rarely comes equipped with a how-to guide.

Though, if that love goes sour, the pair is punished for eternity for the treachery of turning their backs on such a sacred gift. Neither Sophie nor Donovan knew their loophole to fate's design carried such consequence and have, so far, had no reason to fear it."

"This loophole, it's permanent. That's what you're getting at. No matter good or bad, the connection, it'll never go away."

"Yes."

"Even if they remove the Soul Magic in this life and recycle into another life?"

Vincent shrugged. I took it as he didn't know, a bad sign since he knew more than anyone else I could ask.

Shit. Shit, shit, shit! I slumped into my seat. And now Donovan can't feel Sophie. It was already starting, and Sophie and Donovan were clueless about the consequences of letting it worsen. Sophie would've said something if she did.

The SUV's steady heat dried out my eyes as I lost time thinking of what we might find by the time we dragged Sophie and Donovan from their cells.

8

PROCEDURAL AND PRACTICAL

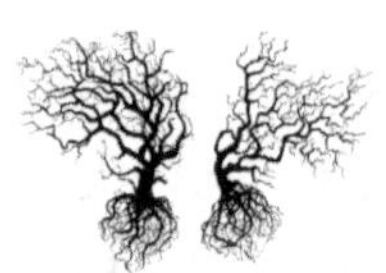

Kim

All eyes were on us when we re-entered the Ballard Estate's attic, expectant and in anticipation of results. They shifted into disappointment when it became clear we didn't have Sophie and Donovan with us.

Most seasoned by Magic politics knew to expect it, though Sophie's family coven—especially her mother—held out hope. Lu shed fresh tears from bloodshot eyes at the prospect of whatever horrors she imagined her daughter enduring at the hands of an enemy she knew little about. Unfortunately, whatever Lu's anxious thoughts cooked up, they probably weren't far off.

I stood by as Ranlyn relayed the grim details as before, and as before, the Conception Rituals were omitted from the group update. The fact the disgusting ritual was repeated a second time was atrocious and the Coveners didn't even know about the first time.

The repercussions of the break in Sophie and Donovan's Soul Magic were nixed from the update as well.

All that mattered was that during the Winter Solstice tomorrow, covens would converge on the field outside Diluculo to reopen the Creation and they needed to do everything possible to ensure Loring and Evaristus didn't sneak away to destroy Magics and the Blind at will.

Though I would miss all the fun of welcoming Caine back to the real world, he would forgive me if it meant my skills were being used to save Sophie—and consequently Donovan.

When Donovan was able to connect with Caine across the veil, Caine said Loring was half the Magic he was when we faced him the first time, but still equally dangerous.

Evaristus was the wild card. An ancient Magic who took on the persona of a god and managed to ditch his soul. Outside of the Creation he would turn Magics and Blind into mindless slaves in order to cap off his personal mission of killing everyone in his and Sophie's bloodline. They didn't call him the Puppeteer for nothing, and he was used to being the king of his Creation.

"There's a hell of a lot of us you forgot in your roll call there, Elder." I snapped back into my head. The redness of Blake's cheeks deepened as he confronted Ranlyn. "Most of us were on the field when Loring and his Puppet Master were trapped. Why wouldn't we show up when they try and escape?"

"Even as a supporting role." Leave it to Jared to soften the blow of his best friend's words.

Ranlyn didn't meet my eyes as if he expected me to put Blake in his place, but he got partway before resisting the impulse. "The three Elders you see will lead the siege on the field as Elders have done in the past. Kim will approach others to join her and a valued contact to extract Donovan and Sophie from the Sorrel Compound. Any others unmentioned will not be expected to participate. If you do, your death will not be of the Coven's will."

It didn't take a mind reader to know Vincent would rather collect Sophie and Donovan instead of being in the field, but he had his duty as an Elder to uphold.

Could Ranlyn stop him if he refused to head the charge on Diluculo?

Grumbles through the Sect went unacknowledged. Some, like Blake, expected to be involved and would be no matter what a Coven Elder dictated. Others wanted to provide simple help in a non-front-line role. The difference between the two groups was obvious in the amount of "lets kick some ass!" attitude they wore as if it was the only armour needed.

"Yo!" Adam saw over the heads of most at me with his reedy frame, his dark, short hair a mess, his sunglasses to lessen the impact of soul glows from his Soul Seeing firmly in place. "What about getting back my sister? Who's going?"

"Adam!" Adam and Sophie's mom's voice rose above the crowd. She raced over to her son from Olive's desk where Serena sank into the chair her Aunt Lu vacated, the failed effort to keep her aunt calm exhausting. "You can't be serious about going."

Adam ignored his mom and glared at me, waiting for an answer.

I shrugged. "Hell if I know."

Adam's brows cinched in a clear "are you fucking kidding me?" response.

"What? I'm not that far yet. When I know, you'll know. And I'll consider your stank face your application. Cool?"

Regardless of what Sophie's mother wanted, Adam was an adult. Instead of reminding people of this, he joked that his sister was probably lost and not stolen. The chick was directionally chal-lenged, but even his mother wasn't falling for the distraction and followed him when he went to busy himself elsewhere, using his full name and clenching her hands into fists as she stalked after him.

A replay of Hall's warning reminded me my choice of rescue crew could lead to their deaths. They could literally die trying to stop Loring and Evaristus, too, but handpicking them for this mission seemed like I was amping up their chances.

I also remembered my Sect was counting on me to keep it

together without Donovan around and I was doing a piss-poor job of it.

Whatever. I took a breath in and released it as slowly as I could manage, reminding myself that I couldn't do everything or be everything for everyone and to focus on what I *could* control. Social media might be a toxic cesspool half the time, but it has inspirational quotes out the ass and some of them were actually useful.

Now, I had to act. To take charge and find a way to make the decisions I needed to.

How do I choose who should go where? I couldn't see souls to determine which were strongest. Olive and Lewis could. So could Adam and Sophie's cousin Kassie, though Adam was still busy getting lectured by his mother. Besides not liking Sophie, I didn't know enough about Kassie to trust her.

Lewis and Olive looked at each other after I asked them to survey the souls of the Magics in the attic. Lewis fixed his pants and inhaled deeply. "We understand the responsibility of our gifts."

Olive nodded. "How many do you need?"

"Uhm, I didn't think to ask. Besides the six Tactical Team members already going, maybe four or five?"

They smiled at my estimation and surveyed those around us, making quick comparisons before heading into the crowd and tapping people on the shoulder. In no more than ten minutes, they created a line-up for me to give a once-over.

Olive smiled at hers and Lewis's selections, putting her hand on the first person's arm. "Introduce yourself."

He tucked long and wavy hair behind his ears. "Umm, Cam. I'm Cameron. Which you know?" He side-eyed Olive and myself until I nodded. He was a rather new member, but I knew him. Sophie recruited him, so I always assumed he was strong. She never said why. Maybe he didn't have a speciality gift.

Lewis peered down the line. "Next."

"Kassie." She huffed and shifted her stance with subdued attitude.

"Soul Seer." I remembered her Rene Ruiz off-the-shoulder gown from the Restoration Party. "And not a fan of your cousin."

"Please." She rolled her eyes. "Doesn't mean I'd let Sophie die. Even if she is stupid enough to get caught in the first place."

"Mhmm. Okay, awesome. You're dismissed."

She raised her brow—a perfect match to the other—confident and non-apologetic in her opinions.

"The attitude is not only unneeded, but inaccurate, dangerous, and straight up petty, so you can go."

She glared at Olive as if her great-aunt wasted her time. Olive returned an expression I read as "Not my fault" and Kassie left the group to return to whatever she was doing.

That was okay. I didn't need all of them and Kassie being kicked off the island, so to speak, was better for Sophie. Actually, I totally wish Sophie were here to see me do that.

A cleared throat drew my attention to a familiar face. "Gerard."

"Right. Huntsman like your turncoat buddy Roe, now dead."

His stare went unchanged. "Yup."

Roe going against his coven wasn't entirely his fault since two other Mother Coven Elders convinced him Sophie and Caine would bring down the Coven and begin a civil war. Questioning your Elders was one thing. Denying a premonition that predicted exactly what we were now going through was another. The fact we would be potentially fighting our own people outside of the Creation because they didn't want to open it and risk Loring and Evaristus's evil spreading into the real world, even if it meant saving their own Coveners also trapped inside, was proof enough.

Roe picked his side. All we could do was hope Gerard remained committed when it came down to the fight. If he came with us to the Sorrel Compound, fewer people were in his way of tracking Sophie and Donovan and he could sniff out anyone before they saw us.

I looked to the next person.

"Sloan. Necromancer, from the Mother Coven." This was announced with a voice of precision from the blond, bar-beaten man with vengeance in his stare. "Never met these people and I'd be missing one hell of a brawl in the field, so you better promise me a good fight."

"As long as your objective remains getting Sophie, Donovan, and the rest of us out alive, you can hang back and party all you want. I'm not your mother and you're not in my Sect."

Sloan nodded with an anticipatory grin.

The next potential was young. Jailbait for the common perv and too baby-faced to trick a testosterone-fueled bouncer with a stellar fake ID. She must have been fourteen or fifteen, eyes wide and darting to the floor as if she wished she contained the ability to transform into an ant and slip between the floorboards.

I waited until she met my gaze. "Are you sure?"

Her mouth opened but she didn't have words.

Lewis stood behind the girl with a fatherly hand on her shoulder. "This little one is special. I don't recognise her foggy, grey Soul Colour, but the soul itself is so bright it nearly obscures it. Someone with such strength is an asset, regardless of experience."

Call me impressed. "Do you mind if I ask what type of Magic you are?"

Taking a moment as her eyes hit the floor again, she clenched her jaw before answering. "I'm a Banshee."

"A Banshee? As in a screaming, harbinger of death type of Banshee?"

She nodded. "I guess captive retrieval is better than being in the field with all the dead." Her cheeks flushed as if sorry to assume people would die. "The magic in me is drawn to death and mourns it too deeply. I'd fight with everything I have to avoid that torture."

Damn. My heart broke for the girl's pain already evident in her large tearful eyes. She could be a liability if she didn't know anything else but how to mourn the dead. I didn't question them further and hoped I wouldn't regret not taking the opportunity.

They knew the Tactical Team would lead them, their numbers comforting as the Team was a famous ghost story to most Magics, akin to the boogeyman dressed in black and ready to snap their fingers and dispatch enemies. No one knew Vincent was their leader until recently, making their involvement even more exciting.

When the new team rejoined the others, I was pissed at myself for forgetting to ask the young Banshee's name.

The innocence missing from her young stare reminded me of Andy. Trying to shield him from all the talk of impending death wasn't easy and he spent most of his time on one side of the attic in a virtual bubble. A transparent one of course, yet hardly better than being locked in his room back home. He could move around freely from his bubble, but no other kids were around to play with him, and everyone talked of battle or kept quiet when he was around.

Being so busy with running around with Vincent and organizing the potential death of more of my Sect, I completely forgot about Andy and went to check on him.

I knew I crossed the communication barrier as everyone quieted behind me. I didn't realize how loud the group was. "Hey, bud."

I sat next to Andy on his small cot. Bosco got up from Andy's other side and came to greet me, tail wiggling.

"Hey, Kim."

"What's happenin'?"

"Nothing." He put down his book. "I'm bored."

I laughed. "I bet."

He was a kid. He shouldn't have been here at all. Less than a day was left before we would challenge an enemy we should have shut down permanently instead of trapping them for another day. No pre-battle party like the last time and nothing more to do but be sure my supplies were ready and to get some rest, even if it didn't mean sleeping.

Andy deserved a break from the monotony and so did Bosco. Both were fed and sheltered but were bored and emotionally neglected.

I pulled Bosco into my arms. "How do you feel about snow angels?"

Andy's eyes lit up and he was running for the attic exit before I could stand up off the cot with Bosco.

Snuggled in our winter gear, we went into the estate's backyard. Andy jumped into the snow and started waving his arms and legs for no reason other than good clean fun.

I grabbed his hands and helped him up so he wouldn't smudge his design. He laughed and made a few more. I didn't realize it represented his family members until he told me, saying he hoped to see his mom and his grandparents soon.

Jumping into the snow and making my own snow angel saved me from blubbering like a baby. With his grandfather murdered and his grandmother joining his murderer's flock, I hoped Andy would see his mom soon, too. She hadn't been saved from Evaristus last we connected with Caine, and now Donovan wasn't able to warn Caine that his time to save her was running out.

Still on my back, I lobbed a chunk of snow at Andy. It hit him in the chest and spraying his face while Bosco jumped to catch the debris. Bursting into a belly laugh that echoed into the quiet of the surrounding acreage, I knew I made the right choice focusing attention on Andy and hoped if something bad happened or if he never saw his mother again that in the future, he could remember his time at the estate as one with a little fun.

"Can we make a snowman?"

"Only if I can dress them."

"What? Snowmen don't wear clothes."

"*Pfft.* Mine do. How else are they supposed to impress their snowpeople posse?"

Andy thought I was weird, but it didn't stop him from getting down in the snow and rolling the largest snowball he could manage. I got some extra clothing from Olive and gave Andy's creations some style before Andy's nose and cheeks blazed bright red from the cold.

Chilled yet somehow sweating in my Burberry now probably ruined from the tunnels and the snow, I chased a glass of ice water with my famous herbal hot chocolate—with added caramel for sweetness Andy loved—and some mint chocolate chip that was getting freezer burnt in the deepfreeze.

Hours passed as snacks turned into *Snakes and Ladders* and at least a dozen games of *Go Fish* and *Crazy 8's*.

"You know, you're a bit of a cheater, Berisford." Andy laid down the queen of spades, making me pick up five cards. Again. The kid was kicking my ass.

Using his last name made me think of Caine and what he might be doing inside the Creation right now. Hopefully surviving. He was trapped in a type of hell before, but not like this.

"It's not my fault you suck." After a sinister giggle, Andy laid down a card to cause me to miss a turn then another to pick up more cards, rolling on his side on the cot and belly laughing until Bosco crawled all over him, licking and sneezing in his face, the snorting and laughter filling the rafters with joy.

Pushing away the playful Pug and wiping slobber from his face with his sleeve, Andy waited for my turn before making another move.

He laid down another card. "I'm glad you don't have spots."

Mild shock slapped me upside the head. The gasp I wished I hid better startled Andy enough to make him look at me like he regretted saying anything. No spots meant I would likely survive tomorrow. Relief took me for a loop. "I'm glad too, actually."

More cards were laid as I fought asking a child twenty questions about his gift of seeing the spots and everything it entailed.

"Thanks for telling me." Smiling, yet unsure of how tense it looked from his end, I didn't want to make a big deal of it in case he felt weird, but an earth-sized weight was lifted off my shoulders. Of course, the future can always change, but you don't get that kind of guarantee often. "I bet you're seeing a lot of spots with this group, huh?" It wasn't very smooth. A part of me hated myself for asking.

Andy shrugged and kept his attention on his cards. "I guess."

Specifics of which Magics here were going to die would have been nice. "More than five of them?"

He nodded with a twist of his mouth and changed the suit in the game to hearts.

I laid down a seven of hearts. "More than ten?"

His young eyes surveyed the crowd while I did my best to act natural with the most unnatural conversation I could ever have with a six-year-old.

"More than ten." Andy refocused on the game without understanding the gravity his gift added to battle.

Death was not an unknown concept to me. Helpless as Loring's sick obsessions left Aunt Lacey bloodied and tortured after she enriched my life as my mentor and Sect leader was almost as bad as my mother wasting away in slow motion. While my sister, Anita, opted to deal with mom's sickness as far away as she could be, I was left cleaning bed pans and sponge bathing a body of cold sweat foreign to the woman it poisoned.

I knew I could ask Andy to point out each Magic with the spots portending their deaths, but the knowledge was no cure. Telling someone they were going to die was no brand of chemo and, unlike Sophie and Donovan, chances were their Soul Shepherds wouldn't break whatever rules Aunt Lacey did to revive them like when Sophie and Caine faced Loring and Evaristus the first time.

Hiding the fact I was filled to my curled lashes with envy that Sophie interacted with Aunt Lacey again was easy when she was preoccupied with trying to escape the Creation and drowning herself in the emotions of hers and Donovan's connection now that she'd given in to it. Or did. Who knows what it meant for them after all this?

I laid down another card, then picked it up as Andy claimed he changed the suit to clubs, and I was too stuck in my thoughts to notice. He kept playing as if all was normal. To him, I supposed this was.

Organization was my control. When I saw my mother's ending coming, I forced myself to speak with her about her wishes and then delved into seeing them through. Procedural and practical, cold to some, but it worked, and it was what I wished I was doing right now. Instead, I played my next card, changing the suit to spades and contemplating who would be responsible for the Sect if Donovan and I didn't survive the Sorrel Compound.

The Sect couldn't disband after all the years Aunt Lacey kept it going. The Sect needed to continue to practice no matter what.

When Andy couldn't fight his heavy eyelids anymore, I left him to sleep with his Pug guard. Members would stay behind in the attic to be available if needed for healing or collaboration of escape measures, and to ensure Andy's safety if all went to shit and no one he knew survived. Realizing the high likelihood of this occurring, I had to prepare for that as well.

Stepping out of Andy's bubble of quiet, my ears were hit with a mecca of people talking over one another. Each were hyper-focused on the tiny details of battle: where people needed to be, primary targets, focused abilities, and layers of strategy. I should have been involved, but I had another focus.

I found members in my Sect standing in a group, excited and chatting. Fox devised a solution for maximizing any leftover Magics' powers, keeping those unwilling or unable to fight on the frontline far from harm's way, yet still able to contribute.

As a Druid, Fox channelled certain powers and amplified them through others with active abilities. The plan was to surround the battlefield with Magics, siphon a portion of their magic, and use it as a catalyst to filter healing, protection, and even specialized abilities to those in need. No one knew how much of a bump it would give their comrades, but they were pumped to be able to help.

This diminished those left behind to care for Andy as Gwen was my top choice and she was planning on being a conduit with Fox.

In the field, far enough away from the action that escape was possible, I stuck with my original plan and shared it with Gwen.

Gwen took a literal step back from me. "I can't run a Sect."

I closed the enlarged gap between us and grabbed her hands. "Believe me, it doesn't take as much as you'd think. You wouldn't have to deal with Donovan, for one. And two, you've been in the Sect longer than I have. You know the rituals, know our people, and your power gives you great insight. I was given the title to assist Donovan. Aunt Lacey's parting wish or I wouldn't've taken it."

Her eyes widened as if she didn't realize that's how it went down. "What about Louise? She's been around longer than any of us."

"And has good reason to let the Sect fall." Reason being her husband Henry's death while trying to break into the Creation the first time, but Gwen understood without mentioning. "The Sect members don't need to be mothered and fattened up with her latest soufflé recipe. They need that too, Louise is an invaluable member, but they need a leader more. If we screw the pooch on this thing, shit is going to turn nasty, and all Magics not ready to call Evaristus Master will have to run and hide."

Her expression steeled as if she hadn't thought of this possibility.

"Hopefully at least one Elder or high-ranking Mother Coven representative will survive and be equipped to run it and keep everyone safe. Even if they do, we need one of our own to lead. You can handle that."

She chewed her bottom lip in contemplation.

"Your hesitance is further proof you're the right choice, but you don't have time to mull it over. You're either willing to pick up the reins or you're not. No hard feelings if that's the case, I know what I'm asking, and I don't have time for fickle."

"Right. I guess you don't. Fine. *If* it comes to all that and you and Donovan can't do it, I'll step up and do what I can to keep everyone safe. Only as a last resort. I read tarot. I don't public speak."

"And you're a Prophetess. Don't undercut your worth."

Gwen's cheeks nearly matched the colour of her hair as she strong-armed me with a crushing hug while I prayed Gwen wasn't among the "more than ten" with the spots.

I wouldn't be around to see Fox's plan succeed or epically fail, but I didn't have much faith in it being enough to overthrow the big bad coming down on them. Not on its own.

Now, I needed a babysitter.

Only a few were staying behind and no one Andy knew well. Fox's option removed all of the Ballards from the equation. Most, at the very least, released their power even if they'd never truly felt or used it, and apparently this was enough for Fox, so not even they were available. Before the ticking clock ran out, I had to choose someone.

The vacant gaze Sophie's mother wore like an itchy, yet functional, sweater was a combination of anxiety in overdrive and the lemon balm Serena spiked her tea with. It allowed her to slow things down and think, but all she was doing was worrying. Someone facing their one child being in the hands of power-hungry enemies with magical powers, while the other child was drumming his fingers raw on anything he could touch as he thrummed with anticipated war, didn't mean she was up for taking care of someone else's kid, but maybe it would distract her a bit.

If Sophie and Adam survived, this Christmas would be Lu's most treasured holiday. If one or both of her kids didn't come home, it would be forever altered and mourned every subsequent season.

"I have someone reliable to leave Andy with." Vincent entered my peripheral vision, looking down at his phone.

He must have read my mind.

"I was going to—"

"The plan to leave some in the attic is naïve. Andy's safety is a high priority for Sophie, as it must be for us. The attic is not the venue to ensure this. Sophie's mother will feel safe within the familiar walls of the estate until Evaristus turns her into a Puppet before a prolonged death for being his relation. What happens to the child is much worse and not a death you want on your conscious."

"If we lose, you mean."

He peered up from his phone to meet my stare. "Always prepare to lose."

The seriousness with which he said this made me want to slap him, but he was right, even if I didn't want to think about the devastation of losing.

"Fine, I'll tell people to go somewhere else, though I have no clue where. I think most are going anyway. Who do you have for a babysitter?"

"A woman I have known for many years." He was looking at his phone again and turned to leave.

I grabbed his phone from his hand and shoved it into my back pocket. "I can't leave Andy with someone random. I'm already taking a chance that Hall isn't going to fuck us when we infiltrate the Sorrel Compound."

"Hall is—"

"A Recondite Magic, like the Apporter, so sorry if I don't trust your gut. It's one thing to put my ass on the line, it's another to gamble with Andy's. Tell me where he'll be."

"The Magic's name is Moira, an Alchemist who works for me yet is more akin to family. She resides in a location Sophie is familiar with and one I cannot repeat. Not because I seek to be mysterious but because I am bound by strenuous levels of security ensuring it an impossibility. If those in power of such permissions clear you, you will know. For now, a modicum of trust will have to be extended. I would never put a child in harm's way."

I believed he would do anything for Sophie. If that meant safeguarding Andy, he would do it. "Fine, but how do we get him there since no one will show me where it is? And where does Sophie's mom or anyone else go if they can't stay here?"

"The boy is easy as has already been there. Allow me to arrange details for any others." Vincent put his hand out and I gave him back his phone, his attention glued to it before I could say anything else.

Leaving this in his control made me antsy. I felt like I was passing the responsibility onto someone else instead of dealing with it myself.

Seeing Andy to safety kept me from overthinking the details of infiltrating the Sorrel Compound since I wasn't leading that charge either. Vincent's super special Tactical Team was taking point while

I led them with my guiding light and prayer not to be killed the second I hit Sorrel territory.

My only hope was whoever was looking after Andy was a friendly face without a hidden agenda.

The estate swelled with more and more Magics, some coming and going quickly, intent on getting information or supplies and then heading off for other preparations before needing to go to the field. The attic possessed everything you could think of but couldn't outfit an army. Olive's generosity was paramount. If someone needed something, it was given freely no matter how much those twin aunts of Sophie's complained there would be nothing left for the family. Olive was happy to ignore them, and they were happy to distract themselves by caring for the furry little worm used on Donovan to connect with Caine across the veil.

It kept getting plumper. The white, fuzzy hair along its back bushier by the day. Donovan should be happy he wouldn't need it shoved up into his skull again. I doubted it would fit.

Olive's generosity extended to the estate as a whole. If someone needed private space to work a spell, they picked one of many bedrooms or if they needed the equipment to whip up a potion or concoction, they used the kitchen and anything in it. Though, some like Blake and Jared only needed the fridge full of energy drinks and the backyard to stretch their Elemental powers. The estate didn't have many neighbours, but there was enough to ask questions if he created tornados. A bit of wind and bolstering the already falling snow was enough.

Stuck in my head, the bathroom door opening sent a jolt through me. I didn't know how long I was in a trance of thoughts waiting outside.

Lu exited the bathroom, eyes red and swollen, and rubbing her temple.

"I've got some natural herbs for that headache. Nothing habit-forming and low on the allergy spectrum if you're worried about reactions. Also, nothing too witchy. Good ol' mother nature."

She hesitated, fighting, what I assumed, was the decision to use my solution so she could be of better use if needed and having enough of everything witchy and weighing how long she could hold out. After seeing Sophie have a few vomit-inducing skull bangers, it wouldn't be long before Lu was laying down in a dark room somewhere.

"No pressure," I added. "I assume you're sticking around. Catch me if you change your mind."

Lu nodded and stepped aside so I could use the bathroom. "Wait, Lu. Umm, Sophie wouldn't hate you for not going after her. She really wouldn't."

The quiver of Lu's chin worsened before she averted her eyes and shook her head instead of saying whatever her body wouldn't let her say without more tears. I didn't need a response and she might not have needed my validation, but I had to say it.

Quitting with the deep stuff before Lu started hyperventilating, I offered the headache solution again. This time Lu agreed to have some in her tea since it was the easiest way to get things down right now.

A handful of minutes later, Lu was leaning against the kitchen counter with her warm cup between her hands. Her shoulders visibly lowered with a heavy exhale. They had been tucked up by her ears for hours.

She rolled her neck side-to-side with her eyes closed. "Thank you, Kim."

I sipped my own tea, without the Blue Skullcap. "You're welcome. Not all us witches use our abilities and knowledge for war. Sometimes we use them for a timeout."

Lu's relaxed smile and steady breaths were a win.

9

OWNER AND OPERATOR

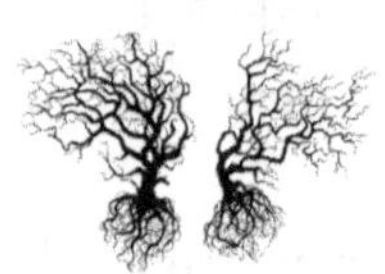

Kim

Returning from the kitchen, I saw a bedroom door on the second floor a tad open and a familiar loafer-tip inside. When I went in, Vincent stood in the midst of an otherwise empty guest room.

"Sorry. Door was..."

He was standing and staring at nothing, not paying any attention to me.

Fuck. Was he a Puppet? No. He couldn't be, right?

I shut the door behind me, still with no reaction from Vincent.

"Vincent?" I touched his shoulder and felt like I was sucked into the sun. A sharp burn and bright light overwhelmed me. "Whoa!"

"Kim?"

"What's happening?" I couldn't see anything through the tears flowing down my cheeks.

A familiar chuckle proceeded me being hauled off of my ass and onto my feet. "You sure know how to make an entrance to a private party."

I swiped at my eyes and blinked as fast as a hummingbird's wings until I could see enough to spot Hall's smiling face and Vincent's not so smiling one.

Above us was a bright sun shining down from a blue sky empty of clouds. Beneath us was an open field of wildflowers and nothing more for as far as my blistered retinas could see.

"The field party looks a lot different than ones I remember in high school. Where are we?"

Vincent huffed. "Back at the estate where privacy is interpretable."

Hall chuckled again.

"Don't be testy with me. You were literally standing alone in an empty room and staring at a wall. I thought you were possessed. I touched your shoulder—"

"And waltzed into my head." Hall widened his arms to indicate our surroundings. "How lucky am I to benefit from your intrusion?"

His head? Great. "Cut the cute and tell me what's going on because anyone else could walk in and find us together being weird in an empty room."

Hall clucked his tongue and shook his head. "Wouldn't that be a scandal?"

"Kim..." Vincent fixed his glasses, "in my rush to ensure privacy I overlooked locking the door. Now that you are here, understand we do not have much time as Hall, too, is someplace else in the midst of his own vulnerability."

Hall shrugged. "A private bathroom works much better when leaving the compound is impossible."

"Did something else happen? Don't tell me you're being a flirty asshat instead of telling me bad news."

Hall raised a playful brow. "Who said I was flirting?"

I exhaled, Hall's games annoying me. "Vincent, what the fuck is going on?"

Hall chuckled. "Settle, kitten. I came with an update on the particulars of the growing situation. However, I cannot obtain access to certain materials regarding which Sovereignty hand will be by Tobias's side during the Creation opening."

Vincent seemed upset that it might not be his brother. Sibling issues I got, but I didn't want to kill my sister. Maybe sit her down and force a barrage of memories of Mom throwing her guts up in the grips of her disease since Anita was hellbent on retaining her memories of "the good times" leaving me with all the ugly baggage.

"Furthermore," Hall looked to Vincent, "Tobias doesn't have the discus."

Vincent squinted at Hall. "You are certain of this?" Hall nodded. "Chase?"

Hall folded his hands in front of him. "I believe so."

"That doesn't make sense." I waved off a small bug flying in my face. Apparently, this place was as realistic as real could be. "How did it wind up in the Sovereignty's hands? Hinapouri and Miklos went through the trouble of joining forces with the Berisfords all to torture the info from Sophie to steal it from the Ballards, only to turn around and play into the Sovereignty's self-serving plans? They must have worried about being lumped in with the people causing the civil war and brokered some kind of a deal."

"Seems likely." Hall didn't have anything more to say about it and Vincent dipped into his thoughts.

"Should I even ask how Sophie and Donovan are doing?"

"You can, though my answer would be much the same as last time. No, the Conception Rituals were not replayed a third time, though the two of them are still recovering from the experience in their own ways. Most not positive or healthy. The quicker we can make an extraction, the better, and the sooner reconciliation can begin."

"You mean before their Soul Magic tears apart and they hate each other." I saw the underlining negativity of his words, even if he didn't want to say it.

To illustrate my point more, he nodded with a bit of a helpless frown. Hall could help us break them out of there, but he didn't have the power to fix their love or erase their memories of the rituals. Actually—

"No." Hall interrupted my thoughts, able to hear them in this place. "It's my head, so I can hear everything in yours. And while I don't wish them the pain they have been forced to endure, erasing the memory is worse. They deserve to know what was done to their bodies and who is responsible for it. One day, children will be born from the rituals. If they come looking for their father, Donovan will deserve to understand how they came to be."

My turn to nod. Crazy to think Donovan might already have children if this wasn't the first time it happened to him. I didn't want to pull the cover over their eyes. I just wanted to protect them in some small way.

"Not that way." Hall's tone was a little sad, hammering home his opinion on the matter.

Hall took a couple of steps towards Vincent, touched his shoulder, and then came my way. Vincent looked to be in his thoughts still, but he wasn't moving. It was as if Hall set him to pause-mode, just like how he appeared in the room back at the estate.

"My old friend has left the conversation and is back in his body next to you wherever you two are, equipped with what little information I could provide. While I hate for you to leave, I look forward to seeing you soon in person." He tucked a piece of hair behind my ear that was blowing loose in the light breeze. "Anytime you want a discreet meet up, you are always welcome."

"Inside your head."

A smile stretched across his full lips. "Anywhere you want."

Before I could respond, the weight of his large hand on my shoulder booted me from the field and back into the estate's guest bedroom where Vincent was looking at me, waiting.

"Please be careful."

A shiver ran through me at the loss of the penetrating sun, now back into a Canadian winter wonderland.

"What? I didn't do anything."

"Not yet."

"*Pfft.* I have a—"

Vincent shook his head. "Not my concern. Nor Hall's. You are a strong woman with full dominion over your body and who you share it with. My concern is not your current relationship and what heart-break it may cause, but the danger of Hall's lifestyle and how easily one may become a target in his stead."

Vincent went to open the bedroom door.

"You mean others he's cared about were killed instead of him because of the undercover work he does?"

Vincent nodded, left the room, and I followed him towards the open attic access door wondering who died instead of Hall and how long ago it may have happened. Vincent made it sound as if it was his wife or someone close to it. What a shame for Hall.

Magics were standing in the hallway and eyed Vincent and me leaving the same room. I ignored their side-eyed assumptions to go upstairs and check on things, including work on a possible reason why Hinapouri and Miklos gave the Sovereignty the discus. If that's what really happened. Hall even said he wasn't positive. I shoved thoughts of the Viking aside as I didn't need opinions of a man I wasn't going to have a future with getting in the way of saving Sophie and Donovan.

Though, I should call the man who was in my life in case the mission went sideways.

———

Ranlyn was staking out the field looking for opportune placements for portals so our people could drop into the field. To our benefit, most of the surrounding trees were Pine and created perfect hiding places to gather defences when they landed. Since Ranlyn was profi-cient at portal making and out of range, I watched Vincent dealing with anyone and everyone calling with questions and expecting answers. He let many calls dump into his voicemail to tackle when he could and glared at Veata for not sharing the responsibility of the ones he did take on.

When Vincent hung up from another call, I approached. "Cursing Sophie for talking you into becoming an Elder yet?"

He made a noise not quite a laugh. "In some moments, yes. Though inside the current timeframe, I am simply overjoyed to be in the position to access all resources to ensure her safety and eventual return."

"Ensuring sounds pretty cocky considering what we're up against."

"I supposed it appears as such. Hatred built on an empty stomach is best left for those who deserve it and the Sorrels and those in my family surely do. While they have immortality, they are not infallible. I will see them freed."

"Or I will. Unless you plan on being there instead of on the frontlines."

"Is the Sorrel Compound not a frontline of sorts?"

I couldn't argue that even if his answer didn't solidify his whereabouts when everything went down.

His phone rang again, preventing me from digging.

The frantic voice I could hear without it being on speaker was one I didn't know.

"Moira?"

The person who is supposed to look after Andy? Has to be. It's not a common name these days.

Whoever Moira was, she was whisper-yelling into the phone, but I couldn't hear everything she was saying. Someplace was infiltrated. Her home, maybe?

"What's The Chiff?"

He spun at me with such fierceness, I recoiled. "Shit. What? What'd I say?"

Vincent moved towards a less populated part of the attic and then to the attic entrance, stopping before actually leaving as if his thoughts were as frantic as this Moira person was.

He stopped moving and I could hear her speaking again.

"Neilan found me. We're hiding but they're going to find us."

Vincent was breathing too fast and removed his glasses in a helpless way as screaming and crying spilled from the speaker on the phone.

"Can you proceed to the forest exit?" Seconds passed without an answer. "Moira!" Loud muffles and more screams came from the call. I didn't know what was happening, but it was bad.

"I don't know what to do." The shaky voice on the phone was so heartbreaking it brought tears to my eyes.

"Moira, can you proceed to the forest exit?" Vincent reiterated.

"Not without the—"

"I know the incantation," Vincent interrupted. "Be there. I will meet you outside. If you are not present when I arrive, I will find you." The background noise wasn't as loud as before. Maybe this was a good thing. Or maybe less people were alive to cry for help.

"It was your defecting Elders, Vincent," Moira said with certainty in her tone. "I thought no evil could breach The Chiff's defences."

Vincent paled as I covered my mouth against wanting to scream at something, anything. "Fight your way to the exit, Moira. I will be there. I promise."

Vincent ended the call, took a breath, and stuck his phone in his pocket. "Listen up!"

The group in the attic quieted, though anyone would after hearing him yell. He was usually uptight and composed.

"The Chiff has been infiltrated." Gasps came from a few in the room, but most looked at me and each other for explanation. "The Chiff..." He shook his head. "It is a name I should be unable to utter because of the painstaking precautions to prevent word-of-mouth, thus solidifying my theory an insider tore open one of Magics' best kept secrets and destroyed thousands of lives in the process. Unless you have been thoroughly vetted against all sources of Tainted affiliation and are formally invited, you would know nothing of its existence.

"Some living within the safety of the dwelling have never stepped foot outside of it and have never found cause to fight as most of you have. At this very moment, our former Elders, Hinapouri and Miklos, are targeting these innocents with unfathomable ruthlessness, tantamount to attacking a nursery.

"I need bodies to assist where we can. Anyone who can transport others, anyone. I need you now."

Adam stepped forward. "What about the Creation and getting back my sister? She an afterthought now?"

"We have time. But please, we must hurry. Some will be escaping into a freezing cold forest in a place unfamiliar to them."

Was there really enough time for this rescue mission when two others were already in the plans? I wanted to trust Vincent, but he was losing it and maybe not looking at things like timelines very clearly.

With the cars we did have access to, we could fit a rather large group with or without seatbelts. Not to fight; to save the few we could.

I let Jared drive my car in favour of going with Vincent—I wanted to know everything that was happening the instant it was happening and wasn't letting him out of my sight. Adam took Sophie's Barracuda, Serena jumped into the aunts' VW bus, and Lewis drove his own. Sophie's mother's vehicle was in the driveway, but Bosco and Andy still needed a way to escape if we didn't return in time. Including Vincent's SUV and some others I didn't know as well, we had ample room to stuff people in, though I didn't know what we would do with them once we saved them.

If reopening the Creation didn't spark a war, ex-Elders attacking a place most people didn't know about that housed countless Magics on the bright side of soul glows, this sure would. I didn't know how Hinapouri and Miklos are justifying going this far. It didn't make sense to kill innocent Magics in order to save innocent Magics.

Running through every red light and stop sign, Vincent didn't slow when he spoke to his SUV's system to "Call Nora". Again, another name I didn't know.

On the second ring, a deep voice answered.

"Who is this?" Vincent illegally passed an emission-poisoning minivan.

A deep laugh came through the SUV's system, its owner one who half-surprised Vincent, though I didn't recognize the voice.

Vincent inhaled, his grip tightening on the steering wheel. "I see."

"Do you?"

"Nora was the insider," Vincent said this with confidence. Insider of where wasn't mentioned. "Why would she betray her own? Her family has run The Chiff for generations."

Okay, so the owner and operator of this secret place turned on her people. Disloyal assholes can't learn to choose a side and stick with it.

"Did you kill her?" Vincent asked the voice on the line. I still didn't know who it was.

"Yes."

The mysterious, pompous voice held zero remorse. Though, if Nora and the voice were on the same side, why kill her? I wanted so badly to ask questions, but the voice didn't know I was listening in, and I wasn't about to announce myself if Vincent didn't.

"Good."

The laugh sparked again. "Why you believed The Chiff dwellers could offer sufficient safeguarding against Magics like Evaristus or myself..." They paused in astonishment. "It's pathetic, brother."

I clasped my hands over my gasp and then fiercely mouthed "Brother?" at Vincent. His attention panned back to the road and navigated around traffic as my brain spiralled.

The head of the Sovereignty conspired with our ex-Elders and attacked a place full of non-Tainted Magics, let in by the person who was supposed to keep the place safe.

Oh, man. We were so fucking screwed. Everything kept getting worse and worse. Kind of made me want to retreat to Hall's little slice of heaven with nothing to worry about but sun exposure and a bug or two buzzing in my ear.

How were we supposed to keep anyone safe when all the people in charge of doing that were the ones killing them off?

Plus, by the way Vincent reacted, he believed his brother. What if this Nora person didn't set things up? How was Vincent so sure she did?

Vincent didn't respond to Chase as his gaze shifted mechanically at the traffic he swerved through.

"You should seriously reconsider, Vincent," Chase said with a song in his voice.

"I appreciate your condescending proposal, Charles, nevertheless you have in no manner—"

"Blah, blah, blah. We can't afford to bypass assimilation in this new world, and yet, you insist on the old ways, boring me to death with the same response, never stepping outside of your perfect diction even in anger. Join this century and live a little." He laughed in that pretentious way to the silence on our end. "Better yet, brother, work with me to define it. Very soon the Magic population will be needing a leader to turn to. Who do think that's going to be?"

"I agree leadership will be sought but I guarantee you, this person will not be you nor the Sovereignty and I will not be a part of either one."

"Bold statement."

"I beg to differ, Charles. When they seek this leader, the Sovereignty will be extinct and the offices and court rooms you serve will be chaired by Magics of worth. However, I have decided I will not kill you."

Chase full-out laughed at this. "How very kind."

"Instead, I will imprison you and keep you alive until you have suffered every brand of torture and degradation you have caused innocent prisoners under your reign."

Chase laughed again. "Hey, there's the spirit, brother. I knew Father's blood was in those veins after all."

At this, Vincent shook his head as if he disappointed himself and disconnected the line.

"To steal a saying from Sophie, what the fizz was that, Vincent? We're literally driving towards your brother hoping he won't be too pissed to get his hands a little dirtier."

"I couldn't hear any background chaos on the phone. He may not be in The Chiff."

"He said he killed Nora. Would she not be there?"

He scoffed. "And he probably did end her life. Or more likely ordered another to kill her while he played witness to ensure she understood the true culprit behind the death sentence."

"Or he lied and kidnapped and tortured her instead."

"I have no sufficient answers for you, Kim."

I knew he didn't, but it didn't stop me from wanting them.

Whomever Moira and the others were, I hoped they were at the meeting point so we wouldn't have to go inside and face Vincent's brother. The time for family drama was around the Thanksgiving table, not right now, and not when the drama resulted in needing to cover up murder.

Everyone parked their cars by the road, but The Chiff's secret exit was only accessible on foot. No one told me where the normal entrance was. No one said anything about it, though if the place was as huge as it sounded, you'd think it would be easy to find.

I zipped up my coat and, at a run, followed Vincent and all of the others who came to help through the trees. No matter what the man did, he did it in those damn loafers and he did it with better control and speed than I did. I couldn't feel a sense of power, but it didn't mean he wasn't using any or at least that's what I told myself every time I slipped around on the slick snow.

I had been in these woods before, mostly as a kid and once on a date that turned sketchy. I never saw a door or anything.

I stopped short when Vincent bent for something, spouting off a few words I tried to tuck away in my brain for later. A metal door revealed itself. He spoke another short incantation and the sound of metal sliding was muffled through the door. He grabbed the handle just as it was being pushed open from the other side. Everyone in the woods poised to attack.

A terrified, wide-eyed, and very dirty man exited first and recoiled when he saw us, his deep-set eyes lingering on mine.

"You are okay, Neilan." Vincent extended a hand to the man who shifted to elation as he recognized Vincent.

Right behind the man was an older woman who practically fell into Vincent's arms in sobs as the man and Vincent helped her. She looked body-worn, emotionally exhausted, and in need of an inhaler. I'd be surprised if the woman ever battled a day in her life. Same with the man.

People really lived down there?

More followed after them. Not as many as there should have been considering Vincent said thousands were in there, but it still ended up being far more than our cars could accommodate. Fortunately, some of them were more worldly than others with family or people they could contact to find safety, even some who agreed to take in displaced Magics.

Others must have seen the group escape as more people rushed the exit like panicked ants. They didn't wait for instruction or guidance, they just took off.

Damn. Why were they so dirty? Was it from whatever happened down there? Their clothing was torn and filthy layers of whatever somewhat fit their bodies as if it was one big homeless shelter down there.

Their escape seemed a little too easy, but I didn't want to jinx it. They were clearly attacked, though none of the enemy followed them through this exit. Did they not know about it? Maybe they let them go for a reason. What that reason could be was over my head since I didn't even know why they were down there. If the message was that their hideout was no longer an option, it was a clear one.

"Shouldn't we go down there and make sure others don't need our help? What if they're hiding or injured?" I couldn't leave without knowing something was being done.

"A team will be sent down to assess need." Vincent stood over Moira who was lying on the ground as she caught her breath. "Chase and his people would have left long ago, though others may require aid."

"They flooded the bottom levels and deactivated the spelled doors so no one could access the higher levels." Moira then went on a coughing fit.

I've never been to this place, but I got the gist of what she implied and pictured the scene of the movie *Titanic* when the lower levels were filling with water and people were trapped. If it was anything close to that, I was going to lose it. Vincent shook his head, eyes closed, and lips pursed when Moira wasn't looking, not exactly helping my visual. Any Magics on those lower levels were already gone and no one gave me any indication how many that could be.

After getting Moira and Neilan plus another couple of people jammed into the back of the SUV and into the other vehicles while some Magics went into The Chiff to see what else they could do, we headed for the Ballard Estate. Vincent called on the Tactical Team and deployed them to assess the situation and do what they could with those who already went in, reminding them of the original plans still in motion without repeating it in front of the others. Last thing we needed was for the Tactical Team members to die when they were supposed to escort me in and out of the Sorrel Compound.

Another call came through, and this one he answered by hand. I braced for something else happening to shit on our parade as he stayed quiet and listened.

Vincent said nothing and ended the call. "We need to make a stop."

10

SHUT DOWN

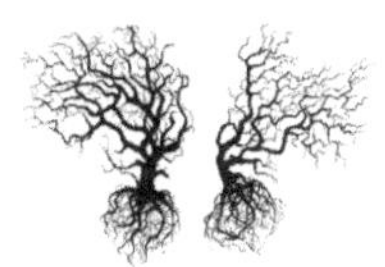

Donovan

Why won't he just kill me? Since my last steps off the compound brought me to Fox's as a teen, death was all I waited for. Always looking over my shoulder and living life like it was already over. With all the talent and resources at Tobias's fingers, taking his rebellious son's life would have been as easy a target as the pool table jockeys I used to swindle. So why didn't Tobias pull the trigger in some club alley?

He probably loved me contemplating my death every waking hour.

I paced and flexed my fingers before clenching them over and over again, staring at the door. Eating, showering, even taking a shit wouldn't keep me from being Johnny on the spot when a visitor barged in. And they would come in unannounced whenever they wanted to.

Any future I cooked up involved me in a coffin or caged like an animal. Now, with Sophie...She changed everything.

Where was she? I pressed my fingers into my chest where I

usually felt our connection. The space was now empty of anything except regret for not killing my father before now. I couldn't feel her at all. When, exactly, did it stop? I couldn't pinpoint the moment while my father made me do what I did. She had to know that I didn't want it, she had to.

Fox explained Soul Magic's pitfalls, but surprise, I never thought it would happen to us. Never thought something wise ol' Fox warned me against would come true. Maybe we wouldn't live the life I hoped we could, but cutting me off, shutting the connection down, she couldn't do that to me, could she? No. Something else has got to be happening. Tobias did something to her. Keeping her alive but incapacitated? I don't know. Something.

Hell, I never deserved her anyway. Not in this life. Probably never in the others either. Her detesting the thought of being connected to me in anyway...She didn't know what that would do to us. I never told her about the dangers Fox warned me about. I never told her of the Conception Rituals. When she saw some of my past, it was all the physical torture and humiliation sitting out front, overshadowing the psychological scarring squatting in the swamp of my memories. Now Sophie actually thought I wanted those brainwashed—

I forced myself to stop before the memory of Tobias's "fun times" caused me to break more things. Though most everything left was indestructible. If only I retained a morsel of my power, I'd bulldoze through the door and Sophie's and...and what? Considering the reaction I expected from her, it made the bologna sandwich in my clenching gut scramble for an exit strategy better found than my freedom.

The sandwich found it and tasted like ass coming up, washing my tastebuds in stomach acid and stale, bland bread they probably scraped the mold off of and grazed butter and mustard on for a dash of flavour. It could have been laced with something that would knock me unconscious again, but if they wanted me, nothing I could do would stop them, so I may as well eat.

Keeping it down was a whole other deal.

After my heaves became dry, I laid on the floor and stared at a crack in the cement ceiling, feeling just as damaged.

I closed my eyes and searched for Sophie again, willing her to talk to me, begging for her to break my loneliness, and help me feel anything other than what I was feeling right now. And as I had every five minutes since she slipped away, I found nothing and got nothing back.

Where was she?

11

EASE THE PAIN

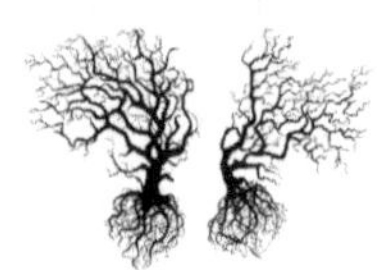

Sophie

Puking was my most potent enemy. It skipped hand-in-hand into my cement box with its bestie Migraine and together left me a rocking heap on the not-cold-enough floor. A windowless room was heaven. If only I could control the damn overhead lights causing auras to sting my strained eyes without any souls around to blind me. The blanket wasn't thick enough to hide under and added to the sweating.

Angry "whys" and angrier answers, and then reverting onto myself with angrier "why nots" flooded my non-consenting introspection as I pressed the thin scrap of pillow around my head and cursed it for the little reprieve it granted until my arms didn't have the strength to hold the vice.

If I could only pass out, I might wake up migraine-free and ready to defend myself since I was now in this alone.

Donovan was who he was. That tag was the theme of his existence and should have been a tramp stamp Fox tattooed in technicolour. The brash attitude, the cockiness, the self-serving opportunism. All of which now translated into another conquest serving his precious ego. I couldn't blame the other vaginas or maybe dicks in this equation when my genitals were no less innocent of falling for his ploys.

"Can you hate me that much?"

My eyesight whirled and bled objects into one before settling and focusing on the middle of the room where Donovan stood. The question may have been but a whisper, but I heard him and wanted to rip the unapologetic glare, equipped with those dimples, off of his face.

"How can you not hate yourself?" My words were slurred in my ears.

I could barely hold my head up to keep staring at him, the pain was pounding so badly and making me nauseous.

When Donovan bowed his head, I nearly felt sorry for making the dig, until his eyes reconnected with mine and were filled with nothing but his mocking, asshole attitude. How? How did I fall for his shit so easily? I hated myself for being so gullible to believe he was more than a charming douchebag.

Distracted by my starved, clenching stomach and pounding skull it took me a moment to realize Donovan was gone. This happened a few times now. Initially, I thought I was dreaming, until he picked up and smelled a stale sandwich I refused to eat. My stomach growled at the memory of inspecting all the meals that came before and went uneaten.

Now gone, those dimples evoked fresh reminders of our past intimacy, making my skin shudder as if it could shed off my bones and scurry off into the corner. I hated those memories knowing everything he pretended to enjoy from me was used to enjoy someone else.

The animal coat came in and took the uneaten food away. He paused, looking me over on the floor in a flash of hesitation where he seemed to waffle on wanting to say something, yet kept to himself. I never entertained a conversation either since he was trapping me here. Gorgeousness didn't change a Tainted soul. The room took all my powers, even my Soul Seeing, but I didn't need to see Caveman's soul to know he was likely Tainted to his core. His station in the compound said enough and pegged him as another pretty face who would relish the chance to manipulate me.

Plus, I was not in prime fucking mode at the moment. And if he was into this mess, he was not a worthy revenge-fuck.

Ugh, those fucking lights.

Their brightness raked my retinas, the tears they caused blurring my eyesight and were the reason I didn't see Donovan leave.

Control over my visitors would be grand and was another reason I questioned Donovan's visits. The metallic door never groaned when he came and went, meaning he never used the door. So how did he get in? Was he that powerful that he didn't need to use the door? Some kind of astral projection or something? Every visit left me a tenderized piece of meat after he had marinated me for four days in his unending pride and triumph for conning me. Or however long I've been stuck here.

As quickly as Donovan left, another visitor popped in, their visit equally seamless, without the need of his physical presence. A voice called my name, deep and gravelly. At first it was easy to assume the pounding in my ears drowned out the sound of the groaning metal door, but as I struggled to sit and lean against the wall facing the entrance, no one else was in the cell.

Again, my name was called. I refused to answer, sifting my mental Rolodex for a face to match the voice and coming up empty.

"That's because you haven't heard my voice before."

Okay. *"Who is this?"*

"Animal coat guy outside your door."

I should've guessed by the deep tone. It suited Caveman perfectly.

His laugh resonated in my aching skull. *"You think like your red-headed friend."*

"You know Kim?" Instantly I regretted the admission. I thought again of what I said and what it could cost my best friend. I was so

overjoyed to hear anything about her I didn't think of the danger it poised to confirm we knew each other.

"We've met a few times. You'll reunite soon." This sounded like a promise. *"Right now, I need you to listen."*

I went silent, easily obedient when being upright took all of my energy.

"The tortures your mate has been through are not his doing. Tobias has completed the Conception Rituals twice over now. If you allow it, the Soul Magic between you and your mate will poison the both of you."

There was too much of what Caveman said that I didn't understand. It wasn't the migraine, he just didn't make sense. Though it was curious he knew about any connection between me and Donovan since this guy was essentially a grunt. Though, if Donovan switched sides, he would have told his father everything.

"Donovan is not the brand." The strong voice rang in my already banging temples making me claw for my scalp. *"Nor has he stepped foot inside your cell. Tobias's trickery."*

Tricks?

I pressed my fingertips against my temples trying to ease the pain a fraction and manage to think clearly and ignore my nausea.

I didn't hear the door open each time Donovan showed up. Could have been a trick. Or this was just a different trick meant to keep me confused. I didn't know this guy. He was one of Tobias's people.

"Listen," the voice redirected. *"None of this is your mate's fault. Once the time has come, you will be reunited with him and the redhead, and we'll leave here when I co—"*

His words cut off.

A groan of metal shot my weighted eyes to the door. Caveman opened it wide dutifully for Tobias. Caveman didn't say anything, but his fierce gaze conveyed a message of warning not even I was too weak to interpret.

"I thought it best to visit." Tobias was fully in the cell before Caveman closed the door with himself outside.

I pulled myself to my feet in case I needed to fight, even though Tobias hadn't attempted to...yet. My jelly-like knees threatened to drop me as I leaned back against the cement wall, cool enough to keep me conscious as my stomach rolled while trying to seem strong and capable with spectacular failure.

"Reports tell me you refuse to eat."

The topic of food reminded me of how long I went without it. Felt like weeks, though was likely not.

When I didn't respond, Tobias went on. "Very well. I won't bother granting you the choice."

Again, no response, though I understood the food option was firmly off the table.

"Of all the families to align yourself with, do you find yourself lucky to be with that of my son's?"

"He's not your son." Ugh, damn him for making me defend Donovan. Fucker.

"I remember the day well."

"I remember the sight of you torturing him well. Forget about the whole parenting thing after you cut the cord? Fathers don't torture their children."

Tobias pushed his hands into his dress pant pockets, his strong chin flush with the floor in weighing smugness. "It's not as if Donovan would die. His genes are too useful for that. He needed only to believe his life would end."

"Why kill Eli?" I jumped topics, eager to talk about anything other than Donovan.

A grin crept. "I thought my reasoning was crystal clear at the scene. Collusion with the enemy holds great penalty. Eli paid not only for his treason against my Coven but for the disappointment he brought to his namesake. The Berisfords have a far reach. No need to dirty their hands. Nonetheless, they were pleased with the result."

"Interesting. You took on a job like a hired thug. Thought you were, I don't know, more important than that."

Silence ensued, he not taking the bait, but I was right. The Berisfords must be a bigger deal than Caine's now-dead father. I wondered how much Caine knew about them.

No amount of arguing would skew Tobias's perspective. My opinion meant dick-all to the man. Why did he bother visiting or talking to me at all? Occupational obligation? Curiosity?

"Any message to pass along to my heir? I plan to meet with him when I leave you."

My daggered stare spoke for me, knowing he wouldn't pass along anything even if I did have something to say to the asshole.

"Alright," Tobias said with a fake smile. "I guess the premonition did nothing to bring upon your victorious ending. More reasons to have weak faith in those wise Elders you dote on." Spinning on his heel, Tobias looked at the door and it opened as if he willed it, though the Caveman knew when to open it up for him. Caveman then allowed his Master to pass by before sealing me back in.

Glad to be alone, I slid to the floor. More so flopped onto the cement as my head swayed as I fought to stay conscious. I was so weak. It hadn't been long, but no food on top of vomiting and dehydration...I couldn't keep this up forever without truly passing out and not waking up again.

I curled into myself and covered my face with the crappy blanket, hearing nothing more from the Caveman.

Tobias was right, I realized. What was the point of the premonition? We racked our brains to decipher it. Much of it happened exactly how it said it would, and unlike what Tobias said, it never guaranteed our success, simply stating that everything we did would lead to a civil war. I'm sure it has or will. The Creation hasn't been opened yet which was the true cause of the break in the Coven. Tobias would've gloated about what happened if it had.

All it did was make us try and change our future, add armament like Fox's tattoos which clearly don't work in the cells, and instead landed our asses straight into Tobias's creepy awaiting hands anyway. Hinapouri and Miklos saw this fight coming and tried to stop it. We couldn't let them kill us, and no fucking way was I leaving Caine in the Creation to rot with my egomaniacal ancestor. But was the rest of this worth it? We even made a truce with Donovan's mother. Or he let me think he hadn't seen her since he was a child. Probably another manipulation tactic.

We would have been better off not knowing a thing about the stupid premonition, which meant if the others went ahead with the plan, Caine wouldn't have a clue we were busting into the Creation and the survivors would be blindsided, possibly not making it out at all.

My brain hurt too much for this much thinking.

The sheer stupidity of believing I could pull off something so complicated was pathetic. Or pure ego. Either way the hit of "you goddamned moron" slapped me around until it left welts. I'm a bartender, not the "change-the-world" kind of chick my schoolbooks outlined others in the psychiatry business. All of it. Pure ridiculousness.

This realization sunk me deep within myself. Not as in reading my soul—I wished I could, the distraction would be blissful—but more of a sinking depression that beat me down with every passing monotonous second.

Time passed before I could concentrate on what Caveman said. Did he really know Kim? Or was he an Olson replica and pretending to be on my side as part of the Sorrel Compound spa package? Why defend Donovan if he was messing with me? Caveman has been mute since then and there was no way to tell what he would've said if Tobias hadn't interrupted.

It was the first time in what felt like days that my curiosity shifted to Donovan in any form other than detesting his existence. What was he doing? Tobias insinuated he was also in a cell, but was he? I sure as fuck hoped so.

What tortures did the Caveman talk about? The Conception

Rituals for one. I understood the insinuation behind the moniker but how was blissful sex torture? Donovan loves sex and I felt what he did. During the dozens of orgasms he dragged me through, with whatever coven extras throwing themselves at him, he enjoyed every single one of them. Maybe he was their new Master and taking up the robe meant mounting his subordinates in a show of dominance. Far too *Animal Planet*, but not out of the realm of possibility. Tobias didn't specify he was seeing Donovan in a cell. He could be in his newly acquired throne room getting a pedicure by a pack of naked debutants.

If so, he could move around as he pleased and sneak into my cell whenever he wanted, however he wanted, be it in person or some type of projection. Was it possible him visiting was an illusion like the Caveman said? Tobias was powerful enough to pull it off, but so was Donovan, and it would be easier for both of them if I laid here and wasted away.

At least if I died, I could steal Donovan from this life and fuck over Tobias's plans.

12

———

WIN-WIN THEORY

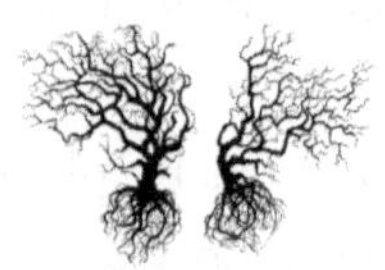

Donovan

"She refuses all sustenance." Tobias stood comfortably in my cell looking around at the destruction I created with casual curiosity. "This doesn't matter since we can heal her from starvation though she finds the mote of rebellion worth committing to."

"Worth more than your commitment in keeping me around? Why create more of me when I want nothing to do with you? You're not afraid those bastards will turn out like me and tell you to shove your throne up your ass?"

Tobias shrugged. "All young minds can be molded."

"Apparently not mine. Guess I'm as special as you thought I was." I was sick of the sight of him. "Why are you here again? You haven't seen me this much my entire life."

"Thought I should visit before your transfer."

This created mixed excitement in my gut. No matter where I was going, at least I wouldn't be here.

"No curiosity for your next destination?"

"Do I get Air Miles?"

The edges of Tobias's lips twitched. "No. Only a new cell far less padded than this one."

The Sovereignty. Had to be. "We have people inside the Sovereignty. You sure you trust they can keep me contained once you hand me over?"

Tobias smiled and glanced at the floor before taking a step towards me. "Hold on to that hope, son. You will be lucky to see the spoils of your heirs as old men, let alone the outcome of the siege for Evaristus's release."

Since people didn't age in the Sovereignty cells, he may be right. I never wanted kids, never got a chance to decide if I did, and now I'll have scores of little buggers who won't know how unwanted they truly were—at least by me.

"They will know who they share blood with, and your incarceration will be a warning to them if they refuse to fall in line." Tobias was pilfering my thoughts. "And while your years are over with Sophie, if even a wayward Sovereignty guard or nurse decides you're worth their entertainment, you will never sire more kin. I have made certain of it."

Certain? How can he be certain? Wait a sec..."You sterilized me?" The question left my lips in a mere whisper.

"No sense in allowing you to father a bloodline other than those of my flock. I have what I need. Think of it as my going away gift as you should never again be burdened with the likes of an heir. You're welcome, son."

Always available to kick a broken puppy, Tobias passed along his proclamation and left.

He made me infertile. Of all the things he could do to me, has done to me, that piece of shit took away my biggest choice and one he has always lorded over. To be a father when I wanted it and not because a Coven needed an heir or a splash of new DNA to stave away inbred mutations. I didn't even want kids, not now, probably not ever, but to make it so that I can't…The tremble in my hands vibrated until I punched the wall over and over again.

Bones in my hands snapped, fresh blood splattered, it didn't matter. I wanted to get out, needed to get out, not even to escape. Dying while my hands were clenched around my father's throat was a perfect way to go.

I sagged to the metal and mattress when my energy gave up and my body couldn't handle it anymore without the ability to heal enough to continue hitting things.

Tobias took everything from me. And soon, the Sovereignty would give me another place to gnaw on the leftover bits. As long as they kept me breathing and the world wasn't destroyed from underneath my cell floor, the infinite amount of time I could spend locked in a Sovereignty cell was unimaginable.

An odd sensation in my chest caused me to palm my sternum, it spreading the length of my fingers. What was that? Anxiety about the Sovereignty cells? I forced my breath to steady and bring my heartrate down. Before I could identify it, the sensation vanished.

While taking a piss, as I wasn't given a timeline for this transfer Tobias mentioned, it occurred to me that I felt the sensation before. Not until I was lying on my back in bed did I realize the feeling was Sophie.

She reached out.

Goddamned piece of shit, how could I have fucking missed it? After days of her giving me the cold shoulder, she finally sent out feelers and found what? Nothing, because I was a prick who couldn't learn to pay fucking attention.

"Come on, come on." I sat on the edge of the mattress, a desperate palm to my chest searching for that string, the connecting thread that bound us, but she wasn't there. No matter the exertion I applied, no matter the torrent of anger I stirred, it was useless. Of all the heinousness I managed to snake my way around, this was something she controlled. I couldn't reach her unless she wanted me to.

Hands tied from not being able to see or speak or even feel her was driving me insane. Our lives weren't supposed to be like this. They weren't in different lifetimes. We were on the same page before and now we're not even in the same library. And this stupid fucking cell kept me from tearing through the compound to show her how messed up that was. Maybe kill Tobias on my way before they cut me down. If it didn't mean ending Sophie's life, I would have.

A morbid idea sparked. Not the first time, yet the wheels were turning faster on making it happen.

In death we recycle. We would find each other again and truly be free of Tobias and the mindless quest to kill the un-killable Evaristus. Not to mention Loring. They may all be dead when we resurface. Or they may be running the planet. Forgetting about what was done here was gravy on my mashed potatoes. On the other hand, did not feeling Sophie mean she broke our connection? Would we recycle together again or were we truly done?

Crashing through the imagery of how I could murder the love of my many lives was the cell door reopening and slamming shut behind...Rosemary?

"Why haven't you left?" Rosemary sneered. "Of all the times you've been imprisoned here, you chose this time to sit idle?"

"Sit idle? Do you have any idea—?"

"Yes. I do." Rosemary's interruption came with a pointed stare. She knew about the Conception Rituals.

Embarrassment flooded me and sent me pacing. At least she wasn't in the crowd.

"I can't leave Sophie and I don't know where she is." I could see Rosemary assumed this and she didn't look happy. "I'm not leaving her with him."

"You would murder yourself instead? I'm sure she could love you after knowing that."

Shame railed through me. I just wanted the pain to stop, for Sophie too.

"Ending pain, I understand too well. We all reach deep levels of desperation at one time or another, which is why I'm here. The timeline changes every hour and it's been long enough. Tobias has used you up and has no reason for keeping you alive."

"And you thought waiting until after I was 'used up' was the perfect time to step in?"

Her brows stitched together. "Yes. Before he got what he wanted he lorded over this door day and night. Now, he has other priorities and was dumb enough to think I didn't still have contacts in the compound."

Still. She waited.

My parents weren't of the normal variety and never would understand how fucked this was. "I thought we were being transferred?"

"And you believe Tobias would hand over a rival that's eluded him for over a decade? You are a trophy worth shelving. Tobias may have brokered a deal, but he has no intention of following through if it means letting you out of his sight. We leave now before they euthanize you publicly. This time, Tobias would bleed you and Sophie to dry husks in ritualistic celebration before the flock without a Healer on standby and deal with the supercilious Sovereignty later."

Either way was a win for me. If we were tortured to death, we would be free to recycle. If we botched the escape and died, again, we would be free.

"How do you think Sophie would feel about your win-win theory?"

Forgetting only my power was mute inside the cell and not hers, I steeled. "This life you gave me is shit shovelled through a meat grinder. I think any future version of herself would understand."

A twitch of something close to guilt was smothered quickly. "You underestimate her love for her family. Your parents may have been flunkies but hers deserve her in this life, wouldn't you agree?"

Without waiting for a response, this time Rosemary grabbed for the door and walked out as if casually entering the grocery store. I hesitated at the threshold to survey the hallways that stretched at my flanks, remembering the institutional yellow of the walls as it was then instead of the institutional taupe it was now.

"Now?" asked a big man I remembered being at the Conception Rituals and outside my door. He was angry enough I bet he skinned the sheep he was wearing himself.

Rosemary and the man continued to argue as I approached them in bare feet on the cold floor.

"Neither the Tactical Team nor the others are in position. You expect the two of us to pull this off?" The closer I got I realized how big the man was.

"Not ready to pull your cover, Reconnitor?" Rosemary stepped up to the guy like he was wearing a clown nose.

The man's eyes narrowed. "Vincent—"

"—works too damn slow. You want something done, you do it. If he prefers his precious Charges in pieces, then he can take his time."

"His what?" Did she mean Sophie and me?

The big guy's expression tightened, and he closed the gap an inch to glare at Rosemary. She side-eyed me as if she slipped up about something.

"His Charges?" I repeated with invitation in my tone for her to fill me in.

Rosemary was unwilling to explain and pressured us to move along. She may think it was over, but I was circling back to this conversation once we found safety. Whatever Sophie or me being Vincent's Charge meant, it was another thing the shady asshole was keeping from us as Sophie would've mentioned something about it to me before. I huffed and followed the thud of the big guy's leather boots.

Rosemary stopped when we reached a clear-walled room.

I gasped. Couldn't stop myself from it. I didn't look at my own cell from the outside. How crafty. They were constructed so the prisoner couldn't see through the walls, but everyone outside the cell could observe everything. They looked and felt like cement on the inside. From the hallway, it appeared as clear as glass.

There she was. The sight of Sophie stabbed a sick hollowness inside of me for her suffering was so clearly all over her. I never saw her so sick. Long hair matted and unwashed, skin sallow. As she sat on the floor against a wall with her knees curled to her chest, it was her eyes that slashed me. They stared into nothingness, half-hooded in exhaustion as dark circles coloured them as if she hadn't slept for ages.

"Migraines." The big guy's voice came from behind me. "Guess it's a thing with her."

More than a thing. She was stuck in this place and in pain she couldn't heal. She couldn't even use a cold cloth or turn off the lights.

Her pain was all my fault.

No matter how much I wanted to hold her, I couldn't force myself to reach for the door. The big guy did it for me, pushing passed Rosemary and swinging it open. From then, I couldn't imagine looking Sophie in the eyes. I glued mine to the floor and listened, wishing I possessed the power to mess with time and erase all of this.

"Time to go, Soul Seer." The big guy didn't lower his voice, and I wanted to punch him. He knew Sophie had a migraine.

Nothing was said in return. Was she too weak to talk?

"Nah, Chase will have to wait to get his hands on you. How about wherever you call home instead?"

The big guy could hear her thoughts. She believed she was being transferred. Tobias must have told her the Sovereignty was going to take her, just as he told me.

Some scuffling came from inside the room. A quiet mewling noise from Sophie was heartbreaking enough for me to bite down on the inside of my cheek to stop myself from looking up and running to help her.

Then Sophie's bare feet came into my periphery along with the big guy's boots as if he had to support her every step to help her outside of the cell.

She inhaled and moaned like the cell wasn't equipped with

oxygen. Being clear of the cell must have reinstated her power. Maybe even healed her migraine. If she hasn't eaten since we got here, she would still be weak, but it was a start.

Fuck. Feet from each other, unimpeded by the cell, and still, I couldn't sense her or the connection. Whatever she was feeling, emotionally or physically, was hers and hers alone.

A small gasp from Sophie and my head whipped up in a reaction I couldn't help, but she was staring at Rosemary.

"It's okay. She only looks scary." The big guy was doing what I should've been able to do by reassuring Sophie she was safe, but I couldn't force myself to do anything except look away as Sophie seemed to trust Rosemary wasn't going to attack.

13

HUNTING PARTY

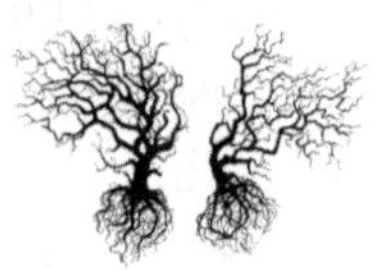

Sophie

Being in Caveman's arms wasn't a bad place to be as I somewhat trusted he wouldn't hand me off to Chase. Even if he did, it was better than this cell, and at least I could find comfort in his burly hold.

An inch outside of the cell and my power was restored, triggering my healing ability, my migraine bleeding away so fast my knees nearly buckled. Even my stomach muscles unclenched, and my diaphragm expanded for a full breath without feeling the need to hurl. I was still starving and so thirsty, but the pain itself was taken down a few notches.

Rosemary! Fuck!

Donovan looked up in a momentary shock when I gasped and then turned away from me as fast as he could while I focused on his mother.

Caveman kept his hold on me as my instinct was to run away. Maybe he sensed it. He seemed like the hunting type. "It's okay. She only looks scary."

He had a sense of humour. How nice.

With a couple of blinks, the soul glows around me were back. Wouldn't help keep me from getting another headache, but now I could see who would be helping us and who was getting in our way.

Caveman's soul was a tad murky. He worked in the compound, but his soul didn't look how I expected. Far lighter than the Apporter. Not Tainted, yet a hint of something was there. He must be a great actor for his soul to survive this line of work. Why work for Tobias at all if you don't play for his side?

Rosemary's soul was as it always was, dark as fuck and billowing around her like a vampire's cloak.

Curiosity found me glancing at Donovan. No Taint on his soul. Meaning he didn't have any extra hate or evil in him, but it didn't mean he didn't do evil things. Instead, he wore a familiar face I saw before on another guy who treated me as if I was disposable Tupperware. Guilt. He knew what he did, and he was too much of a coward to own it.

I pushed my revulsion down enough to focus on Caveman leading us. It was either that or I would've beat the living shit out of Donovan and trapped him back in his cell for his daddy to have fun with.

Everyone but me knew their way around. This didn't stop me from staying in front with Caveman and pretending the map was seared into my brain, Donovan consigning himself to the back where he wouldn't have to interact with me.

Ahead of us were offices. Thankfully since we were a small group of Magics, we could manoeuvre the halls relatively unseen, at least in this section. However, Donovan and I being barefooted and in matching prison outfits would cause questions. They weren't black and white striped or neon orange, but a white t-shirt and grey jogging pants were still somehow a heatscore.

When we hit a particular intersection of long hallways, Caveman stopped and took a quick and effortless second to call a cover spell over us.

According to Caveman, the compound employed Tainted Magics serving as living security cameras. Beings with the ability to see past Magic intervention such as cloaking, even detecting bodies through walls or underground, perfect against intruders or escapees. For now, Caveman used his skills distracting certain guards with idle conversation or sending them on false errands, even chancing to use memory alteration when we slipped up with something too obvious to explain away—something Caveman was remarkably swift at, no incantation needed. This may have spoken to a Persuasion gift, but I couldn't see a colour in his soul glow besides its brightness and silver sparkle of immortality.

The Sorrel Compound itself was more than a grand single building, comprised of the main structure of various offices including physical training and health facilities as well as the cells. Out buildings still stood in our way of freedom, which meant going outside. Neither Donovan nor I wore winter gear, so the first cutting steps into the snow were lip-bitingly harsh.

Caveman swung me up to carry without making the offer first. Apparently, as far as he was concerned, Donovan could suck it up. Without the energy to protest, I didn't fight it but was happy when we reached a small building and Caveman quickly unlocked the door with a spell and slipped me to the floor inside.

The room was long, no bigger than my apartment living room and filled almost to the roof with food crates and general supplies. We ducked to the floor as Caveman stood vigilant at the small windows. This was when I realized I couldn't feel as Donovan did. The guilt he felt the instant they freed me from the cell should have poisoned me, but I felt nothing.

How was he doing it? Did he think I was too stupid to read facial cues and figured hiding his feelings all together would take care of everything? How long could he do it for?

"Now," Caveman commanded and hauled ass, pulling my attention from Donovan.

We stood to follow, taking a chance we could dodge anything

unseen. After a step, blood rushed to my head. Or maybe to my feet. Not eating catching up with me. Blackness dotted my vision and sapped the little strength left in my knees. Shit went sideways and I hit frozen ground with a thump I barely felt in the scraping ice against my skin.

The overwhelming, undefeatable weakness held onto me for too long, longer than usual, and longer than we could afford to perfect the timing Caveman was going for. I was used to fainting from vitamin B12 and iron deficiencies when poverty and stress ruled life with my ex. The muscle spasms, the laboured breath, erratic heartbeat, deafness, pitch-black blindness, the body channelling all its resources into survival mode to keep the heart beating and rebooting the brain. At least that's what it felt like. I waited out the silence as my unseeing eyes jutted around, seeking something, even if it be the enemy.

Moaning warbled in my ears as noises filtered back, my eyesight still a wash. Was it me? No. Too low.

Polka-dotted portholes of scenery came back as Donovan was also pushing himself to his feet, unsteady, yet fighting for his equilibrium as we were all back inside the storage building. What was wrong with him?

I did the same, standing in a panic of what may be coming after us, tilting on unsteady feet.

Donovan reached to catch me as I swayed—a knee-jerk reaction I pulled away from.

"Don't." Saying I was fine would've made more sense, but I was surprised my voice was working at all. No way I wanted his hands on me. He's lucky it's all I said.

Whatever his reaction was to my dismissal, I didn't see it, though I caught movement in my periphery from Rosemary, her son stopping her from coming at me. After twenty-four years of zero contact with her kid, suddenly she's ready to throw down for him? The woman didn't make sense.

I took the anchor that was the Caveman's huge hand and saw the guy peer back to Donovan with sympathy in his light eyes.

Was Donovan jealous? As if he had the right. Though, Caveman was the perfect specimen to knock Donovan down a peg or five. Petty was my new favourite colour, and I was all for painting the sky with it.

"Hold up." Caveman squeezed my hand, stopping me.

"Why?" Rosemary protested. "We need to keep moving."

"I need a minute." Caveman took his cell from his pocket. He whispered something I realized was a spell. When he took a few steps away and we couldn't hear him, I figured it was something to disguise his voice. Maybe he didn't want Rosemary to know who he was talking to. His heavy, furrowing browline and clenching fists meant it wasn't a good phone call, but it was short, nonetheless.

"Ready?" Rosemary asked impatiently as he hung up.

Caveman growled a response and hoisted me up into his arms again, moving for the door of the storage building, it opening without his touch.

A bracing wind whipped against me, causing me to curl into the Caveman's animal hide, it's musk-like scent stuck in my nose.

When I could peek through the blowing snow, emptiness stretched between single or double-storied white buildings. Not exactly military-esque, yet nothing inviting lived in their curb appeal.

The perimeter also wasn't what I expected. No barbed wire, guard-laced towers, or electrified fencing, although I got the feeling we would need to tread lightly through the open field, or a wrong step could be our last.

"No iron gates?" I asked.

Caveman's chest rumbled against my side. "Too obvious for Tobias's tastes."

A few more steps and Caveman stopped and mumbled something in another language. When he opened his eyes and saw me squinting at him through the fierce wind, he said, "Just another security code."

Without explaining more, Caveman moved forward while I did

nothing but shiver and wish Tobias's prison gear included shoes so I could stand on my own.

Thick treeline flanked our left, while the right followed an open road where designer suburbia ignorantly shovelled their uncracked sidewalks and heated driveways opposite the compound. Begging these blissfully Blind to take us in would be a quick hop across the road but didn't promise safety. Even less so for the soccer moms and golfer dads. Tobias would interrupt their secret Santa parties and kill them mid hot chocolate sipping. We needed to run as far away from Tobias as possible and find somewhere to hide.

Caveman stumbled a step when the ground trembled beneath his boots. Less than a heartbeat passed when the tremble became a pitching vibration so loud I panic-searched for trees or the houses being torn to pieces.

Rocks and dirt shot up into the air all around the property-line, followed by stone pillars growing more than twenty feet over our heads from the earth like mutant sunflowers. The pillars buzzed with energy but were yards away from each other.

"Can we—?"

I thought the space between the pillars was empty, until a warble of magic caught my eye and distorted our view of safety. No Magic could miss the strength of power pouring from the stones. The unspoken "You're not going anywhere" was enough to jolt a prisoner back into their cell without being dragged back.

"How are those not terrifying to the Blind?" I yelled over the trembling earth still settling around us.

"The Blind see nothing we don't allow."

Caveman squeezed me tighter to his body and spun to the voice who answered. A yard away from Donovan and Rosemary stood the ever so helpful Apporter, Olson.

Rage flooded me and burned in my skin, my heart thumping at the sight of the piece of shit trash bag of a Magic who kidnapped and brought me here, who tricked everyone in the Mother Coven into thinking he aligned with them, who probably took part in Aunt Lacey and the other Elders' kidnappings, tortures, and murders, and who let a psycho like Tobias stick me in a cell. This was all his fault. Everything. Everything was his fault.

"Hello, traitor," Rosemary called to the Apporter. "Present to ensure your hard work in opportunistically acquiring Donovan and Sophie wasn't wasted?"

Olson cracked a grisly smile. "Yes."

"I need to hand you to Donovan," Caveman whispered to me.

"I'll stand on my own." My feet were already freezing, so it made no difference when they sunk into the snow. No way I was letting Donovan lay a hand on me.

Caveman kept his voice lowered. "I already told you it was not his fault."

I glared up at him. "If that were true, he wouldn't've enjoyed himself so much."

Caveman stood, the crease in his heavy brow deep before he refocused on the more pressing danger.

"You can try," Olson's voice projected above the wind, though I didn't hear what he was referring to. "I promise your failure will be your only success." His lips creased into another ugly grin. "Others will come."

"We won't be here." As Rosemary carried her confidence on her shoulders, the snap of her power cut the brisk air so quickly it melted the snow between us and the Apporter.

Olson disappeared and then reappeared in the sodden grass and returned a hit that sent Rosemary soaring into the empty space between the stone barriers with incredible accuracy. She hung in the air. Foam spilled from between Rosemary's teeth as she seized. Donovan cried out in genuine horror for his mother, calling her by name, but the shock was all his. I felt nothing but the panic of what to do next.

Olson moved on to his next biggest threat—or at least the largest. Caveman anticipated an attack and sprinted for the Apporter as the Apporter came for him. Olson disappeared and reappeared a step in front of Caveman, my animal skin wearing bodyguard grabbing Olson by the collar like the man was a misbehaving child. If Olson was taking off, he was taking Caveman with him. Neither man disappeared, Caveman opting to give Olson a knuckled nose-job with three hard and fast fists to bust open the Apporter's face nice and wide and painting his nose, mouth, and chin in a macabre red.

Olson wrenched himself away from Caveman's hold, half-way disappeared, and shoved his form straight through Caveman's body, reforming on the other side in satisfaction as Caveman fell to his knees in a pained huff.

I screamed a curse in surprise of someone putting Caveman down. I didn't hear my own voice as I should. As if I was too struck by the horror of watching one of the biggest men I've ever met be taken down with what looked like minimal effort, the large lump of man in animal hide now gargling on what sounded like a shit tonne of blood.

The Apporter appeared directly in front of me. A move that shocked a lump in my throat as my gasp was too scared to shriek. Olson towered over me. His broad frame oppressing as I trembled from more than the shitty, uncooperative weather. The crackling of power ripping through Rosemary's body was still background noise behind me, but all I saw was the unsuppressed evil Olson hid expertly from the Elders clouding the space around us.

Nothing to hide now.

I struck out at the traitor, enraged at the pain he caused the people I loved.

Olson grabbed my arm. My hit was more of a glancing punch from a dream where you couldn't gather the strength to push a snail out of your way let alone beat the shit out of someone the way you wanted to.

The asshole chuckled low and squeezed my arm as I tried to hit him again, feeling nothing but my under-developed and exhausted muscles fail. Somehow his touch was cancelling my powers. I didn't see him mutter a spell, but maybe I missed it. I struggled in his grip and got nowhere. He squeezed tighter until I slumped in pain.

"I wouldn't touch her, Sorrel." Olson's husky eyes flicked over my shoulder. I managed to turn my head to see Donovan inches from tearing his mother down bare-handed, "unless you want to kill yourself and save me the trouble."

Donovan swore in frustration, then paced and raked his fingers through his hair in desperate hopelessness.

The center of my chest tingled with something close to sympathy. It radiated up my throat, grating the veins there making it hard to swallow. If it were my mother, I would be frantic, but Rosemary was far from my mother.

Donovan turned and glared at me with a hard stare. I couldn't help but slink away from him, using the pretence of Olson's threatening closeness.

"Where's...." Caveman croaked, regaining attention to the fact he wasn't yet dead. "Where're the Sentinels?" For Caveman to eke out the question it caused him to wheeze and choke up more of his insides. Perplexing as to why he bothered with the question at all.

Who were the Sentinels? Did he mean Vincent's Tactical Team? I had never heard them called that before.

Olson allotted a glance teeming with irritation for Caveman. "Performing dutiful rounds as instructed until further notice."

Okay. Not Vincent's people, but Tobias's.

With the stone pillars activated, every single one of Tobias's people should have swarmed us. I guess Olson was looking for brownie points by handling our escape on his own.

For whatever reason, Caveman wasn't dead yet, and I couldn't reach him to try and heal him with the backstabbing SOB Apporter sapping my powers from me while in his grasp. I didn't know if simply getting Olson off of me would restore my power, but I sure as hell needed to get away from him.

I must have shifted my weight to clock Caveman's condition around Olson's shoulder because Olson's grip tightened like a vice and made me cry out.

"You should worry for yourself, whore."

"Whore? Yeah, okay, buddy." I may have slept with Donovan while still with Caine, but that was all because of the emotional loop through the connection. Neither of us knew what was happening. Whore. *Pfft.* Olson knew all of this and thought "whore" was a scathing insult. Try again, pal.

Olson telekinetically tore Donovan off his feet and into the air away from his mother's still seizing and unconscious body. With a telekinetic pull, Donovan was skidding in the snow until he stopped at Olson's feet, his back road-rashed, skin a screaming red with pins and needles as it doubled across my back. The only thing keeping me from collapsing was Olson's grip on me.

Donovan kicked and bucked on the ground but couldn't escape Olson's magic hold.

"You two are too valuable to lose." Olson bent to physically grab Donovan.

Donovan must have realized if the bastard got a hand on both of us, we would get nothing but an escorted trip back to the cells. So, before Olson got his mitt on him, Donovan used his momentary freedom to roll out of arm's reach into a defensive crouch.

"I hope you don't think it's that simple, Sorrel."

"You've met my father. I can handle you." Donovan's cocky grin begged for Olson to accept the challenge. If it meant Olson letting me go, I could maybe access my power again.

"You're not in the position to barter," Olson countered. "I've got your whore." Olson jerked my arm roughly and jarred my shoulder. It hurt but I didn't strike back. Doing so without a plan would secure my death. "Though, I suppose you two are a perfect match considering how many of the Coven you've passed your seed onto."

This strummed a sensitive cord as Olson intended it to. Not in Donovan, as this may have caused him to attack Olson and the Apporter likely wanted Donovan to come closer so he could nab him as he did me. Instead, the dig created a distracted anger within me. Donovan didn't deny the claim, nor did he look to me at all to convey any type of sympathy or remorse.

Of course he didn't. Can't emote what you don't feel.

"Who thought Traitors were so talkative." Caveman forced himself up from his position as a bloody heap to his knees, coughing. He kept trying to stand, but would fall and be worse off for the attempt, looking like shit someone dressed up in a coat. "Shouldn't you be off squealing to your Master instead of manhandling little girls?"

Olson glanced behind him at Caveman. "Die with honour, Hall. You lived with little of it and failed to free these poor excuses for saviours. Move on to your Valhalla with dignity. A more important future lay ahead."

Olson yanked me towards the compound. If he couldn't apport me back to the cell himself, then he took the chance Donovan would follow us as not to leave my side. This was exactly true.

Donovan couldn't let me go back there without tearing Olson's arms off. He didn't need to play hero or try to win back my affections, if he even wanted to, but my capture and death meant the same for him. The Donovan I knew would preserve his life over anything else. Maybe the Apporter knew Donovan well enough to know that as well.

Seeing the light-coloured building beaten by wind-whipped snow, I thought of the cell and what happened to me within its walls. Everything inside of me punched into panic mode.

I dug my bare heels into the snow, grabbed the arm Olson was holding with my other hand, and pitched my body backwards with abrupt ferocity, lifting my feet off the ground to let my dead weight trip him up.

Olson's grip slipped on my wet shirt sleeve. His nails were long enough to dig through layers of skin in a hiss of pain as I fell onto my back splashing into the ice water pool Rosemary's magic created. Before Olson could re-establish his hold, I scrambled away from him towards Caveman. He still laid in the snow and flirting with unconsciousness flat on his back. I grabbed a hold of his lifeless hand and burst forth healing power, shooting it from my whole body to encapsulate his.

Caveman grunted with the invasion of my healing force and fired up into a seated position, the veins in his neck and temples protruding, fists clenched in front of him.

Oh, shit. It worked!

Blinding pain ripped through my scalp, slamming me onto my back. The scream that cut the cold air was enough to alert the whole compound as I grabbed at Olson's wrist, trying to lessen the pain.

Growls and hitches in angered grunts came at me from a distance as I flailed my legs and fought to spin around onto my knees for leverage as Olson dragged me through another foot of icy water and snow.

I kicked and thrashed as my skin threatened to let go of my skull. A building force blew through me, cramping in my back muscles and burning in my hands around the wrist of my captor. They were ripped from me when growls and yells rushed at us, bowling me over, and tearing Olson's grub-ass hands off me, snatching locks of knotted hair as he went.

Caveman and Donovan were picking themselves up off of the ground when I could track where everyone was. They must have simultaneously tackled Olson from opposing sides, one focusing on me, the other on the traitor. If they collided with each other, they didn't show it. Both focused on the Apporter, Caveman retaining eye contact with Olson with a hand towards me as I scrambled to my feet, braced and ready for retaliation as Olson tried collecting himself.

The Apporter straightened, looked down at his hand, arm, and then body instead of attacking.

Anticipation hung in the chilled air.

The sleeve of Olson's jacket thinned in spots as if being eaten away by acid. More fabric was chewed away at his chest as his fingers grazed it. The burning and melting grew. He growled like a pissed off lion while more fabric fell to reveal his red and blackened flesh.

Caveman launched himself at the Apporter while spouting off a spell. To do what, I had no clue, though it caused Olson to roar at Caveman's contact. The asshole spun with a sharp elbow to Caveman's jaw.

Unphased by a hit that would have spun my skull on my neck like in a cartoon, Caveman roared a deep-chested war cry and heaved Olson like a Scottish Caber Toss straight into one of the stone pillars keeping a still unconscious Rosemary stuck in its crackling warding. The stone's mortared seams busted into rubble and dropped her and Olson to the ground amongst the debris.

Donovan ran to his mother and fell to his knees in the snow beside her, shoving large pieces of rock aside, and pulling her into his lap.

Why he felt anything for her made no sense to me. She abandoned him like a mama turtle at birth and left him to his sadistic father's devices, and here he was tending to her as if she spent every day of his life doting on him.

The other Humpty Dumpty was knocked out as well. Caveman kept a close eye on Olson as Donovan was focused on his equally broken mother.

It appeared as if Donovan was trying to heal her, though I didn't think I felt anything.

He turned to me with a questioning stare. It was the first time he braved meeting my eyes. After a second, I realized his courage was only because he wanted something from me.

His audacity made me return a hollow laugh. "She's alive. Couldn't miss the spillage of her tar-black soul glow if I tried."

Donovan turned his attention back to his mother, finished with his use of me. Whatever reaction he felt for my unconcerned tone, he kept to himself. Another thing I couldn't feel.

He bowed his head with a hand on his mother, maybe trying to heal her again. I couldn't tell and didn't care whether she lived or died. Rude? Probably, but she was Tainted and wasn't here for me in any other way other than the possible inconvenience of her son dying if I did.

I looked away from the dodgy mother-son team to Caveman who jerked in motion towards the Apporter.

A flash of Olson standing was all I got before the Apporter fell back on his specialty ability and disappeared, dripping flesh and all.

Donovan said his mother's name, regaining my attention, as she was trying to stand and survey her surroundings, her long dark hair a mess and grey from stone dust. She stumbled on debris or maybe wasn't fully herself yet, her dutiful son there to steady her before she gathered herself as if she didn't want his assistance.

Caveman cursed in another language. "I bound the bastard's apporting abilities, but it didn't stick. We need to beat the path. You mobile?" He growled the question at Rosemary who gave an insulted, yet clear-headed nod.

He took off in a run between the busted stone pillars, the rest of us close behind. My feet were frozen, yet tingling with some fraction of power staving off frostbite. It was like running on spiky clouds. If it meant losing both feet, I was cool with a marathon *Forest Gump* style until I dropped as long as I was not returning to the innocent-looking compound and back into its not-so-innocent cell.

Fuck that noise.

"Where are we going?" Donovan asked yet kept up pace.

"What? You don't trust me?" Caveman was joking or so I hoped.

The Apporter called Caveman a traitor, so he was as much a conman as Olson. Maybe we shouldn't be trusting him.

Caveman chuckled. "Lewy should be waiting for us in the tunnel."

"Lewy?" Donovan didn't know and neither did I.

"Vincent." Rosemary clarified with venom in her tone.

Relief hit me like a warm bath. Vincent was close by. If we could get to wherever this tunnel was and to him, he may understand what happened and how to keep Olson from getting at us again. Plus, if Vincent knew where we were, then he knew about the Apporter being a traitor, so the rest of the Elders and the Coven did as well.

For the first time, I thought of my family. Shit. Did they know

Vincent was coming to my rescue? Did they know what happened to me at the Sorrel Compound? One look at my mom and I would know if she did or not. Ugh. My brother knowing would be, I don't know, weird? Gross? How was a brother supposed to act when he found out that sort of thing? Most would kick the ass of the guy who cheated on his sister. Dad would most likely be in the dark. Better that way when he didn't have any power to do some ass-kicking of his own against a Magic.

We moved quickly through a wooded area. It reminded me of exiting The Chiff while trying to get rid of Sovereignty assholes. Maybe that's where this tunnel was going to bring us. I would feel much safer being down there and suddenly understood why so many picked hiding out inside its dirty little cubbies instead of dealing with the Tainted above. Right now, those holes in the wall looked mighty tempting.

I kept checking behind us. So far, no one was following, but I would bet both of my frostbitten baby toes that Olson disappeared and immediately went to his Master. How long would it take for Tobias to scrounge up a hunting party?

Caveman stopped at a tangle of naked branches and spoke an enchantment. The branches unwound themselves and scurried like snakes in the frozen soil before revealing a burrow deep in the ground, black as night inside without allowing any light to guide our steps.

I was happy to be anywhere other than the constant retina-piercing light of the cell, but complete darkness caused a knee-jerk step backwards at the terrifying prospect of going down there, especially since it meant trusting Caveman, Donovan, and Rosemary weren't setting me up by convincing me to trust their promises of safety by mentioning Vincent. For all I knew, they were conspiring together to get me away from Tobias so they could hand me over to the Sovereignty.

Rosemary led the way, not exactly debunking my theory since

she seemed so familiar with wherever we were going. Donovan followed behind without hesitation.

I tried to enter last to keep an exit in view, but Caveman waved me forward with a "Get in" so I did, resolved to be fucked if my paranoia became a sick reality.

One jail cell was probably the same as another and I would fight not to be shoved into any if I could help it. Taking out myself, or at least threatening to, might work. Though, if Donovan found a way to break the connection, they may not see it as such a great threat. Whatever he was feeling right now, I couldn't sense him, so maybe he weaseled his way out of our attachment.

I took a step at a time in the blackness without seeing how many or where the next step was. With frozen and tingling feet, the only way to judge hitting the step was a jarring in my knees which also glided on jelly-like cushions of semi-feeling from all the running.

Lights snapped on in the distance, flickering at first, and illuminating a long and skinny tunnel ahead of us barely above Donovan's head.

Once the lights were steady, Rosemary and Donovan took it at a jog and Caveman urged me to keep a faster pace to catch up.

Drops of water hit the top of my head. I flinched like a jumpy turtle, but my protesting feet kept me moving towards what was now hurried footfalls coming at us from the opposite direction.

Could it really be Vincent?

It was impossible to see past Donovan as his height and shoulder width dwarfed the tunnel around him. Though, Caveman behind me was worse off. Of course, I wasn't close enough to Donovan to see around him, leaving space a car could park snugly between us. All I got were sweaty and mossy concrete walls, a dirt floor, and those pounding footfalls getting closer and closer.

A tightness in my chest forced me to swallow hard to keep it from choking me. Probably anxiety.

Donovan looked back at me as he kept moving forward. Not a full turn around, as his eyes never connected with mine, but he definitely looked. Even seeing his one eyebrow, it cinched and judgemental, was enough to know he was pissed off.

Pfft. As if he had the right to be pissed off at me for anything. Fuck him and his pissy attitude.

"Sophie?"

I didn't have to search over Donovan's hunched shoulders to know the voice was Kim's. Shuffling and complaints echoed through the tunnel, but it was unmistakably Vincent's uptight and mannerly grumbling.

No shit. They were really here! And not only Vincent, but Kim, too.

Knowing they were close and that I was really free from Tobias and not going to the Sovereignty cells super-charged the impulse to race through the tunnel two-fold.

The complaints grew louder as did the shuffling of feet until Donovan was surrounded by arms, and I could see the top of Kim's red hair at his shoulder. He didn't raise his hands up to hug her back. Kim held him tightly and moved on quickly, spinning him until his back pressed against the swampy wall so she could squeeze past him to run to me.

Tears rolled down her cheeks as she crushed me in her arms.

Questions Kim asked didn't even make it to my comprehension. My best friend's tone was one of elation, but I couldn't focus on her words. I wanted her to keep moving so we could get back to the estate. Instead, she squeezed me to the point of wanting to puke.

Trembling overtook my whole body. A moment after the others raised voices filled the small space, and I realized it wasn't me. The tunnel was vibrating.

"We need to leave! Now!" Vincent's warning echoed; his voice detached as I didn't lay eyes on my immortal friend yet.

Kim grabbed my hand and dragged me along in a sprint, as it seemed like the earth overheard our panic and was using it to fuel its anger by shaking worse. Chunks of the ceiling hailed to the ground, batting me in the head and piercing the bottom of my bare feet in the scramble. Thunder cracked above and busted through the ceiling, the trickling hail now a storm of rock and dirt spraying us in a fog of dust.

Hearing was shell-shocked, eyes arid and caked with dirt. Kim pulled me along again before I could see what was coming through the roof. A mound of earth blocked the tunnel, light falling onto us through a gaping hole.

"Back this way!" Caveman yelled and Kim and I hightailed our asses back the way we came.

Donovan, Vincent, and Rosemary were on their own, but they were headed further away from the enemy, not closer.

I grabbed a handful of Caveman's hide in the pitch dark and held on tight, moving as fast as I could with Kim gripping my other hand as we rushed blindly for some type of escape.

The tunnel could have simply collapsed, but with how Caveman was locked into mission-mode to find an exit, that type of coincidence was not a factor in this life anymore.

Tobias's Sentinels found us.

Caveman's hide shifted higher as he climbed the steps. My toes hit each rise as he recited an incantation, and we were back through the tunnel entrance.

I made it up and free of the hole, immediately on alert as Caveman's eyes held a hard stare and a warrior's stance as he lifted his finger to his lips as if to shush us.

We saw the faint figures of Magics in the distance through the trees filing into the hole after us. They didn't see us pop up from where we started.

Caveman closed his ice-blue eyes, lips moving in a spell. When finished, he waved a hand to motion us to follow him. We headed through the trees, not back to the compound, but not in the direction the tunnel followed either. I figured—or hoped—we were under a cover spell and tried to pick my steps, but we were moving quickly and my feet were thrashed. Using more power than what Caveman managed might have alerted the Sentinels and I wanted to get as far away as we could, so I didn't try and heal.

Once we gained some distance from the tunnel site, I figured we were relatively safe because Caveman wasn't trying to quiet his every step anymore.

"What the fuck was that?" I pushed some healing power into my feet and felt some momentary relief. I would be lucky if I had any toenails left if I lived through this trek. The first flip flop season might be awkward.

"The enemy," Caveman responded without stopping or looking back.

"Thanks, Tips," Kim countered as gruffly as it was given. "Which one? And where are we going?"

Good question since there were a handful of enemies these days.

"The traitorous Apporter sent Tobias's Sentinels. Without the tunnel, we need to circle wide in hopes of missing the enemy and rendezvous with Vincent and the others."

Kim pushed a branch out of her way. "What if they were captured?"

"Then we move on and regroup."

What else could we do? Staying behind to get caught with them helps no one. If they caught a big fish like Vincent, no doubt the Coven would know about it immediately. Tobias wouldn't keep something so monumental quiet for long.

"Here." Kim handed me her scarf. She tried to give me her coat as well, but she wasn't dressed much better than I was and at least I could heal, so I told her to keep it.

"Are you okay?" Her voice was low, though Caveman probably heard her.

I nodded but Kim's expression told me that she didn't believe me. "I guess I look like a bag of shit."

"No, no." She wasn't a good liar. "Paler than usual, which is saying something. Besides the blood and dirt, translucent isn't your colour, Soph." Kim was better at forcing a smile. "Nothing a quarantine-style wash down can't fix, but..." She paused and stepped closer, her voice dropping even quieter. "I was more worried about your eyes." I was confused but Kim wasn't beyond being blunt. "They look sort of, I don't know, vacant? Like, too much is going on inside to focus outside even though we've got a lot of shit happening right now."

A shake in my chin threatened to take me over as Kim was right. I began to crumble, the floodgates opening a pinch more than I wanted to allow. A couple of tears took a dive onto my chilled cheeks before I wrestled the rest back into place and shut that shit down. Now was not the time.

Kim put her arm around me and rubbed my back as we kept walking, hoping to convey support, but I couldn't handle her touching me.

I created distance between us by pretending to be distracted while trying to step over a fallen branch. I couldn't look up at her to see if she saw through the ruse.

"It's okay. Just breathe, Soph."

The mechanical nod in response came with nothing beyond the surface. I couldn't muster up the emotion without losing it completely and wasn't about to freak my shit in the middle of the forest during a high-stakes escape that could result in me getting dragged back to that place.

And if I was recaptured, no way in hell could I survive if I was breaking down all the time. I wasn't giving Tobias the satisfaction.

"Donovan will be okay." Kim's assumptions were far off.

"Please. Donovan has proven he can take care of his own needs."

Her expression and the stutter in her step said, "What the fuck happened?" but she didn't ask aloud, maybe sensing I wouldn't answer her if she did.

Caveman glanced over his shoulder at Kim but didn't comment. Did he speak to her telepathically?

Whatever. Any explanation I could give her would only embarrass her and make me want to punch things. Neither helpful right now.

14

———

BEYOND MY CONTROL

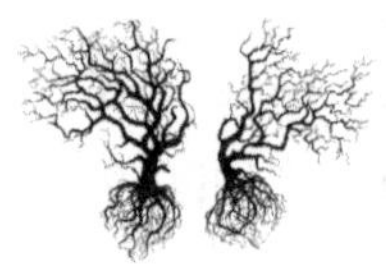

Donovan

Why couldn't Tobias have kidnapped us in the summer? My feet ached with every step, the cold biting my skin, as we ran our asses off out of the tunnel door.

A tunnel that would have been really fucking grand to know about back when I was trying to escape the compound years ago instead of dredging my broken ass through the forest.

No one followed us. Sophie, Kim, and the big guy were cut off which meant they would have to go back the way we came or out of the hole Tobias's people punched over our heads. Sophie was still alive because I was. Or maybe the connection was so fucked that didn't matter anymore. I kept thinking I was getting some emotional runoff from her. Maybe not. Or maybe she was ignoring everything she felt, and it was masking the connection?

Her fainting put me down, so something was still connected, but she pushed me away, disgusted by the thought of me touching her for the simple purpose of helping her.

Not that I could blame her. I was disgusted with myself as well.

In no time, Tobias ruined what happiness I worked for after years of getting through long nights of the shit I needed to survive.

Everything about this life being over and starting again in another time period sounded pretty damn good.

Rosemary stepped in front of me. "How about you give this life a chance to improve before you pass on it."

Wow. First time for everything. I never felt the true scorn of a mother before, and Rosemary wasn't treading lightly. Everything with escaping the cell and fleeing the tunnel happened so quickly I forgot my mental fortitudes but tightened them up before mommy-dearest could question my follow-up thoughts.

"What are you talking about?"

I didn't miss Vincent's question, but all I saw was my mother's eyes trying to beat me into submission.

Since we didn't answer him, Vincent continued on, muttering about needing to find the others.

All for a search party instead of a brow beating, I took the path Vincent created and started following him back in the direction of the tunnel. We stayed above ground and remained hyper-aware of our surroundings.

"They can find their own way back," Rosemary argued as we left her behind. She followed only to continue the discussion of why we should be taking off in the SUV. "I know you love her, son, but you no longer carry the obligation of responsibility over Sophie's life."

Of all arguments to take on, she chose the wrong one. I nearly growled at her but kept moving instead.

"You still feel nothing?" Vincent asked, receiving the same non-answer as my mother. "Is it all her?"

Vincent wanted answers I didn't have.

Rosemary scoffed. "She doesn't deserve your heart anymore then her power."

The glare I shot her was deadly, but Rosemary was Tainted, likely used to worse, and didn't flinch.

"You know nothing of what Sophie deserves." Vincent would always come to Sophie's defence. "This is Soul Magic, Donovan—"

"I know."

Vincent straightened and rested his hands on his hips. The fact I knew was a clear surprise for Vincent. I hadn't told Sophie the risks of Soul Magic, but neither did Vincent or Sophie would have mentioned it.

"This will poison the both of you. You have to try—"

"Try what?" I stopped and faced off with the man who thought he knew everything. "Before I felt nothing through the connection, I felt her undiluted hate. I felt her betrayal and I felt our love crumble. I can't reach her to change any of that any more than I can go back in time and assassinate my father instead of ignoring his existence."

Vincent was persistent. "There has been no chance to address the truth. Once you can talk—"

"What would I say? I can't fix this. I can't make it not have happened. It happened. It's over." I went on walking, needing to move as the rest of me was thrumming with anger.

"Is this about the Conception Rituals?" Vincent asked from behind me.

My fist clenched further, and I forced myself to keep walking. "Fuck off."

Rage bubbled and craved another go at breaking Vincent's face. Rosemary wouldn't interfere.

"Donovan…" Vincent caught up with me. "We can make her understand."

"*I* don't fucking understand!"

"Why should he have to explain himself?" Rosemary piped in. "After what he's been through, she should be grateful he's not a babbling idiot."

Vincent shook his head and must have been tired of speed-walking as he landed a heavy hand on my shoulder in hopes of stopping me.

A surge of power raged through me into Vincent and landed him on his ass in the snow and dead treefall before I ghosted onto him and punched him in the face. Registering moving so fast came after I felt the constriction of Vincent swallowing as I lifted him to his knees by his throat.

Blackness.

Rocking in moaning agony, the sudden darkness thinned to reveal the cloud-covered sky and trees.

What happened?

Shit. Attacking Vincent landed my shot, until he retaliated. Judging by the damage of the tree trunk beside me, he introduced me to one or more. A twitch in movement caused a lightning strike of gripping pain through my collarbone, some ribs, something in my face, and knocking a couple vertebrae out of alignment. My legs didn't want to move, but I wasn't paralyzed. They knew shifting around equalled agony and opted to forgo the exercise.

Peering from where Vincent tossed me, I saw Rosemary trapped in some type of box. Bluish in colour and preventing her from coming to my aid, though she furiously fought against its gel-like walls.

Vincent stood over me before I could find the strength to heal. His expression was one his enemies must have feared for its casual brutality.

He reached towards me. I flinched in anticipation of a hit until breathless pain and sinking despair cocooned me as Vincent ripped my soul from my body.

A vacuum of fruitless hopelessness with no end overwhelmed and set me on fire. I can't take it. I can't do it. He was doing me a favour. Just end it.

"I know what you feel." Vincent held my soul in his Soul Extractor grip, his gaze not meeting mine as he couldn't see the soul outside the body, but it didn't matter. "I hear the pain in your mind and see as you do in your thoughts and could leave you in this state to watch your body rot while you drift around these woods until you turn mad without hope of unveiling a minute sense of peace. No ending to your insanity and no connecting with those who pass through." The look on Vincent's face was the calm, psychological killer type insane. "The only reason I refrain from doling out this fate is for Sophie as she may suffer the same endless days an—"

"But you won't."

Rosemary's voice cut into Vincent's. In my dissociative yet locked-in agony state, I saw her behind Vincent with a blade at his throat. She cranked Vincent backwards to meet her height for full effect of the threat.

"Put my son's soul back into his body or I'll open your throat so wide you could store your pretty polished loafers inside."

Vincent smiled. "Back down. If I fall with Donovan's soul extracted, no amount of force will insert your son's soul back into his body."

Rosemary sheathed her blade though I didn't see where it came from or where it returned.

Sudden reinsertion of my soul back into my body was literal ecstasy. The moan that escaped me was beyond my control. No glass of the smoothest whisky or actual ecstasy compared to the sensation riding through me and sending me in the satisfying fetal position if only to convince my soul never to leave me again.

I took a minute on the frozen ground to let the feeling have its time to play without a care that the experience jacked up my heart now beating itself into a slurry inside my chest.

Vincent knelt at my side, a mix of tough love and resolve in his stare. "If forced, I will repeat an extraction, and I will keep you suspended in that state as long as I feel it is required."

I closed my eyes to Vincent and lay in the snow and treefall, feeling my broken bones ache with every breath.

"Why do you not heal?" Vincent's eyes widened as if he knew a reason and didn't want to say it.

Shattering earth interrupted.

I shifted and strained to see what happened. Vincent and Rosemary stood braced for battle as I collapsed back into position where I could still see what came for us. My neck and collar bone screamed while the back injury pulled like a crusty rubber band ready to snap.

Props to the Extractor.

Memorable voices exchanged words. Fuck me. Why not add Tobias to the mix? Oh, and throw in his Sentinels. They may as well finish me off. If ever there was a time to take advantage, now was easy pickings because I was pretty sure my legs weren't carrying my ass anywhere.

The handful of primed-for-war Magics behind their Master were hungry for a brawl, the power in the forest swelling as they stood dirty and silent, aching for the call from Tobias to put their skills to good use. Blinking, I realized my father was much dirtier than his flock.

Damn. The fucker himself was what came through the roof of the tunnel. He was probably waiting below for the right time to pop up as well once we were busy trying to fight each other. He'd get a kick out of us attempting to kill each other.

A catching breath stung like salt on a burn in the center of my chest where Sophie's and my connection made itself known.

Sophie? Are you there? A blip of recognition told me she was. How did I get through? Was she injured too?

A bitter resentment streamed back at me and then she was gone.

Jesus-fucking-Christ. Every time I tried to connect, I found a new way to feel like a piece of shit. Why did I push so hard?

The acidity of her response bled into my veins. Broken and torn skin, muscle, and bone shifted, re-broke, and re-stitched into their proper places on the peak of a ragged healing attempt. No one touched me. Sophie must have healed herself, consequently healing me, since I didn't make the effort.

However hard Sophie worked to cut the connection off, she wasn't fully rid of me yet. Almost, but not quite. Wherever she was, she went through the same beating and partial soul extraction Vincent gave me and wasn't about to lay around on the frozen ground. She took care of herself, probably to ensure she got away to safety and without worry of how or why I got my ass kicked.

Again, as with Caine after Sophie and I slept together, my actions precipitated harm against her. Yes, I could argue it was Sophie's fault we slept together, but I knew she would have never been under my roof by choice and was essentially manipulated into the situation. I was the prick and pushed Vincent to the brink since he never would have needed to teach me a lesson if I wasn't being the moronic aggressor I always was. My temper had buried me in shit before, but now with Sophie paying for my inability to keep my head straight.

Shit. It was better if the connection was broken.

Getting up, I lifted and turned my feet uncomfortably to their outer edges as they were no longer numb to the freezing snow. With no shoes they would numb-up once the burning worsened.

Stepping closer to the group, they were cordially chatting about handing me over to Vincent's brother Chase. Tobias admitted to refusing to do so "Just yet". To me, this translated as a part of the deal that must have been changed in Chase's favour.

"You chose to negotiate with my brother," Vincent said to Tobias. "What caused such trust to believe his word was concrete?"

"A man's word used to mean something," Tobias replied.

"In times past. This is modern business with the oldest of charlatans. Agreeing to dealings with the Llewellyns includes small print to the point of invisibility. The liability always falls on the signee to locate, through whatever spell, incantation, herb, or their fourth-generation grandparent necessary to uncover these invisible clauses that fall within the terms and conditions and not ever something a Llewellyn would make one aware of. Like many before you, Sorrel, you have been swindled."

Tobias's taut expression tightened further as Vincent went on. "Listen and comply if you wish but if you happen to ever set your hands on Sophie and Donovan again, Chase will stop at nothing to burn your compound, with every inbred bastard you conceived inside, to the ground and enslave or dump you into the Sovereignty prison system to be used over and again however they please."

"Is this so?" Tobias asked without a hint of intimidation in his tone.

"Not unless you got your hands on them. And I promise you, you will not."

The guy beat me like tenderized meat and now he's protecting me? I could never get a full read on Vincent. It was probably why I didn't particularly trust him, never able to tell who I was dealing with, though hurting me meant hurting Sophie which was unlikely his true goal.

Vincent would probably kick his heels up if the connection simply disappeared without consequences.

Tobias gave a grimy smile and looked at me. Knowing him as I did, Vincent's words did nothing but delay attack and motivate Tobias in challenge to prove Vincent wrong. Maybe Vincent was hoping for a fight.

Something felt off.

The edges of the mouth on the Sentinel closest to me creased ever so slightly into a sly grin. Enough of a tip-off to turn my defensive power into high gear in time for the Sentinel to launch crackling power at me, while I brought my forearms up to block myself from the hit.

Tobias must have given the guy a telepathic command.

The Sentinel didn't expect anything but my risen arms, as if to block a boxer's strike, and charged like a bull behind his own attack.

Moron. My block deflected the Sentinel's hit at one of their buddies, taking them down in a roar of pain then redirected in a punch of anger, ploughing into another brawn-without-brains aggressor and throwing him into another Sentinel, and then a tree.

A three-fer, I thought as I braced for the next hit.

Like the impatient Sentinels, the energy inside me was angry and bellowed for the chance to play, the anticipation twitching my muscles and sharpening my sight onto likely targets in front of me.

The drive to use my power hadn't been this prevalent since before Olson turned us over, but it was still impossible not to think of Sophie as I put myself in danger once again and I wished that Rosemary, Vincent, and I were with her instead of in front of my fuck-face father and his lick-the-tip followers.

The strength this gave me filled me to the brim as I thought of ripping every bastard apart, knowing that once we got passed them, that I would be with her in some capacity. I couldn't say anything to make her smile and nothing I could do would erase the time spent within the compound, but if we were probably going to die in the endgame anyway, all I wanted was a chance to see her again.

The closest Sentinel showed teeth in a snarl and posed to strike, until somehow the landscape abruptly changed yet stayed the same.

15

LET IT GO

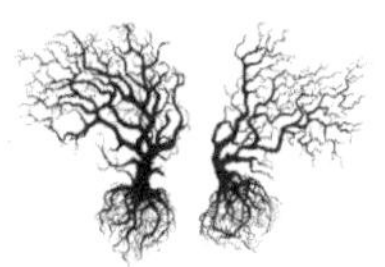

Sophie

Healing should have come easy but this one took a lot out of me. I swore the ache in my chest was indicative of internal damage and that was what propelled me to finally heal. I didn't tell Kim or the standing-in-awe Caveman about the sensation in my chest. How could I when I didn't know what the hell it was? Had to be Donovan, right? Logically, who else could be nagging me with unspoken questions? It disappeared when I healed, so maybe it wasn't.

Whatever that was—being thrashed around the forest like a dog toy, bones crushed, and then...Well, I don't know what happened. Tobias or his goons hadn't found us and Kim and Caveman didn't see anyone touch me when despair and sinking dread took over. No, something deeper, darker, like a draining poison. If I lived to be a thousand years old, I never wanted to feel this again. From the black hole to the shock of gratitude and bliss...I could handle a little more of that bliss. If that's what substance use resembled, fffuuucccckkk, I was best to keep away from it because it was delightful.

But what now? I was healed, yet still soaked to the marrow and laying on the frozen ground content to lay there and disappear.

Kim was kneeling close, Caveman hovering. "You've taken us too far off course, Viking."

Kim was right, Caveman did look like a Viking.

Caveman huffed. "I know where I'm going."

"Do you? Because you've taken us far from Vincent's SUV, which is that way."

"No—"

"As per my guiding light power, yes, it is."

They argued back and forth as I continued to want nothing to do with them or anything else.

A rush of panic drilled through me. I sprung to my feet.

Caveman dropped into a defensive stance. He scanned our surroundings with a hand in front of Kim to cover her if needed, though she was focused on me as if I might grow claws and attack.

Pain sliced my gut. I hinged over in pain, confusion, and bloated anger. My back ached something fierce as my insides twisted sending me close to projectile vomiting if the agony didn't subside right fucking now.

I didn't realize I was on the ground until something jabbed through the skin of my knee. Too exhausted to do anything about it, I gave in to the pressure as my insides crawled and my throat threatened to collapse without oxygen.

A scream rung my eardrums. Kim's.

When I could finally breathe again, Caveman was apologizing to Donovan.

To Donovan?

"What happened?" Vincent straightened himself from a crouch. When his eyes hit mine, he ran to me and helped me to my feet. "Are you okay?"

I didn't respond. I just fell into him and held on. This was the first time I saw him again since he'd been holding me in the attic before I disappeared and showed up at my elementary school where the Apporter kidnapped me. I choked back a sob as Vincent repeated the question, one I still couldn't answer. He separated himself from me. I unwillingly let him go, but I held on to his arms as he smoothed my greasy hair from my face. I couldn't look into his green eyes, knowing if I did it'd be the switch to the waterworks, and I was too tired and too vulnerable to let go.

"Can you do it again?" I heard Kim ask.

Vincent shifted us so he could see the others better, but he kept an arm around my shoulders, maybe knowing I needed the support.

"How could you have transported us?" Rosemary asked and I realized that Donovan was somehow responsible for them showing up.

Running a hand through his messy hair, the other on his hip, Donovan's eyes were on his thoughts, drawing him inward. Whatever he did, it wasn't happening again anytime soon, and that look meant he didn't know what happened in the first place.

"Maybe it was Fox's tattoo work again?" Donovan guessed. "I might have activated it."

"Well, you zapped us closer to the compound." Rosemary was quite pissed and disappointed. Awesome parenting. "With Tobias on our asses, we've got a lot of ground to cover."

Kim's eyes widened. "Tobias?"

"Yes," Rosemary responded curtly. "The tunnel party-crasher was Tobias and his Sentinels dropping in to see why he hadn't received an invitation."

Made sense when considering the beating and horrendous sinking feeling I experienced. Something so potent definitely stank of evil to me.

"Let's move," Rosemary added with impatience next to her son, who I noticed still refused to look at me.

We needed to get going, though Vincent argued his SUV was compromised. Tobias was no moron and would find it or already ordered Sentinels stationed nearby to pounce when we arrived. Meaning, we needed someone to pick us up at a safer location.

Vincent called someone and then told me to climb onto his back to save my frozen feet. "Eventual healing does not stave off long-term damage, if you have not incurred some already. Donovan is walking still, so you will feel the residual effects enough as it is. No need to double the probability of irreversible impairment."

How could I fight that logic? Once I was on Vincent's back and comfortably in place, I didn't care as much as I thought I would. I liked the sense of safety and familiarity that came with him. Caveman was a tank, pure muscle and brute and the stuff steamy fantasies are made of, but I didn't know him like I knew Vincent. My long-time friend may have safeguarded his secrets, but his concern for me was genuine and that counted for a lot.

———

After a while, one tree after another bled into identical colours of bare, brown branches or green evergreens weighed down by the snow in the pitch darkness. The moon created enough of a light source for a night vision spell Rosemary cast over the group, Vincent keeping true to his footsteps with me still on his back without tripping. One of them may have used some kind of cover spell, but I wasn't sure, just happy to be getting farther and farther away from the compound. Bedding down wasn't an option. We needed to get out of the woods.

We did have to stop a few times so Donovan could fully heal his feet. This was confusing since healing used to happen automatically when the damage was no worse than a papercut.

Something was different.

Vincent's phone went off again. It did quite a few times. Though I was close while hanging off of his back monkey-style, I couldn't hear a voice on the other end. Soft talker or another spell, I didn't ask, and Vincent never mentioned who it was or said anything definitive enough for me to gain the gist of the conversation. Best guess was assuming it was someone who could help us.

No matter who it was, he never slowed down and carried me

easily one-handed when needed, using his shoulder to hold his cell in place.

"Location?" Now Vincent was looking around as if he expected someone to pop out from behind a tree.

A red laser beam hit Caveman square in the chest. He froze and snarled at the red dot.

"Location perceived." Vincent closed his phone.

The laser dropped from Caveman's chest as an agile female with sharp features and cropped dark hair stepped into the open, one I recognized as a part of a group who went after the demon Gualichu at the mall.

With the gait and posture of a soldier, the woman moved aside and Lincoln followed another familiar Magic, though it was odd not to see him next to his love, Anne-Claire. Maybe his hard expression was because of her death. Whatever it was, Lincoln was fit to fuck someone up.

Four more members revealed themselves, making the team up of six kickass Magics all in black gear camouflaging them in the dark forest.

"What the fizz? How do I bag your job?" They were clearly elite Magics with power beyond their genetic gifts.

Vincent peered over his shoulder at me. "You only need to ask."

New career path, here I come.

Vincent referred to the first woman I saw as "Jessabelle". She smirked at my response in a way Lincoln couldn't muster, her sense of humour surviving Anne-Claire's loss as she approached me.

"How about we get you into some boots first, yeah?" Jessabelle moved as if mighty comfy in her own tactical set. "Ismail...." She called to another team member, one with tanned skin and black curls who looked more like a history professor than a soldier. Instead of a sweater with elbow patches and relaxed-fit jeans, he was clad in black tactical gear ready to take on any enemy.

At the sound of his name, Ismail spun a pack that crossed his chest to the front, pulled out a pair of boots Jessabelle called for, and threw them over to her.

"First piece of the uniform." She held them up for me.

I took the black leather in hand. They were heavy and warm from being tucked away in Ismail's pack. It took a few failed attempts to get my red and irritated feet situated, my toes tingling with pin pricks even worse as I pushed a bit of healing power through them. Pulling the laces tight, they fit well enough. Maybe half a size too big but would be fine with a good pair of socks and some inserts. Nothing akin to the lamb fur peeking out of Caveman's boots, however, they were new, and mine to work in.

I looked badass.

I slapped Vincent on his muscled shoulders. "You're a good mule, but my legs were going numb."

"Anything for a lady," Vincent returned with a gentlemanly nod.

"How far until we're clear of these trees?" Caveman didn't whine but, as with everyone else, wanted to know.

"Not far," Ismail told him. "The way ahead is clear."

"Excellent work," Vincent said, and Ismail nodded to Vincent in a way that portrayed a respect for a commander. "Bronya..." He called to a woman with gleaming blond hair in a high ponytail.

Try as Bronya might—and she wasn't trying that hard—she couldn't keep her eyes off of Donovan and I didn't need to try and check her mind to see what she was fantasizing about. Blatant eye-fucking outside of the club or bar scene was awkward as fuck and this chickie was slathering it on Donovan so thickly she could have used a butter knife.

He was ignoring her, though maybe they had been together before. He did fuck Anne-Claire and other Magics, so not exactly a stretch.

"Bronya," Vincent called again, and she snapped to attention. "Assist Lincoln and Gregor and circle back to ascertain if others have followed."

Bronya gave an affirming nod and followed Lincoln and another man with a rusty-coloured soul into the trees before disappearing. Knowing what all the soul colours of the Magics protecting us was unnecessary, I was simply ecstatic to see souls that were bright, meaning strong and sufficient enough to help us. Being a part of the Tactical Team was now an organic drive and tickled my curiosity of what other kind of missions Vincent sent them on.

Making our way out of the trees came without further attempts to end our lives. When the trees thinned, we came up on two ultra-sized black SUVs occupied by a few tagalongs from The Chiff. I didn't hear the whole story except for Vincent to say that The Chiff was infiltrated, his voice low as not to upset Moira and Neilan, both looking nervous and elated we returned for them. Moira was quick to hug me, her eyes glassed over as if she hadn't stopped crying since it happened.

Some squeezed into the open cabbed trunks. Neilan moved to the other SUV, his lanky form best fitting in the trunk. When Donovan and his mother got into a vehicle, I jumped into the other one. I didn't need to be in an enclosed space with him.

In the open forest was one thing, confined in the cage of the SUV and sharing the same limited breathing space would have suffocated me. The thought of it choked me up. Next to Vincent in the farthest row back of their SUV was much more conducive to retaining my cool. At least I could count on his stiff shoulder to lean into. He didn't seem to mind and let me know we were headed back to the estate.

People chatted, but I didn't have the energy to engage. Caveman and Kim sat in the row of seats in front of Vincent and me, arguing over Tobias's next move. Caveman was confident the Creation would be Tobias's priority. Kim didn't believe he was done with Donovan.

"He left us to the woods when grabbing his son would have been easy." Caveman leaned across the expanse of the seats as if he and Kim were drawn together. "Tobias plans ahead. When the Creation is cracked, he knows his heir will front the army meant to stop him. No need to take Donovan out in the privacy of his backyard when the glory of an audience awaits on the battlefield."

Narrowing her blue-green tenacious eyes, Kim looked like she was thinking of a comeback yet had nothing and knew it.

"There you go again, kitten." Caveman's deep voice was all purr. "When you think like that, it tickles my imagination. Frog must be well-cared for."

I watched Kim in profile recoil at Caveman reading her thoughts, thoughts I could only guess at, though weren't difficult to decipher. Kim was embarrassed or maybe pissed off and took back her personal space, crossing her arms and righting her posture, busying herself looking out the window to her right.

"Maybe not," Caveman muttered with a half-smile in satisfaction.

Before he managed to upset her, the initial transparent sexual tension emanated not only from Caveman but from Kim. Maybe she was fighting it—the guy was sex on toast—and may not have been happy about it, but Kim couldn't hide it.

Immediate thoughts of Donovan and how we were in the beginning came to mind. I should have listened to my gut back then instead of getting roped into his bullshit. I hated it so much it made my chest tighten with anger or anxiety, something that worsened with every breath instead of loosening up.

I pressed my hand into the spot in my chest that ached, willing it to calm down as cramps in my ribs were stabbing at my lungs.

"*You are safe now.*" Vincent's voice in my mind was meant to be soothing, as was his hand on mine, but it did the opposite. I felt trapped.

My head was a torrent of "I know" and "I'm fine" but I didn't feel fine and couldn't create either thought to project to Vincent, nor could I block Vincent from getting into my head.

"*What happened to you will be avenged.*" The promise spoke of great devotion I found hard to believe since Tobias was not an easy target to bring down. Many would relish a chance at him, Donovan and Rosemary included.

The ache in my chest worsened and I turned my head from Vincent so he wouldn't see my pinching reaction to it.

It took a moment for me to be able to turn back to him.

"Being on the Team is a good fucking start."

His shoulder against mine rumbled with a chuckle. *"As stated, a position is always open for you."*

"Good. I accept."

Vincent smiled and nodded.

Next was one of those thoughts I would rather have kept under the fog. Needless to say, the fog was too thin to obscure the hatred I harboured for Donovan. It flushed to the surface with that burning in my chest. How I could be so stupid to fall for the charade, again, was insanity.

Same betrayal, different guy, far worse outcome.

Why he bothered to pretend he was someone he wasn't was ridiculous and the fact I defended him and our relationship to the bitter end was an embarrassment as bad as the betrayal itself.

How did the past-life versions of myself put up with this? Or did I use up all the fairy tale romance in those lifetimes? The spell that bound us to each other had to become a curse at some point.

"Do not allow this tragedy to harden you." Vincent shifted to look straight at me, confusion darkening in his green eyes, judgement as thick as his glasses. *"Such thoughts carry more danger than you comprehend now. I will not sit idle and watch you destroy yourself."*

"I'm not trying to."

"Trying is not the element I fear. It is the allowance of twisting the unknown into the bases of your excuses."

"Excuses? Stop trying to dictate how I feel." The last part of my message made Vincent flinch from the volume alone. I didn't care. Immortality didn't mean you were all-knowing and it sure as hell didn't mean your opinion was greater than others.

This wasn't said directly to Vincent, but I didn't attempt to conceal it. After that, I found untapped energy to keep my gaze out the window. Seething beneath my skin was an edginess sending me vibrating in my seat. I chewed on my nails, my knee bopping involuntarily. Of all people, Vincent was going to side with Donovan? To fight for us to be together again as if nothing happened?

Kim turned around in her seat. "What's wrong?"

"What's wrong? Everything's fucking wrong."

Kim's brows cinched together in attitude, making me want to scream and get the hell out of the vehicle.

Power hit me, energy cramping deep inside me, engaging my stomach muscles, and forcing me to double over, my nails biting into the leather seat in front of me.

"Gain control of yourself."

The direction came from Caveman. It didn't matter who said it, anyone who felt my power going wild had something to say about it. The raised voices fighting for space in the small vehicle was gasoline on a bucket fire, clouding any escape.

"Let it go," a female voice was encouraging me with thick sensitivity. I knew if I didn't lock my power down, I wouldn't have a choice, because whatever this was would take me over by force.

"Pull over!" Vincent's voice commanded the driver. I didn't feel the SUV slow. How could I when my blood was pumping at race car speeds.

"Sophie?" Kim planted a hand on my arm with ample pressure, trying to grab my focus.

I snapped up to stare at her in warning to back off as I couldn't form the words. She recoiled.

"Your eyes...." Kim scrambled away and unclipped her seatbelt.

"Sophie...." Vincent grabbed my shoulder, trying to look at me the same as Kim.

This did it.

"Don't!" The force of my voice hit Vincent in a shockwave, throwing him against the window. It spider-webbed behind him.

Vincent grabbed at his head and tried to peer at me, his lips moving, but I couldn't hear him.

I was over the bursting stage like a Seedling, no? What the shit was this?

Not my power, something else was happening. It undulated under my skin and made me wheeze in big gasping breaths.

I clawed at the throbbing veins in my throat and arched at the surges of power or whatever was attacking me from the inside. I couldn't sit still, yet couldn't find my feet to take off.

Was Tobias around? Chase? Could they be outside doing this to me?

My screams drowned out voices around me. Only one voice broke through with impossible clarity.

"Let it go." The voice repeated itself, breaking down my will with every murmur.

Holding back from that voice was too difficult of a struggle. The pain worsened the more I tried to find a way to conquer it.

When I couldn't handle it anymore, I did what the voice said, and let it go.

LONG AWAITED

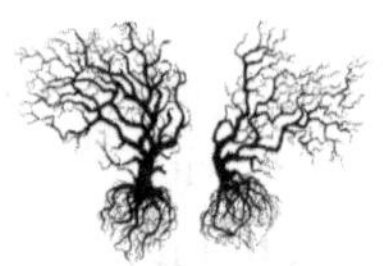

Donovan

We were making good time, but the trip was painfully quiet, and I couldn't focus on the route Lincoln was taking. No crappy music filled the air space, no petty conversation...even a boring one would have been something to keep me from thinking about our trek through the forest.

I did everything I could to ignore the emptiness I felt without the connection. Sophie was now bent on joining Vincent's crew the second he mentioned it. The smile it gave her wasn't right. So much hardness, claws and fangs, Tobias locking her up causing damage.

I knew the feeling.

The steel in my bones and emotional dissociation in my daily grind was a heavy load. Except when I was riding high on anger and a justified sense of revenge. I could gut my father slowly for manufacturing yet another case of desensitized fury on someone so innocent.

I shifted and scrunched my toes in the boots Ismail gave me. They pinched my toes a bit. At least my feet had a chance to thaw without the constant thrum of power as I tried to keep them from falling off.

I wanted to be happy for Sophie's decision to join Vincent's Tactical Team, but all I saw was a fast pass to the darkness I told her I would never let her be mixed up in. No, actually, I told her I would follow the path with her to try and save her from it. I never expected she would be walking the path with hate for me. How was I supposed to follow her when she doesn't want me anywhere near her?

Her revenge was justified—I wanted it myself—but it might not end there for her and she may start fighting evil just long enough to see it up nice and close. The ache for justice would become so bad maybe she muddied the lines before becoming the enemy she hunts. A future blipped into existence and all with the handover of a pair of black leather combats. So easy it was a damned cliché and I felt unending shame for setting things in motion.

My breath caught and I cleared my throat, thinking I was about to make an ass out of myself by crying in a car full of people. Some jagged emotion was there, but not mine, and it was mostly physical. An ache? A pressure from something pushing from the inside, trying to spring out of me like a rabid grasshopper.

Fuck. Did Tobias do something to me? Insert some kind of magical time bomb with a delayed detonation?

I dug my knuckles into my chest. The physical pain distracting me from the inner pain, but only for a second, and not good enough to make it go away.

Was it Sophie? It didn't really feel like her. If that was her, something was wrong.

The pain surged. I clutched my gut and sat froward as something intense rattled my insides.

"Donovan...?" Rosemary's voice was a flutter of concern I batted away. Her closeness and being stuck inside this fucking metal box made it worse.

I wanted to escape. To get away from the pain. Just to move and ease whatever the hell this was now flowing from me in waves of heat.

"What are you doing?" Lincoln checked over his shoulder and in his rear-view as he drove, trying to see me.

"I'm not...." The sensation pouring from me was choking.

The gnawing pain grew and kept growing.

It was Sophie. Did she feel what I was feeling? Was this our connection dying?

"Why are they stopping?" Arden's voice caused vague interest. Who was stopping? Was the vehicle Sophie rode in stopping?

No, we were stopping, the slowing of the vehicle making me want to jump and roll before the tires quit turning.

"Go!" I tried to push them, but I couldn't focus. Couldn't tell them to gain their attention from the SUV in front of us, couldn't push them away from me.

I was going to lose it.

A rush of oxygen left me in a loud exhale as if it was sucked out of my lungs. I tried to grab onto something as the air wouldn't come back. I couldn't breathe. My chest burned. My ribcage a half-second from cracking down the middle.

I crushed someone's hand in mine, but couldn't look, knowing it was probably Rosemary.

Pressure built so great I thought my chest and skull might detonate in an explosion of power. I tried to brace for it, unable to speak to warn the others.

Suddenly, I felt nothing. No pain or pressure. No urgency. A snap of a finger and nothing. Sweating, but I felt normal.

A silent beat passed with everyone looking at me in confused expectation of something big not happening as it should have.

A massive explosion of energy attacked the vehicle, bursting the windows into bullets of glass that rained in on us with the bang of the air bags deploying and the tires popping.

My ears rang as I tried to shake off glass fragments and squint through airbag dust. Everyone was alive and unharmed as we filed into the street to the sound of the wailing car alarm and noticed the other SUV in the exact condition as ours.

Kim was in the ditch spilling her guts in back-arching heaves as the big guy stood over her, on watch over her or for enemies, though not exactly holding her hair back. The other Magics hinged at the waist with their hands on their knees or paced aimlessly in something close to shell-shock, Moira with a hand to her chest like a heart-attack was seconds from putting her down.

"Someone explain what just happened!" Rosemary yelled over the alarms as those who could met between the vehicles.

The alarms quit as Lincoln popped the hood and yanked a wire into submission, the other silenced as efficiently. We didn't need the attention. Though, the only light source were the headlights, so these stayed on, but at least they weren't flashing anymore.

Ears still ringing, I headed to the others since Rosemary's question hadn't earned a response. The expression of shock, or maybe disgust, Vincent wore kept me from asking again. With Sophie's back to me, I could only see Vincent's focused stare locked on Sophie's face.

Why the fuck was he looking at her like that?

"Hey!" Rosemary called again, she empty of patience.

This captured attention as Sophie turned towards my mother. The minute she did, I realized what it was Vincent was freaked about and knew exactly what happened.

Her eyes. They weren't hers. Too light, almost gold. "Nya."

The name evoked a smile. One Sophie wore yet didn't create.

That was what I felt. Aunt Lacey's daughter-in-law finally got sick of riding shotgun and took over in the driver's seat. The pain I felt was Sophie's last struggles to try and stop Nya from taking her down. She didn't want this. She could have let Nya slip into the lead as Caine sometimes did with Gareth, but she didn't. Sophie fought and lost.

"Why take her now?" Vincent's voice was filled with a surprising hopelessness as Kim finally stopped heaving and she and the big guy joined the group. As far as I was concerned, Vincent's question was odd. As if it confirmed Vincent knew it was going to happen at some point.

Nya turned to Vincent. "I suppose waiting would have suited your needs. Mine were better served under my control and not the Seedling's."

"Your needs?" My words struck out at her. While Vincent was hopeless, I was enraged.

Nya spun to me as Vincent lifted a hand as if to warn me to be patient with the personality now riding Sophie like she finally broke a wild horse.

"Yes. My needs." Nya repeated as if being rational. "However, with what I have extrapolated, my needs will be satisfied as well as your Sophie's."

"How do you figure that's possible with you possessing her?"

Nya took steps towards me. Even those steps were not Sophie's. "Your Sophie was too weak to accomplish that for which she desired. An enemy such as her ancestor could never be fought and won with such inexperience. You must know this. The soulless cannot be killed. Therefore, we must stitch a soul to Evaristus's vessel before ending him is possible. In full strength, I shall overthrow the reigning power as well as accomplish my own ends."

"Great. Now that you've let us in on how to get the job done, give Sophie back her body."

Her lips pursed. "Much remains incomplete and in need of rectification while I have the ability to achieve a long-awaited objective. In short...No."

My fists tightened. I stopped myself from attacking, knowing instead of taking down Nya, I would succeed in hurting Sophie and not much else. I've caused Sophie enough damage.

"And you think you can live on forever in Sophie's body and the ones who love her will not force you out?"

Choosing not to answer Vincent, Nya focused on me. "You can try to rid the vessel of my presence. I wonder if such a task may dissolve your appetite to learn my takeover was only made possible by my vessel's hatred towards you."

I froze and couldn't speak.

"Shall I repeat myself?"

I stayed quiet.

Nya squared her shoulders to me using Sophie's stolen eyes to berate me further. "Your betrayal permitted my strength to govern the vessel, the weak will of Sophie proving my time was imminent. The once reigning soul has now shrivelled in the prospect of losing herself to the overwhelming damage and anger your actions cultivated. Admittedly, she may have recovered from her heartbreak, however, I have waited long enough."

What Nya said was a kick to the nuts I wasn't walking off. This was my fault? My fault? The thing in front of me was no better than some alien body snatcher. Sophie may have hated me but how could I leave her like this?

"Now," Nya stated casually after effectively administering the blow, "we are close to the estate. We must continue."

Nya took a step towards the closest vehicle, touched it, and a hitch of power filled the air around us. Something prickled my skin, caressing it, and dipped into me like fingers along the power inside of me. Tugging within me as if something was suckling on the deepest parts of me, equally uncomfortable and embarrassing. And then I realized it was Nya siphoning my magic. The others twitched and moved with a bit of discomfort. Not only me. Nya siphoned off us all as glass refilled their panes, tires inflated, and any dents smoothed. She did the same to the next SUV as we all stood waiting for her to finish.

No one seemed to enjoy the process any more than I did, but it didn't exactly hurt, and she got the job done quickly.

I didn't feel weaker for her taking from me. She needed a jump-start and did the rest on her own.

The SUV was restored to factory line perfection.

"Let us continue our journey." Nya's power leached from the air as she hopped into the passenger's seat of the SUV Sophie was originally in and closed the door, awaiting the rest of us to fall in line.

I searched to Vincent in hopes of a plan, something that wouldn't kill Sophie like every thought running around in my head full of chaos and fury.

Instead, the man looked at me in understanding of what I felt, but waved me off as if warning me against doing anything, and then followed Nya's lead by getting back into the SUV.

That was it? We were just going to go with this?

Kim was pissed and holding back tears, but got in the SUV after the big guy bent to her level and said something so low I couldn't hear. Whatever it was, it motivated her to join the others in the vehicle. He looked back at me without saying anything and followed Kim.

How? How could...? Thinking coherently was impossible as I stood in a suspended sense of panic and despair. I thought my chest would collapse. It took Rosemary to physically push me by the shoulders to get me back to the vehicle so we could continue on to the estate without letting the other vehicle, with Nya inside of it, get away from us.

"How could I have lost her?"

This time I spoke aloud receiving no answer from Rosemary. She and everyone else were equally dumbfounded at the turn of events with absolutely nothing useful to offer. The rest of the drive I spent inside of myself thinking over every single thing since I first met Sophie up until Nya took over.

What if that last occurrence of the sensation was the last time I ever felt Sophie through our connection again? What if I couldn't get her back?

17

IMAGINATIVE DESIGNS

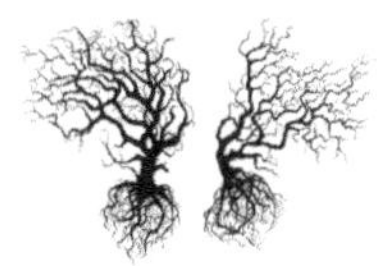

Vincent

Walking through the front door of the Ballard Estate should have been akin to a triumphant return from battle with the innocent victims tucked within my steadfast embrace to be handed off to their awaiting family, but I was empty-handed with only an inch of room to breathe as my chest trembled, too tight and filled with hopelessness and regrets of failing Sophie yet again.

When we crossed the Ballard's boundary wards, Nya was left unaffected. No blast of pain, which meant she was pure of heart and soul. Enough to fool the wards in ways others balancing the line of good and evil could not. Nya's soul was good. I suppose I knew this, yet understanding how such a self-serving soul could remain unTainted was beyond my grasp.

Rosemary remained on the driveway leading to the estate since the wards would not have read her soul for anything than what it was. The Tactical Team from both vehicles, as well as those from The Chiff, were commanded to stay vigilant, keeping Rosemary company and the family from panic as the others' presence in the attic would have evoked immediate emotion not needed when introducing Sophie back to them would not be as they hoped.

Most in the front rooms of the Ballard Estate were bypassed without a faltering footfall while we headed for the members gathered in the attic. The sally port of sorts was left open, the attic door ajar with everyone flowing freely from room to room. Enough Magics were present to create a formidable offensive against Nya if needed, but without the directive, the Team understood they were on standby.

Coming up the stairs, we breached the upper door, and my muscles went rigid in wait for the familial reaction. I noticed Nya had no qualms with so many Magics surrounding her as she strode into the space with a posture Sophie never found necessary to attain.

The first to call attention to Sophie's return was the last person I wanted to see her.

Andy. The boy who lost too much.

As Nya walked unbidden towards the back desk, maybe expecting to find Olive—it was unclear how much of Sophie's knowledge Nya contained—Sophie's name rang out in childish excitement, and the boy ran unbridled towards her. Donovan caught Andy up in his arms, preventing the child from getting within proximity as Andy struggled until Sophie turned to him. A small gasp escaped his lips as he backed down from his fight, was let go, and stood too close to Donovan in fear of what he was seeing.

Donovan's eyes didn't meet Nya's, instead held vacantly to the floor, glazed over in suffused grief as he held Andy by the shoulders.

Hearing Sophie's name, the others of her Sect came running but stopped in their tracks as they, too, saw Sophie's unnatural golden eyes.

"Firefly?" Olive's fragile voice questioned the creature she observed. As a Soul Seer, it scared me to think of what she must have seen. Understanding the difference of what her talented eyes witnessed, Olive sighed and put a hand to her chest. "Nya."

Those in the attic questioned this and talked over each other.

"Who gave you permission to possess her?" Olive's dark eyes, now too unlike her great-niece's, were wide in shock.

A frenzy of voices around the room pitched in disbelief of someone else being in Sophie's body.

"Permissive accountability will not give your Firefly governing reign of this body."

Nya's tone was nothing like Sophie's. Defiant, sure, but no sass, and too formal. Much more like the way those spoke in a time I grew up in and no longer holds space in this century.

"What will?" Adam challenged, Sophie's brother also seeing what most others could not.

I shared in the brother's need to make Nya answer for her actions, yet what could be done without harming Sophie? Until Nya's plans were revealed, and her magic tested for hints of vulnerability, attempts to overtake the ancient soul would be fruitless.

From where I stood, I saw Nya smile as if what Adam stated was laughable, or maybe she read the full threat in his mind.

"Is she still...in there?" Sophie's Uncle Lewis asked as every Magic in the attic circled in closely. It was his way of assessing if their Sophie was alive or dead, calculating if they would allow Nya to breathe air into the body of their family member another moment.

Nya hesitated. "She is."

"How do we know you're not lying?" Denise stepped forward with her usual abrasive attitude. It was one instance I did not mind the "bitch routine" as Donovan labelled it many a time. "You took over Sophie's body like some type of Puppeteer or demon. Trusting you is the same as trusting evil to have a sudden attack of conscience. Not fucking likely."

"I am no evil," Nya assured to no one's belief. "My presence within this sanctum proves this. Given the circumstances, trust must be earned where a grievance has been afflicted." Nya stopped as if to ponder, then turned to Olive and somehow straightened further. "What do you see, Soul Seer?"

Olive focused away from the unfamiliar eyes of her great-niece to look beyond her anger to Nya's soul. "Before, Sophie's soul was a Seer's green as it should have been. Releasing part of your influence created a magenta to...dance around her soul. It would seem, you were actually encircling her until your opportunity presented itself."

"Precisely." Nya's confirmation added to the group's fury. Even ones such as Sophie's cousin Kassie who was not particularly fond of Sophie, was restraining herself. "More importantly, what do you see now?"

Olive's lips pursed as her eyes welled with tears. Lewis answered when Olive's words failed. "Sophie's Seer green is barely discernible, not dancing or plotting, just a hint of green ambient glow."

I looked to Donovan, finding it impossible not to gauge his reactions. If anyone was going to strike, it would be him. How much could he endure? A distinct air of rage around him hung like a fog, as if he was controlling himself from strangling Nya.

Taking the chance in hopes Donovan's guard was otherwise preoccupied, I caught a glimpse of his open mind. A whirlwind of thoughts collided, echoing over each other. What I overheard was disturbing.

She's trapped in there. It's my fault. I brought her into this. What do I do? How do I get her back? What if I can't? Ending this is the only way. Ending her is the only way. This life is killing us slowly. I can save Sophie the torture and kill Nya. It's just Sophie's body. I'll find her again. I always find her.

Over and over again, Donovan conjured images of killing Nya, how he would do it in the name of saving Sophie from the hostile takeover to reunite with her in another time.

"Listen, boy," Nya's voice pulled me from Donovan's mind as his dark and tortured eyes peered up at his target. She heard Donovan's thoughts as well. "Your Sophie was able to penetrate even the strongest of minds when evoking *my* strength. Do not grant yourself the supremacy of believing you can override my power, nor cut me down in the fashion your imagination designs."

Nya took a few steps closer to Donovan, who refrained from flinching or cowering. I concentrated on retaining composure without my power swelling in defence of Donovan as well as against however Donovan may retaliate and put Sophie in danger. I could not lose them again.

"You may be this girl's soulmate," Nya's tone made it sound as if she believed it to be so, "but I assure you, you are not mine, and you being one with the vessel will not free you from this life if you choose to kill me. Doing so will only end you both and leave you floating in non-existence until I allow otherwise by disposing of this body. Your attempt is your fate."

"Enough." Olive's shrill voice cut through the tension. "You may be able to set foot in this house, but you are not permitted within this sanctum. Choose another room to dwell in."

Nya paused as if contemplating whether or not this gathering of Magics was enough to enforce upon her anything she did not authorize. "Your request is irrational. Under strained conditions I can appreciate your fragility. Though segregating me will not benefit the coming battle."

"You're fighting alongside us?" Adam asked for the collective.

Nya's head cocked to the side in an uncharacteristic move for Sophie, her cold gold eyes sober. "Is my cause any less noble?"

"Your cause?" Adam questioned with growing irritation.

"You just busted out, how do even have a cause?" Denise finished for him.

Nya flashed a grin. It meant to conceal her true intent.

"Gareth." Weakened dissociation discoloured Donovan's tone. "Her cause is to reunite with Gareth."

Nya's smile grew until she showed off Sophie's teeth. "Yes. Yes, it is."

18

HELPING OR LEAVING

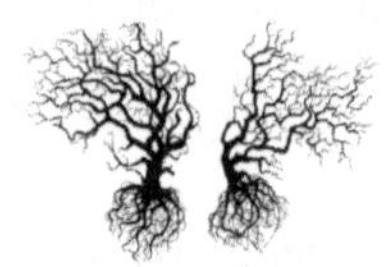

Donovan

When Sophie's family and the Covens couldn't handle seeing Sophie walking around without it really being Sophie, Nya was sent to meander the whole house if she wanted, though was forbidden inside the attic. To ensure she didn't cause any damage, Vincent ordered two Tactical Team members on her at all times in shifts, while the remaining four did constant rounds of the entire estate once they returned from dropping The Chiff survivors off at a safe house meant to protect Magics in times of crisis.

Rosemary was granted admittance, however. This earned some snide comments from the peanut gallery, but everyone dealt with her with more favour than the newly released vessel-napping ancient.

Haunting memories landed me on my back in some bed in one of the estate's rooms. I didn't consider it hiding, not by cowardice anyway. I needed to collapse somewhere private. After drudging through the forest, I was physically exhausted, but it went deeper than that. No one in the estate slept on a routine and caught naps when they could, ready to go to war when the Elders unhooked their leashes and led them to fight outside of the Creation. Needing rest was an easy excuse to be alone. Which I did as soon as Nya was banned from the attic. Kim and Vincent knew enough to pass along any other information people needed. I refused to stand there and repeat it.

Being behind a magically locked door didn't stop the commotion crowding the halls. Every single one of the Magics in the place clucked on about how Sophie was "possessed". No wonder I couldn't block them out. They didn't think anyone who overheard might be doing everything in their power to shut down thoughts of Sophie, and how what's become of her was all their fault.

Fuck. This is all my fault.

What Nya said kept coming back to me. How she could have only taken over Sophie because of my betrayal.

Sophie hated me. Truly hated me.

Waves of emotion kept crashing into me. Sleep was a faraway joke. Whenever I closed my eyes, I saw her disgust when we left the cells and the memory of her beautiful brown eyes morphing into their hostage gold.

When the images hit, it was a sure case for self-loathing to move right in and slap me around. Instead of protecting her as I promised I would always do, I put myself in a different car away from her because I couldn't handle the guilt her absent emotional tie caused me. Another thing beyond her control that she was forced to pay for.

Despite my self-deprecation, I tried to force a good memory I could hold onto, trying to think of the last time those eyes shone happily for me.

The attic.

Fox's tattoos were fresh. The added ingredient dulling my visions and giving us some much-needed distraction from the horror of watching my father murder Eli. Sophie's playfulness and hint of inebriation was evident in her soft-lipped smile and hooded dark gaze, the heat between us a crackling tension of tamed need since we were surrounded by others. All I wanted was to be inside of her, to make her moan in crazed echoes, but was happy with spending the time feeling her skin beneath mine without the invasion of my visions. It was a sliver of unapologetic and selfish indulgence for the both of us.

The expected ache this memory caused killed all the temptation within it as I couldn't freeze-frame her expression before it twisted into Nya's cold retelling of how her possession was my fault.

Opening my eyes to the blank ceiling, I cringed, my muscles tensed. The lust-filled fantasy with Sophie was overridden by the imposing nightmare of the Conception Rituals re-enactment. The contraction in my groin evoked disgust as pure hatred for my body's betrayal as I lay on that slab being milked like a stud horse. It was enough to end this wretched life and everything about me in it.

In the attic, before everything went to shit, I craved the neediness sex with Sophie sated. Now, a hug from her—actually her and not Nya—filled with trust and the same need to give and take comfort from the person holding you, would overwhelm me with gratitude. She knew what I needed and how to provide it. I wondered if that would be the case without the connection. At one time, I thought it would.

Something tickled my ear. I swiped at it, my hand coming away wet. In all the numbness I felt to keep me from tearing the house around me down to the studs, somehow, I was crying. A heavy depression filled my bones. I wanted to sleep for a century, to feel absolutely nothing so I didn't have to wonder what Sophie was going through right now, but I couldn't even find the energy to pass the fuck out.

Until the first Conception Rituals, I had never been with a woman sexually let alone with a woman and her fifty friends and family. Fox tried his best to stop me from approaching sex with such disconnect once I became active, so did Aunt Lacey. They understood why I fucked my way half across the region. At least I retained control over where I stuck my dick. I just didn't expect it to become such a need. Having to do it, sometimes more than once a night, multiple partners and never sated as the need became stronger, while the gratification it brought faded further away.

That lust was never sated until my first time with Sophie. If it even fell into the same category. It was a blur and unintentional, not the predatory stalking in a darkened club. When Sophie woke up and ran away in a panic, I remembered thinking that I didn't want anyone but her ever again. I would have done anything to have that split-second of wakefulness with Sophie naked in my arms before reality sledge-hammered its way in-between us.

Even with Caine on the fringe, Sophie brought a peace into my world I never would have guessed existed until I felt it.

"Caine...."

I sat straight up in the bed. A brain pin popped into place, and I thought back to my capture and the side-lined possibility. Could I do it? Could I connect to Caine without the slimy fucking worm invading my skull again? Its juices might still be in there. The creature was upstairs, if need be, yet it was worth trying so I wouldn't need to leave this room and have everyone else watching and recording what happened. If anyone would understand the despair of Sophie being taken over by Nya, Caine would.

I settled back onto the too soft pillow, dug a supporting arm beneath my head, and closed my eyes. Maybe all it would do was help me sleep, but I needed to try. The other times I did the Nexus Transference spell, Sophie and her saucy distractions helped. I couldn't think about those now without it drowning me in grief.

With my breathing regulated and my heartbeat steady, I thought back to the incantation Sophie's aunts recited each time. I remembered the words...I think. Most incantations are simple repetitive sentences, so I probably got the gist. Fuck it. What else did I have to do but witness the degradation of the only woman I ever lost my heart to.

Concentrating on what I could remember, I went over these words and recalled the process, reaching beyond the pain of the invading worm and to the existence of the bridge between myself and my ancestor riding in Caine's body. Repeating the incantation in my head didn't seem to be working. I kept doing it, letting the words seep into me like massaging fingers to keep me composed as I envisioned Caine and the pathway through the Creation.

"Enjoying yourself?"

I growled and sprung at the female voice of whomever bypassed my locking spell and was now ruining my experiment.

"Geez!" The startled voice belonged to Ness. "You invade our space and you're getting territorial on me?"

I settled back on my heels as I registered her annoyed expression and our surroundings as no longer being inside the Ballard Estate. Sallow green leaves and branches were thrown around at my feet, replacing the old fittings of wallpaper in the estate's room, the air humid, stifling in my lungs. Water squished between my toes through the fabric of my socks.

"It rained."

"No, it hurricaned." The deep voice was Caine's, but the comment didn't me give enough to identify who was manning the vessel. Gareth was good at being Caine when it meant short sentences. It forced Nya's image and more before I could dampen it down. "What's wrong with Sophie?"

Okay. So, it was Caine. Gareth wouldn't have vaulted away from casually leaning against the tree so fast and Ness wouldn't have been so visibly annoyed.

Thinking of how to word what happened tripped me up.

"She's returned."

I looked up at the guy in shock of how he could have guessed. The tone of voice and turn of phrase should have tipped me off right away, but it took me a second to recognize that Caine was no longer in the driver's seat. Gareth must have read my mind and shot into the forefront greedy for details.

As with Sophie, the shift from self to ancient was swift and unmistakable. Caine didn't spark new eye colour, the grey still grey but peering into them there was no way I could ever mistake these calculating eyes as Caine's. The sight of them, busting the seams of his meat packaging in furious excitement, made my veins ignite like black powder as Ness stood awkward on the outside of Gareth's notice.

"I refuse to speak with you." I made it plain and simple. I was not here for Gareth.

Gareth's hand clenched my throat so quickly I didn't see it until the cartilage of my windpipe crunched and pierced skin. I grabbed his wrist, but he didn't let go.

"I refuse to be managed by the seed of my enemies." Gareth squeezed harder, the veins in my throat burning, straining, oxygen starved. "Where is my Nya?"

"Manage this, prick," I inwardly cursed at the asshole. Without verbal flare, I drove my knee into the guy's balls.

Gareth dropped to the mud floor in a huff as a gasp left a nervous Ness, giving me time to suck on razor blades before I could heal my throat.

I leaned over Gareth. "Even time-surfing assholes can be sacked."

Gareth recovered quickly and rose to his feet.

Ready for a brawl, I rooted my stance, every muscle in my back and biceps trembled in anticipation for a fight I so desperately needed. Fighting and fucking always left me with a certain satisfaction, and since this option was right in front of me, I was taking full advantage. Brisk air stung my teeth I was sucking oxygen so hard. When Gareth's eyes shone darkly below Caine's thick brow, it only took the shadow of a mocking grin to evoke my power in a flush, clouding my vision, leaving only Gareth in strict focus.

Flexing to strike, I salivated for a chance to make Gareth pay. Pay for Nya's takeover, for being one of two people who screwed my life over just when it started to come together. Before a half-step could be pressed into the mud, the power I wore on my skin swelled around me. Different than when I was pissed and it took me over, but this did so without permission, without my command, suffocating me.

Then Gareth disappeared.

Strength in the overpowering atmosphere grew so rapidly it choked me again, stumbling back a step or two as I pressed a fist into my chest, willing my primary system of survival to wake up and do its damn job, but my lungs burned like a motherfucker and my vision went spotty and blackened.

Over my wheezing, I heard someone mewling. No, more of a soothing rhythm. Soothing me? Gareth? No. It was Ness using her illusion ability, this time she dropped us into darkness, blinding us, while talking to Caine to bring him back to the forefront and somehow push Gareth into the backseat.

Why didn't Gareth kill her? Especially if she was so useful against him? Maybe Caine wouldn't let him.

Treefall bit into my kneecap with bared teeth before Ness returned my sight and brought herself and Caine into view as I stood. Ness stepped away, arms crossed, shoulders stooped, and looking as if she wished there was a sinkhole to escape into. Her stone mask slipped into place, but before it did, soft almond eyes were heavy with the negotiating power stronger than her ability.

At least I could breathe again.

"Sorry." Caine's apology was all his own.

I could have let loose on the asshole but not when I saw the self-deprecation in the guy. No ego to beat down equals no fun.

I rolled my stiff shoulders while filling my lungs with crisp oxygen to erase the lingering burn. Shrugging off the apology, I wanted to focus on the point. Until I realized I didn't have one.

"So, Nya's large and in charge?" Ness prompted.

Caine hung his head at the repeat of the news. I understood the feeling, which was why I was here.

"What happened?" Caine asked with obvious strain. "Did Sophie...let her?"

I shook my head. "I can't even kill the bitch." The comment triggered something unseen as Caine slightly twitched and cleared his throat. It was if he was inwardly battling with Gareth to keep the ancient at bay. As if my comment evoked Gareth's anger.

"Was Sophie pushed out?" Caine asked once he gained full control.

The question meant Caine knew that was a possibility. I never questioned if that could happen, never gave it any thought, but apparently Caine had the inside scoop.

"According to the Ballard Soul Seers, she's not gone." Caine's shoulders relaxed an inch in relief. "I'll get her safe before that happens."

Caine nodded as if agreeing to be a part of whatever scheme I cooked up, no matter the details.

"Why aren't you affected?" Ness broke through the conversation, annoyed, presumably at Caine's drive to assist Sophie in any fashion. Or her chilly demeanour could equally be due to Caine's bereavement to Sophie's struggles. Either way, she was not happy.

I looked to a shame-faced Caine, surprised by how much she knew as Caine and Ness were obviously chatty. "No clue. I wasn't with her when it happened, but during the...conquest...I felt an energy overload plus the pain that comes every time Nya's power is tapped. Before my body was seconds from exploding, it all suddenly stopped. Then I couldn't feel anything, and Nya was wearing Sophie like a new suit."

"Wait," Caine said and paused. "You can't feel anything?"

I pressed my lips together. "Actually, it's been a few days since I could."

This was a loaded answer which created questions. Ones I answered with a quick synopsis and fielding follow-up inquiries. No way were the dirty details necessary. By the end of it, Caine was wiping his hands over his growing beard and pacing while Ness turned to a hardened statue. She stared at the ground as if her curiosity stuck her in place while the rest of her begged to be excused. I didn't give her the permission to do so. I wasn't her keeper and sure as hell didn't give a shit about her discomfort.

"There were a few blips of sensation, but...nothing close to how it was." I didn't have to see Caine's expression to feel dread for his happiness for this new element. Apparently neither did Ness as she hadn't glanced up from the mud yet.

"So, nothing?" Caine asked again after a few more beats of silence. This time the question set Ness into a pace, almost at the end of her tolerance.

I inwardly cursed. How many times did I have to repeat it? "Nothing," I said, ready to throw punches if Caine asked again.

"You think Nya severed the connection for good, don't you?"

My jaw clenched so tightly I risked breaking a tooth. Straining with every action, subdued fury boiled in me. "Maybe."

Predictable to the end, Caine thoroughly enjoyed this remote prospect. So much so, he dampened the slightest hint of a grin yet failed to hide the crinkle of his eyes. How Ness stood by was astonishing because she wanted to be anywhere but here. She even gazed towards where I assumed the camp was, though I couldn't see it through the brush.

"Leave then." I couldn't help myself.

Ness's attention whipped my way. "Excuse me?"

"I'm not here for you, and I don't give a shit if talking about Sophie gets your green-eyed monster's cackles all fluffed and makes you question whatever romanticized movie version of *Survivor* you got in your head. So, leave and let me and Caine talk about some serious shit. Or suck it up." Ness's eyes narrowed. "All you know is Caine and Sophie have history. I have more. Centuries and lifetimes more. I'd really like to solve the clusterfuck of how to return to it without your drama."

"I am—"

"Helping or leaving," I interrupted without leeway. My rubber band of sympathy snapped. She could throw a tantrum, try and attack, or leave in a heap of tears, I honestly didn't care which as long as it was done now so I could stop wasting time.

"Helping how?" Ness answered with disdain.

"Not sure. Start brainstorming. I *am* getting Sophie back whether Gareth wants it or not. Whatever you did before to bring Caine around when Gareth took over, it worked. What'd you do?"

Harshness faded as she peered over to Caine, uncomfortable with the conversation. "I just talked to him."

Caine's eyes shifted away from hers. "It won't be enough on the field, if that's what you're thinking," he said to Ness's obvious dismay. "When it comes to the fighting, Gareth takes over immediately. Sometimes I can hold him off, only until it gets hairy. Since his only objective is to escape the Creation to find Nya, last thing he needs is me screwing his plans by getting his vessel killed."

Now it was me who was pacing. "I have no cards to play here." My chin quivered and I mashed my molars together to stop it. I reached for that cold part of myself, the part existing before Sophie arrived in my life and kneaded my rigidness into a soft dough. I accessed this to find my focus. I fumbled a bit, but I found it.

"Everything's changed now," I continued. "The premonition's in the shredder, the fight was already supposed to happen and didn't, so we don't know when it will. We don't possess the discus anymore—"

"What?" Caine questioned harshly.

"Tobias has it. We think. Even the truce my mother set up is void as Tobias threatened to kill me in the cells if she didn't rescind it." Who would have thought I would have a mother who could exercise sacrifice? "We can't even bank on you and Sophie anymore."

"Are the Elders doing anything?" A surprising question from Ness.

I laughed almost sadly. "Besides Vincent, they've got nothing and can barely keep Coven morale from plummeting. And don't get me started on Vincent. He's good, he is. He's also a lying sack of shit with a hidden agenda. I'll work for him, but I don't trust him, especially when it comes to Sophie. His focus is all on her. He would probably do anything for her, true, yet he's still a shifty bastard."

"So, again, you visit with nothing but bad news and no timeline to work with. Why do you bother?" This sounded more like Ness.

"Is that your version of helpful?"

"No. It's my version of telling you to get your shit together before we're slaughtered or have to decide on who to eat before we starve to death. You have problems? Boohoo. You can't solve them from here anymore than we can."

"So, I do what, exactly?"

"I don't know. Force the issue. Bring whoever has the discus to the field and egg them into getting started. Lure them out. Maybe tap into that dark manipulative part of you. A little Taint on your soul would be worth setting free your precious Sophie, wouldn't it?"

"Easy for you to say."

"Easier for you to do. I gotta relieve Felix." Leave it to her to take off on a good line.

"Supportive chick you got there."

Caine didn't comment. He usually insisted on saying "it's not like that", so maybe things *had* changed. The sparkle in Caine's eye when I mentioned the tiniest chance the connection was broken wasn't hidden well enough and it scared me to know Sophie would most likely choose the option to try again with Caine since she hated me now. Why wouldn't she? They only split because the connection divided them.

"Can you lure Tobias with the discus to the field?" Caine asked.

"Honestly, I doubt it, but I'll bring it up and see if someone else's brain is working better than mine." The surreal fogginess was relentless. I just couldn't believe Sophie may be gone and our connection broken. The hollow absence I felt in the cells was survival. Now? I couldn't handle it.

Silence ensued until I said, "I assume Evar's still alive and kicking or you would've said something." Caine peaked an eyebrow as if this was obvious. "Figured so. Nya confirmed we can't kill Evaristus."

"Of course we can," Caine argued. "No one's ever truly immortal."

I shook my head. "Can't kill someone who doesn't have a soul.

I'm sure that's why Evar got rid of his, but we don't know how to jam his soul back into his body even if we found it."

Caine peered at the trees as if lost in thought and muttered, "That's what Bridgette meant." Without explaining the comment, he refocused on me. "Does it have to be his original soul? Or can it be any soul?"

I hadn't thought of using a random soul. "No clue. You'd think it wouldn't matter as long as a soul exists within the vessel?"

Caine shrugged as if the idea meant little, but in the end could be the answer to everything.

"Nice. We'll work on that. For now, stay clear of him."

"Fine by me. Our numbers are dwindling. We can't afford to lose more people, especially if the guy can't die. Besides, according to Aunt Lacey, you're supposed to kill him, right?" I was confused. "When Evar knocked Sophie's soul from her body and she saw Aunt Lacey, didn't she say you needed more power to truly end him?"

Oh, right. How could I have forgotten? "If it's possible, I'll do it, but I don't see how. All Magics want more power. Sophie doesn't have the time it would take me to earn it."

Silence reigned while both of us were deep in tormenting thoughts.

"Before..." I took a deep breath and blew it out shakily, "before everything, before Sophie and I got together that first time...she asked me what I would do if she turned dark-side." I kept my eyes cast down, feeling Caine's heavy glare on me. "I told her...I promised her...that I wouldn't abandon her, and if I couldn't talk her out of it, then I'd follow her down the same path so I could watch over her and protect her until she came to her senses." I saw a flash of us in my basement, books and snacks surrounding us as I gave this promise. "She didn't believe me at the time, but I fully intend to keep that promise."

When I looked up, I met Caine's unreadable stare. I was about to segue into leaving before he spoke up.

"I don't know you the way she does," Caine started and hesitated, stopping me from trying to leave. "I know you love her, even if I've always doubted if you even knew what the word meant."

"Can't say I knew before her," I allotted, then mumbled, "in this lifetime anyway."

The quick head tilt said Caine didn't either.

When the seriousness of the direction the conversation took hit me, it was strong, and suddenly I wanted to get the fuck out. Too much share-time for me to continue handling appropriately. My tolerance for everything Caine-related found its end and if I didn't escape now, things would be said that shouldn't and were going to turn ugly.

"Next time I see you will be in the field," I managed. "With the way shit's headed, chances are a lengthy heads-up before the fight isn't going to happen. It was postponed for whatever reason, but expect it soon."

Caine shrugged coldly, attuned to the frigidness I was emanating. "We're used to waiting. Just be sure Sophie's alive when I get out of this hellhole."

The implications of this boiled my blood. It took everything in me not to force him to explain exactly what he meant. Even if I didn't have the right, even if Sophie came back to herself and never wanted to be in the same room as me, I knew I would always have this reaction. Irrational, territorial, tree-pissing, and club-over-the-head Neanderthal it may be, it was what it was, and I would never be alright seeing Sophie with another guy no matter who they were.

Never.

A pounding in my chest tore the oxygen from my lips and vibrated through my ribcage like a steel drum. Caine looked on unconcerned as I palmed my sternum and vacuumed in a breath of the dankness around me before my knees threatened to buckle. I tried to give a pithy parting word, but a hammer hit my chest again, and this time, before my knees splashed into the mud, I was sucking dusty air looking into a pair of beautiful ice blue eyes that unfortunately belonged to the big guy from the compound.

The sound of my wheezing wasn't enough to cover the room's disquiet commotion and my attention flitted to relieved faces as I coughed.

"What the fuck was that?" Kim was teary-eyed and red-cheeked.

The big guy stood back as his hammering fist was no longer needed. "Get up. We've got issues."

A spike of adrenaline greater than my already crushing heartbeat put me on my feet to follow them into the hallway.

"Don't pull that shit," Kim scolded as we speed-walked down the stairs and through to the front sitting room. "We didn't know where you were."

"Other crap to deal with here, Kim." I pushed through bystanders as the big guy did, all gawking through the front windows.

A neat row of shoulder-to-shoulder bodies were lit by fading and inadequate streetlights, they comfortable in the cold and going nowhere, eerily looking at the estate. I didn't need a Soul Seer's interpretation to know they were playing for the opposing team.

"Why are they just standing there?" Caitlyn asked.

"Waiting for the perfect time to strike?" Blake's guess was likely correct and daunting.

"They're safe outside the active wards," I said with a level tone. "We'll know when the Creation is hit because these bastards will make their move. They probably have a way to deactivate the wards, too."

Kim made a little gasp. "They wanna keep us distracted."

"We need to leave." Someone's shaky voice echoed the opinion of many others.

Others spoke up with much of the same. They weren't safe anymore, they were sitting ducks, et cetera, et cetera. Abandoning the estate left us nowhere to hide during a frigid winter. Aunt Lacey's was no better. No matter where we went, we would be followed. And now, even The Chiff wasn't left as a backup safe zone.

Above the chatter, Olive broke through, shooing them from the threat only yards away but closing the heavy shades. "Get back to work, everyone. We have enough to keep us busy inside."

The crowd dispersed but it didn't stop their mouths from running. I didn't follow the herd, instead I dropped into a chair by the window and mashed my face into my palms. The whine of springs under my ass told me the chair wouldn't hold me for long, yet I hoped the wards held strong far longer.

"What were you doing?" Kim was close, her tone as bitchy as ever. "It took a lot for Hall to wake you up."

Letting go of the exhale I was holding, I leaned back into the creaky chair and looked to Kim to see that Hall was still with her. Since it was only them, I didn't mind talking.

"I was visiting Caine."

When Kim blinked as if I must have been talking about a different Caine, I explained what I did and what we talked about.

"So, we stuck that thing in your head twice for no reason?" Of course, after everything I said, Kim wondered about the worm. I actually laughed a little, which seemed to be her goal, even if it was more an exhausted chuckle.

"Have you heard of anything like that? Soul injection?" I asked Hall since he was clearly the oldest and most experienced in the room.

Hall blinked and shifted his weight in thought.

"How did Evar get rid of it in the first place? Maybe that will help," Kim attempted.

Hall itched his neck uncomfortably. "I've never seen it happen, though stories have circulated. Folktales with deep-seated religious fear and no witnesses from our kind. I didn't realize it was true of Evar until Vincent said Sophie couldn't detect it."

"What did you hear?" Kim asked impatiently.

Hall crooked a smile in her direction as if he thought her eagerness was adorable. If they didn't fuck soon and break the sex-crazed tension, I was going to lock them in a room until they broke the furniture.

"It's possible that a soul dies from years of disuse or even abuse. So polluted with evil it has no other reason to hang around. Of course, they say you can sell it. Contract with the Devil nonsense, but I'm sure that's rumour. It's also said it could be forcibly removed or even spelled from the vessel, but really, as I said, it's all rumour since I've never been present for a soul dying without it leaving the decaying body behind."

Disuse or abuse seemed unlikely to me. If that were the case, more of the Tainted would be soulless, including my father. Selling it? Maybe, but to what type of buyer? And wouldn't that kill the vessel, too? Deduction left spelling or removal.

"By removed, do you mean Extracted?" Kim made what should have been an obvious conclusion.

Realizing we were talking to the wrong person, I didn't wait for an answer, leaving the two behind in search of Vincent. In the kitchen, I found him talking to Lincoln and Bronya.

"Can you extract a soul and leave the body alive?" All their eyes moved to me in my brash interruption.

"I'm sorry...?"

"We can't kill Evar because he doesn't have a soul. Could a Soul Extractor have removed it and left him alive?

Vincent's jaw went slack and his eyes unfocused as he thought under pressure. Adjusting his glasses, Vincent was practically stuttering. "I suppose...well, if you...It may be plausible—"

"It doesn't matter," I interrupted again as Kim and Hall caught up to me. "Can you reverse that process?"

"Reverse?"

"Can you shove a soul back into a body, even if it's not the vessel's original soul?"

Vincent's brows knotted. "In what occasion would I have had the opportunity?"

"I don't need references, a yes or no will suffice."

He crossed his arms. "Typically, I partially extract souls and in a temporary manner. I have never attempted what you are implying, so I do not know for certain."

"Besides," Lincoln stepped in, "whose soul are you going to steal to pull it off?"

"Doesn't matter, I just need to know if it can be done." I looked back at Vincent. "Is there a Soul Extractor community where you can ask questions?"

The edges of Vincent's lips pulled down. "I suppose there are others I can commune with."

"Now?"

Vincent's stare hardened. "When I am done here, yes."

"But how does that solve everything?" Kim asked. "Donovan, you're supposed to do it, right? Aunt Lacey said so. So, if Vincent does all the work, then why do you need more power?"

"I don't give a shit at this point. Whatever Aunt Lacey said or didn't say, it won't guarantee us a win." I turned back to Vincent. "Call. Now."

I stalked from the room without caring about how unimpressed Vincent was with being given an order.

19

CHOSEN. NOT ASKED.

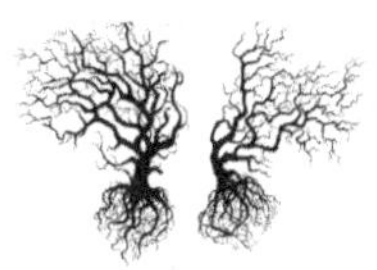

Kim

Watching Donovan run off made my toes tingle with a sense of defeat. Not that the fight was over, nowhere close, but in the beginning, it was Donovan and me in Aunt Lacey's basement partially ignoring each other. Then Sophie and Caine joined up and we became a quad of Magics who found comfort in each other's company, even if half the time some members only tolerated each other. Now, Sophie wasn't Sophie, Caine was trapped and not Caine all of the time, and Donovan was running around in subdued insanity.

Most days, I found it difficult to see Donovan muster a teaspoon of interest in anything. He always maintained a tense calmness or was painfully aloof. This desperate and frenzied Donovan made me uncomfortable. I couldn't anticipate what he might do.

"Comfortable or not, Donovan lacks the capability to lead his Sect with his priorities centered on Sophie alone." Always eavesdropping, Hall chimed in with unsolicited advice. "In his place, you must take control. Your Sect members will have many questions. You don't want one of their deaths to be due to one of their leader's incompetence."

I huffed, getting tired of his meddling. "Is it your mission to spit-shine me into a stellar Sect Leader or are you wanting your own flock to boss around? I mean, you are currently unemployed, but this particular position has been filled."

He crooked a smile, crossed his heavy arms still clad in his animal hide coat over his chest, and slightly leaned down to me, talking so closely his distinct male scent flooded my senses. "I've tasted enough of your mind to know failing your Sect would scar you, so you would never allow this to occur. As one from an unbiased perch, I see a floundering Sect with leaders showcasing their doubt and highlighting their guilt. Feel as you need to privately. To cope, I'd personally ensure your private quarters are filled with nothing except the sweet smell of sex, if you'd allow it." I rolled my eyes as Hall smiled enough to show teeth. "However, on the outside..." He lifted his finger under my chin as apparently my mouth was open. I straightened away from his touch, but he reserved his smile. "...You must retain an air of confidence so thick the brightest of the flock would see nothing but the camouflage. Decide who that member is and rise to their expectations."

How did he do that? Probably years of practice playing with little girl's heads, pushing his muscles around, drawing you in thinking something Holy and profound will come spilling out, and then it turns into a sex thing. The man screamed everything stereotypically masculine, draped in layers of testosterone and unchecked libido. Who did he think he was pulling that shit with me?

He lifted one brow. "Funny how your protests never pass those luscious lips."

"Stay out of my head, Viking." I turned to find someone, anyone. Why didn't he find someone else to bug?

"No need." He followed with languid steps. "I'm mighty comfortable trailing that sweet tail of yours."

I huffed and did my best to ignore him, doing everything in my power to feel anything but flattery for attracting his attentions. Soon all this would be over, and I would see Frog. Forcing his image into my mind helped block thoughts of Hall, but even with him behind me, he was all I could smell, and my body was rebelling against me.

It had been a while since I spent quality time with Frog. That's all it was.

Once I found Blake and Jared, I delegated them the chore of herding the Sect to Olive's empty master bedroom, and damn him, as Hall said, they came quickly, eager for the full scoop, not whatever Vincent covered in the attic. Like a kindergarten class at story time, they listened quietly until I got through what I knew. Hall didn't pipe up at all, instead he stood vigilantly outside the door ensuring Nya wasn't anywhere near us eavesdropping.

Technically, Nya was a Sect member by default since Sophie was, but Sophie wasn't Nya's free pass. When the door abruptly opened, I assumed Hall lost his balls and let Nya in after all his bluster of keeping her clear of everyone, until I saw Donovan.

Peering around the room to see the entire Sect gathered on Olive's large four poster bed and lining the walls, instead of leaving him to guess, I jumped with the explanation before the guy flipped. "I didn't think you wanted to attend another recap considering you lived through your own escape."

Donovan nodded and closed the door behind him and leaned against it.

Taking this as permission to proceed, though I was basically finished anyway, I offered them a chance to ask questions. No surprise, they were tripping over themselves. Most I couldn't answer, like "Why is Donovan's mom helping us when she's evil?" and "Why can't Donovan feel Sophie anymore?" or "Was their Soul Magic scrapped?" or "Can we kill Nya without killing Sophie?".

It didn't help that Donovan stood idly by without offering any explanations when, if anything, he could provide a half-answer. Anything more than I could.

Matt was asking something else about Nya, but my brain was

already fried when a few voices turned urgent. Something was wrong with Gwen. She stood on the outskirts of the Coveners like she was the first one in the room and ended up being pressed into the far wall.

"I ne-ed to...I need to...." Gwen was trying to talk as her hand went from her head to her stomach then in front of her as if her head hurt, was going to puke, and faint simultaneously.

No one missed the cues and gave up their spot on the bed before wearing whatever was battering at the back of her throat searching for an escape. Lying down in trembling shakes, Gwen was covered in a sheen of perspiration matting her ginger hair as the group uselessly hovered. Donovan and I moved in quickly to assess the problem. All I could see was Gwen sweating with her eyes squeezed tight, her movements wild and uncontrolled, no matter how small.

Donovan exhaled. "She's having a vision."

Before we could manage what was happening to her, Donovan leaned over Gwen, grabbed onto her arms, and squeezed her pale skin tightly, his eyes falling distant, and his jaw slacked while filtering Gwen's vision into his palms with his Psychometry.

A sense of power engorged the room, saturating the wallpaper, and tickling everyone's powers with the urge to use them.

Hall rushed into the room, closing the door behind him, and stopping once he came close as if he already knew what was happening.

Gwen gasped and opened her eyes. Donovan did the same. The power in the room eased as the vision passed.

Once the suspended silence dropped like a gavel, every Covener was asking questions and moving around the room in a bit of a panic.

"Please. Everyone be quiet." When they did, I turned to Gwen and Donovan, who were staring at each other. "Anything we should know about?" I was being nice by asking. If they didn't tell me, things wouldn't be so nice.

Donovan raced out of the room, his footfalls slamming against the floorboards in great leaps as he ran off.

"What did you see?" I know I shouldn't have bothered yelling after him, but something completely not good was happening here and I wanted to know now if I should chase after him or stick with Gwen.

I hesitated. Dammit.

Instead of waiting, I followed Donovan. Gwen had enough people around to help her. "Where'd he go?" Priscilla and Lewis were in the hall. They pointed me towards the attic entrance.

Upstairs, too many people were in my way, and I was too short to see over them. Then I remembered I had a magic life hack for that. I took a calming breath and thought of Donovan running into the attic, knowing he was here somewhere, and watched as my guiding light appeared and snaked through the crowd.

Following my guide, it became easily clear once I dodged a few rows of people because I could hear things falling and complaints and whispered agitation. Donovan was rifling through the long shelves that ran along the attic's front wall without concern for what fell to the floor. He moved from shelf to shelf with grim focus and murmured curses in a frenzied search.

"It was here. It was here. Fuck, it was here." Donovan's panic and disbelief was unsettling, but he kept looking, insisting on something being there without being able to find it.

"I'll help. Tell me what you're looking for?" I tried to be calm about it so Donovan wouldn't come at me, but he opted for scraping his fingers through his hair as he continued surveying the shelves.

"What are you doing?" Olive stood on the edge of spectators with the Elders, now looking on in horror at the chaos Donovan was making of her stock.

"Gwen had a vision." I jumped in before Ranlyn and Vincent tried to restrain Donovan. Hall was behind me looking mighty helpful if they decided Donovan needed a timeout. "Donovan sucked it up and ran here looking for something."

"Donovan!" Vincent took a step forward to assert himself, but Donovan was still jutting side to side in search for something on the shelf he wasn't seeing.

"The rock...." Donovan's voice barely registered, but I was close enough to hear as he straightened with both hands clutching at his hair in a devastating frustration.

"What rock?" I didn't see any specific rocks on the shelves. Some crystals, but he shoved them aside.

Donovan was in his own world, not listening to anyone as if the whole crowd behind him didn't exist.

A loud gasp from Donovan shocked the hell out of me as he grabbed for his chest and fell to his knees. I didn't know what to do. He didn't look hurt. Was he having a heart attack? A panic attack?

The others were either held back, chose to stay clear of him, or in the case of a few, were looking on in horror as Vincent stood with his arm outstretched in front of him. At first, I didn't comprehend what he was doing.

I stood yet remained next to Donovan. "How's extracting his soul helpful?"

Vincent didn't look at me. "He is more compliant this way."

Rosemary pushed through the group, invading Vincent's personal space. "Must I unsheathe my knife again?"

Donovan was now hyperventilating. Someone had to do something. The kid couldn't stay this way.

No one was saying anything, not even Vincent, however, his brow was creased as if he was doing something more than letting Donovan's soul hang like drying laundry. Maybe he was reading his mind.

I looked at Hall, who shook his head. I took it as a warning not to intercede, but I was losing patience.

Vincent lowered his hand and Donovan sucked in air as if he had been drowning and then sagged onto the hardwood floor. I leapt forward to try and help him, even if I couldn't do anything. He had enough energy to wave me off yet not enough to push me away from his personal bubble.

Vincent fixed his glasses. "It is no rock. It is a ritual stone. And the vision, I suspect, was not a convenient coincidence, yet sent by someone with the inability to remain on the sidelines."

I tried to hide my excitement. "Are you talking about who I think you're talking about? Please tell me you're talking about who I think you're talking about."

His pursed lips didn't say Aunt Lacey's name, but his eyes did. Aunt Lacey would never sit around and do nothing. Nya may have been her family, but Sophie was too, in a way, and Donovan definitely was. If it was her, she was pointing Donovan towards something helpful. No wonder Donovan was jacked.

Hall was looking at me funnily, curiosity in his grin, but he didn't say anything.

"For which ritual?" Ranlyn asked, not saying anything about the fact his co-Elder Extracted the soul of one in the flock as a means of control or questioning Aunt Lacey's interference.

"It's ours!" Donovan was still coughing as he got to his feet, red-faced and pissed off, then repeating himself even though no one knew what he was talking about. He grabbed Vincent's shoulder and people jumped to force him away, Hall included. The look on the Viking's expression shifted so quickly from "invested bystander" to "protector set to destroy if needed" he appeared to be a completely different person.

Vincent straightened his button-down. "I know where it is."

I still didn't know what the hell they were talking about but Vincent saying so gained Donovan's full attention. "You know?"

Vincent nodded and Donovan's bunched shoulders slumped.

Unsatisfied with being out of the loop, Ranlyn moved towards them demanding an explanation as Veata slowly followed. Right behind them were Fox and Hall. The curiosity didn't stop there, everyone wanted to know, but I stepped into the small circle as Ranlyn was still trying to get the full story.

When Vincent looked around at the Coveners, Hall told him he would cover us so we could speak freely.

It wasn't until Vincent started talking that I realized the others around us were straining to hear what he was saying. Hall casted a privacy spell and people were not happy about it. They could still see us, so I motioned for my Sect to relax, hoping they would cool it so I could find out all I could. If I could tell them about it afterwards, even better.

Vincent spoke to Donovan. The two shared a look I assumed was reminiscent of their past together. "The vision Gwen received revealed a ritual stone with specific carvings."

"What importance do the carvings hold?" Veata asked.

Vincent sighed.

"It's ours," Donovan said again as if he was ready to throw down if Vincent argued otherwise.

Vincent didn't comment on Donovan's insistence. "The vision directed them to the stone, making claim that it can solve the issue of separating Sophie's soul from Nya's."

I raised a finger for attention and pointed at Vincent. "I thought you could already do that? Were we not banking on it?"

Vincent's lips pursed. "When two souls inhabit a single vessel, I can separate and redistribute them, as I did with you and Miklos after fleeing the Creation. In this case, I have no body to put Nya back into and no inkling of what may occur if she is left without one. She may possess another of convenience, if at all possible."

"Is that not why we have Evaristus?" Ranlyn said. "To insert Nya into his vessel so we can take him down for good? Having a soul will make him destructible."

Vincent shook his head. "I cannot work that fast without potentially losing slivers of soul particles or Extracting the wrong ones. The loss of these pieces could leave Sophie half the woman she was or no woman at all."

He seemed to be ignoring Vincent, but Donovan's fists clenched, his jaw working until Vincent called his name and said, "I will not allow that to happen."

He received no verbal reply, and I was getting annoyed with being trapped in this private conversation while still missing the meat of the subject.

Torn by whatever Vincent heard in Donovan's head, he refrained from sharing and continued. "The stone was a crucial element in binding Donovan's and Sophie's souls with Soul Magic." No one said a word, but it was clear the stone was old. "Working with it now, according to the vision, will reach into Sophie and rekindle the connection between Sophie and Donovan as well as strengthen Sophie, coax her in front of Nya instead of being overshadowed in overbearing power. Then Sophie can be a part of her own rescue and work with excising Nya if I cannot do so myself." This negative possibility must be great by the look of sorrow Vincent wore.

What if Sophie couldn't push Nya out?

"I need this," Donovan whispered, then finally focused on Vincent. "I need her."

"I know," Vincent answered as if he truly did know.

Donovan kept an intense stare on Vincent. "You're her Overseer. You have to save her."

Everyone stared at Vincent as his expression dropped to the floor and then shifted in obvious discomfort.

"You are her Overseer?" Veata finally spoke.

Vincent put his hands on his hips. "I suppose I am."

"Why was this never mentioned?" Ranlyn questioned, clearly angry.

"What's an Overseer?" The name was unknown to me in terms of an official position. Sophie definitely never mentioned it and even Hall's forehead creased as though he was mentally confronting Vincent about it.

"Exactly as it sounds." Hall retained his look of scrutiny as Vincent was trying not to look at him. "He's Sophie's eternal caregiver, overseeing her in life, all her lives, to keep her safe and on path. Superb job, by the way."

Vincent's head whipped up with a grisly stare. "I did not ask to watch over her every life she recycles into."

"Overseers are chosen, not asked." Veata narrowed her sightless eyes and leaned onto her cane with both palms. "This is not some menial occupation applied for at your leisure."

"And since they're connected," Hall continued, "you can't convince me otherwise that you're not Donovan's as well."

Vincent was shaking his head. "No one has informed me of this."

"It should be obvious," Ranlyn stated.

Vincent glared at him. "Nothing was obvious. On either account."

"Fix it!" Donovan yelled, making me jump and nearly pee myself when he snatched Vincent's shirt collar in his fist and pulled him in close. The others pushed their arms between them, and Vincent grabbed onto Donovan's arm, but Donovan wasn't letting go. "Overseer or not, if Sophie dies, I will kill you if I don't die first. If so, then in the next life, I *will* see to it that this immortal life of yours ends so you know what it's like to be brought back Blind and terrified of what you are without a millennia's worth of knowledge to keep you alive."

Utter desperation was all I saw when looking at Donovan. He wasn't willing to live without Sophie and was primed to ensure Vincent paid for it if anything happened to her. And nothing about Donovan made me think he wouldn't follow through with his threat.

A wayward thought hit me. I was pretty sure that no one loved me enough to evoke such emotion. Scary to think of what was crawling inside of Donovan's head that he wasn't spitting at everyone.

"*I would.*" Hall's deep voice invaded my brain as the others were continuing their struggle without being so hands on.

The audacity. "*Pfft. Don't expect me to swoon at your obvious attempt at charm. Saying you 'would' is a hell of a lot different than saying you 'do'. And I'm taken.*"

"*Taken by a man you admit could never possess the devotion you crave.*"

"*It's called an idle thought.*"

"*It's called envy. A yearning I can slake. You're too scared to allow it.*"

"*Wrong again, Viking. I'm not interested, nor do I want you believing you have a chance.*"

"*I don't need to alter your mind. I'm already among its fantasies.*"

This Frog will be gone from your life sooner than you think. Not because he is not a good man, but because he is only a man. You require more than he can offer. Fight it now, you will succumb to your heart's demands as sure as your body will."

"My body will not, in any fashion or position, succumb to you. Now get the fuck out of my head." I tried to block my mind. Of course, I wasn't strong enough to keep him from hearing my thoughts, but it was enough to make a clear message that I didn't want him listening in. Arrogant asshole. I refused to entertain the possibility that he could be right and focused on the important conversation I was missing.

"I'm going with you." Donovan's voice came with a growl.

"We may not have the time for this," Vincent argued. "They need you for when Evaristus is released."

"I don't give a shit about Evar or Loring or the Creation. My priority will always be Sophie." I felt Hall's gaze on me as if calling attention to the type of devotion he was claiming he would have for me. "You're not cunning enough to ditch me. If you don't let me go with you, I'll follow, so let's skip the cat and mouse before I remind myself what a scheming piece of shit you are and end you right now."

Turning their backs on the small group, they meant to leave. "Wait!" I yelled after them. "Where are you going?"

"To get the fucking ritual stone!" Donovan spun and pointed at the proximity of where the Coveners were. "Get them to the field and don't say a goddamned word to anyone. We don't need Nya finding out. You think you can manage keeping what's inside your head to yourself?"

I scoffed at him yelling at me, but I knew if Nya wanted information, she would get what she wanted from me before I knew she took it.

"Back down, Sorrel." Hall stepped towards him. Blood rushed to my cheeks as the testosterone in the room swelled and annoyed me to death.

"You have no right to be possessive," Donovan snapped then

looked at me. "Let the Sect fall for all I care. I'm leaving." With that, Donovan turned his back on us and nearly pushed Vincent on their way to wherever they were going to find the ritual stone.

Hall cursed in a different language. "Inconsiderate prick."

"That's Donovan. He can't deal without Sophie and is panicked and desperate."

"Which gives him license to treat others disrespectfully?"

"Hell, no. But put yourself in his shoes. How much would you care about anything or anyone else if the person you loved was possessed and likely to die?" Saying this aloud reminded me I was talking about my best friend and a wave of sadness blindsided me, kicking me in the ribs and getting stuck in my throat.

Hall's forehead scrunched in concern, but I couldn't let it win me over. Sophie wasn't dead. And knowing Donovan, he would fight tooth and nail to make sure she never did.

Unfortunately, it meant Donovan was right. There was a lot of work to do with the Sect in dealing with Caine and the Creation opening. Nya discovering the Coven's plan to solve their issues with a possessed Sophie and a soulless Evaristus was no easy feat.

A concept crossed my mind. "Can that privacy spell you did work on my thoughts?"

Hall briefly considered it. "I think it could. Yet, I'd hate to be mute to that lusty brain of yours."

The low growl in his tone as he stepped in close to me heated my inner thighs. To step away would mean I possessed a morsel of control, but I was stripped of it the second he peered down at me with those ice-blue eyes. This reaction was also caught by the Viking eavesdropper as he gave a sound of satisfaction deep in his throat that equally angered and intrigued me.

Hall made a throaty laugh. "I thought as much. Your body responds even when your heart is conflicted. We'll work on that." He added another salacious grin. "Now, let's try this privacy spell, kitten."

20

FEAR FOR NOTHING

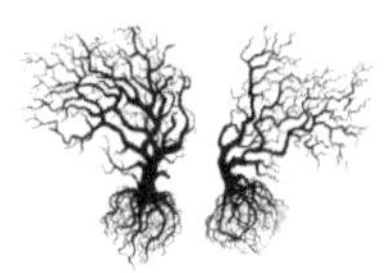

Donovan

"Accompanying me on this venture is unnecessary." Irritation in Vincent's voice was thick, even though he always spoke as if at a formal inquiry. I was beyond giving a shit about Vincent's disposition.

Truth was, I needed a break from the estate. Anywhere. Being inside the same walls as an absentee, animated version of Sophie was breaking me down by chunks. I still wanted to save her and sticking to Vincent's ass might be the only way to do it.

Thinking of her struggle back in the SUV made my sternum ache in twisting anguish and I had to remind myself it was only Nya I was temporarily escaping.

The time it would take to make Vincent understand this was too exhausting to contemplate, so not talking was better for everyone. Especially Vincent. If he tried stopping me from going along, I would have followed through with my threat. The guy knew it. Him questioning it now was a waste of his breath.

Reaching the second floor of the estate with the majority of the bedrooms, Vincent stopped.

"Let's go." I started towards the stairs to head outside.

"No need." Vincent pulled out a small ring of keys from his pocket. "The estate is surrounded. And our destination is not within driving range."

"Fine. Then we hop on a plane. I'm sure we can eke by security without a strip search."

Vincent ignored me and flipped through the keys, landing on a dull gold key. He stepped toward me and grabbed my shoulder, ignoring me further and holding tightly when I complained. German words came from the guy's lips, fast, yet I caught his request to be taken to the "Nest of honoured tributes".

The estate's hallway walls swayed. Others looked on in confusion before the walls changed all together.

Whoa. That was quick. Not only quick, but I wasn't nauseous or dizzy or in pain as with so many other modes of spelled transportation. While bracing in anticipation of something horrible about to overtake me or attack, Vincent was already in search-mode.

The walls of the place we entered existed, somewhere, but I couldn't guess what they looked like. Whatever the Nest of Tributes was it was a hoarder's dream. Stuff surrounded us from floor to ceiling and multiple rows wide. Dusty and unsteady piles appeared random and unorganized. On top of the few in front of me were books, a mangy doll, lack-luster jewellery that spilled over the edges of a tin mug, and newspapers and magazines galore. The tattered cloth of another pile probably added to the grandma's basement smell.

The world's shittiest garage sale swallowed Vincent whole as he wound around more piles of crap stacked over our heads. Following him before I lost him, I could breathe easier when a space of no bigger than five feet square opened up and cured the threat of being a victim of death by fallen box of dime store trinkets. The small space was enough to stave off claustrophobia, but Vincent was still a body's length away in a snaking path searching for something.

Was the ritual stone here amongst all this crap?

"How is any of this shit considered honoured tributes?" I wondered aloud.

Vincent didn't turn around to face me, but his shoulders gently shook with laughter. "You were always good with languages."

The comment was odd, too much of a reminiscent undertone in it to make me comfortable.

"Where are we?" I asked instead of getting into how and who I was in former lives.

Back still to me, Vincent straightened from an old box from inside an older trunk he had been rummaging through. "A storage place beneath a business I own."

Okay. So, we were in a basement. What kind of business could Vincent own that would mean storing this kind of stuff?

Vincent opened a discoloured photo album, found whatever he sought quickly, and handed me a delicate picture. It yellowed over time and threatened to fall apart in my fingers. A gasp left my lips before I could stop it. It was us. Sophie and me before we were Sophie and me.

Soft features escaped the print, unchallenging and devoid of make-up. A simplistic exquisiteness radiated from her as her posture elongated her lean neck and elegant shoulders. Her dark hair was pinned in a high twist, not a tendril escaped, in a style far removed from anything the Sophie of today would wear or even know how to do.

Remarkable. She was absolutely remarkable.

Covered from the collar of frill to thin wrists in her lap, posed side-saddled on grass away from wooden houses in the background in a dress that put her in the working class, I couldn't do anything but stare into those eyes. Untainted by Nya's influence they shone with contented poise, darkened yet ablaze in the colourless photo, smiling with lips romantically gentle.

If I were a millimetre of the man than as I was today, I would have kissed those lips at every opportunity. Younger in this photo, seated beside her, my bare arms slung casually over my knees, it meant we found each other earlier in that life than this one.

Without a recorded date, the fashion of Sophie's dress, and the fact I wore suspenders and a dreadful, short, side-parted hairdo, were the only clues at a timeframe. If only I could step through to this world, I'd wear those ridiculous suspenders to bed if it meant seeing the warm and carefree look behind those eyes again.

When I told Vincent I needed Sophie, I didn't mean to survive in the "two feet and a heartbeat" sense. I meant her being alive wasn't good enough. My survival counted on Sophie being the woman she was at our first greeting on the Coven meeting floor, the one who was half of me for countless centuries. Without that woman, I couldn't pretend to be a semblance of a man, and I would end this life to start another resembling the one in my hands.

"Amsterdam, 1885," Vincent's thick voice declared.

With a nod, I couldn't look away from her as those tears, like all of them, ceased and retreated in fear of what I would do if I dared to let them fall.

"She," I cleared my throat, "she looks...."

"Happy?"

I bit down on my lower lip to stop it from quivering and nodded, still looking at her.

"She was," Vincent said. "That was the summer you met."

If only my presence could give her that brand of happiness now.

"I found her as a child, in that life, when I went to her town on business. Only a kid at the time, I stayed around knowing you would eventually arrive as you had before. I befriended her family so I could remain close. Easy enough considering my financial stability allowed them certain luxuries. Though her father, a proud man, insisted on making his own, he did not object when I graciously offered loaning the monies to begin a business venture where his wife crafted the latest fashions, while he himself wielded wood into furniture and nearly built half the town. Success was never questioned, and they raised Sophie and her brother in middle-class comfort.

"I used to promise her a boy would come and colour her world." Vincent laughed sadly. "She would always complain of the other boys being dull when all she wanted was someone to brighten the sky with every step and bring out the sun until they were old and grey. Funny thing was, the summer your family emigrated from Germany was heinously hot and as soon as she saw you, she claimed you were why."

I swallowed against the squeeze in my throat. "Let me guess, we didn't make it to old and grey, did we?"

Vincent's lips twisted as he confirmed my assumption. "In 1887, during the Orange Riots, Sophie's family attempted to protect their store. An errant bullet struck her in the head." I shook my head at the likelihood. "In the confusion, none of her family was near, nor was I, and you both died."

"Two years?" I hated how thick my voice sounded. "Only two years in that life?"

"Yes."

Taking in a deep breath, I forced myself away from the memory and held the picture out for Vincent while thinking of how it had been less than that in this life and how much had occurred in that short time. "Did you find the stone?"

The question and dismissal of the photo was so brash, Vincent paused in shock before taking it back.

"Here." He showed me palm-sized rock engraved with lettering. "It is runic, Germanic, first or second century is the closest as I could tell, though maybe older. It reads: Hearts beg souls for infinite union." He flipped it over. "Far-reaching onto forever, these souls be granted sought desires."

Looking to the odd lettering, so small and crammed on each side of the stone, I believed what Vincent translated. I didn't know much about Germanic runes, but it was old.

"Here. As stated, it is yours." Vincent extended his closed hand towards me and narrowed his eyes ever so slightly as if bracing himself. When Vincent's fist opened and he dropped the stone into my palm, I was lost.

Scent overwhelmed, atmosphere hugging my skin, untouchably too close. Lively trees, creeping moss, clinging dew on blades of grass, churned dirt beneath my leather-strapped toes. Blackberries, sweet raspberry, tangy lemon, hints of white sage in a meld of a fiery dance of the servitude Elysande demanded, all splayed before us on the remnants of a Cyprus tree as the ritual commanded.

Dark hair flowed down the shoulders of her lavender dress, the back in curls flirting with her knees, her crown sun-kissed in lighter tones. I knelt undeserving before the altar in reverence for the passion that evoked this conjuration of eternal love. No outside power could thwart me from being hers forever. No weapon or restraint could keep me away. Somehow this loveliness before me knew this and stood straight-backed and determined to do her worst. To hide from our makers to fulfill this waking dream.

Elysande said this would help us find each other again, beyond death's notice, against destiny's designs, and we would be stronger with each life's passing. Belief was not difficult, nor was Elysande's success as most powers bowed to her will and begged to be toyed with. Even now. I gazed on in awe of my love. Building energy prickled my skin, hairs set on end in silent witness, teeth grit on the edge of grinding in want as I observed her prowess.

Reaching for another element, stone of the earth, power consumed me as Elysande called for more, causing the stone to dance in the air between us before sudden light engulfed the little stone, obscuring it from view. All I could see was this guarded light with its treasure within it. I watched the light grow and grew further in amazement when Elysande moved the light above us, then back down before circling it around my head and along my back. A charge of her essence sparked the length of my spine, settling heaviness in my chest as she did this, her deep eyes never connecting with mine, though I never swayed from hers.

Around herself as she did with me, she made the light dance at her will, growing with tension the energy called for. Goosebumps raised on her graceful arms. A sweet smile lifted corners of her lips.

"Do you fear the end of this life, Betyn?" Elysande wanted me to answer before the spell's completion, the light still hovering between us.

A timorous expression questioned me, praying I would follow her in this venture. That my love had not grown wings to flee in the opposite direction of this proposal.

"I fear for nothing. Only a single lifetime without you spears my heart with terror. Sacrificing this life for an eternity of others as your mate evokes feelings of overwrought cherishment. Beauty such as yours leaves men searching for worthiness. A worthiness I will never achieve yet I will worship you each day so you know life is greater for you existing within it with myself at your side."

My words dissolved her insecurity evident in her softened stare making my heart aglow. Trust brought her to reveal her secret power and I would have never imagined how beautiful it could be. Now we shared in this power and will for all days forth. This death would pass without awareness. I was eager for when I opened my eyes in my new life and wondered what possibilities it would bring me. As long as they brought Elysande, mirth would forever overwhelm.

Air stirred as the intensity of the energy pressed on my bones, the light Elysande wielded above us that of the sun shone upon us, showering down its power, filling each of us. By the crease at the sides of her eyes, I could tell she too was not immune to this sensation, akin to scurrying insects within my chest. It threatened to expand and take me over. I had to remind myself this was not a true death, merely a temporary end, vital to begin our forever.

Instead of fighting it, I embraced the sensation, permitting it to explore my body and settle where it must. Elysande's arms were losing its hold, elbows bending as if the light gathered weight. Looking to her, unable to move or catch her eye, I did my best to send her a silent message to calm her, to relieve her of worry as the weighty sensation pressed on through my limbs. Taking in a deep breath, I allowed the sensation further control of me and watched as Elysande did the same.

Unknown as to whether my influence caused her comfort, I gazed into the light reaching down to us and surrendered. Washing my sight with the brightest white, I closed my eyes to it and let my head fall back, taking air into squeezing lungs until the weight overwhelmed. Before I thought I could take no more, I sought out Elysande and found her eyes already on mine before the light obscured her all together and the beat in my chest ceased, the light failing with it before falling into darkness.

21

———

PICK YOUR PLACE

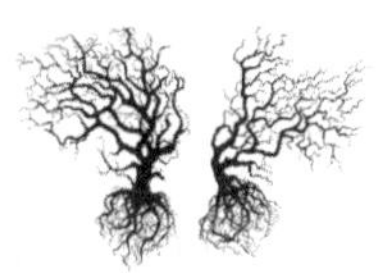

Vincent

Of all probable results, I did not expect this. When handing the ritual stone over, I expected Donovan would be hit with a vision, especially considering his close relationship to the stone, but never did I think it would result in Donovan sprawled on the floor unconscious amongst years of keepsakes.

As the vision assaulted Donovan, and with weak mental barriers in his exhausted efforts to hold back emotion from seeing the picture of their former lives, I witnessed everything Donovan was privy to. In later years, when this treasure was found and carried as a good luck charm, Sophie claimed it was hers, knew it was special, without the ability to pinpoint why.

Since I had not been present in their lives at this momentous event, I lacked insight of how their Soul Magic came to be. Now I knew everything. A puzzle piece to fill the picture left incomplete for as long as I followed the pair through time. Or they followed me. I still was unsure of how I became their Overseer or when as the role did not come with such an opulent vision of explanation.

Kneeling to Donovan's side, I checked for a pulse and found him alive, relieved it did not end with his former self as Betyn even if it meant Sophie's freedom from Nya's prison. Absently, I wondered if Nya too was left unconscious somewhere or if Sophie was affected, hoping the Soul Magic connection existed somewhere deep within her.

The ritual stone leaped from Donovan's slack palm, buzzing past me into my brother's hand.

I stared at my brother and rose to my feet standing in front of Donovan.

"Surprised?" Chase asked with rhetorical delight in his tone.

The question of *"Why are you here?"* lay on my lips, unspoken as Chase would make his intentions clear soon enough.

Chase flicked the stone into the air before catching it and then holding it in his hands behind his back with casual possession. "You are not the only one with purpose in this piece of rock."

"Who within my Coven tipped you off to my location?" Only someone from the Mother Coven could know of the stone and only a few of them could have filtered information back to the head of the Sovereignty.

Chase laughed like the pompous miscreant he was. "My little secret, though not who you would assume, I assure you. They've proven extremely useful. Again, funnelling information wrought with ways to fuck up your plans." He laughed again.

Considering who was present as we spoke beneath the safety of the privacy spell, I found myself hard-pressed to imagine any of them snitching on such a plan when removing Nya and Evaristus benefitted them all. Even Rosemary, who was not present at the time, would not fall that far knowing it may result in her son's death.

The hallway.

Donovan briefly spoke of the ritual stone in the hallway of the Ballard Estate. Endless possibilities. Maybe Nya herself. With what the stone could potentially do to her, Nya was as good as anyone.

"My son the collector." A gruff complaint came from behind a section of boxes.

Unable to see around the piles, visual confirmation was beyond in need. In no lifetime could I forget my father's voice. Glancing to Chase, even his back straightened with nervousness, he too finding our father's presence intimidating.

Around beaten boxes, a man appeared that stiffened the starch in my shirt making me stand taller, knowing this action cast me as weaker in my father's eyes.

Alasdair Llewellyn.

At my age, no one should be able to evoke such a feeling. No matter the location, reason, or in what company, an instant compulsion to wither at Alasdair's feet pressured me to fight for a straighter posture while feelings of inferiority won.

"Why must you insist on keeping every trinket you cross?"

The man in front of me was a black soul of flesh and bone, his shorter stature saying nothing for his formidable presence. I may have been taller but Alasdair's lack in inches was equalized by his sterling hatred for all things sentimental. The sneer he placed on me was enough to shrink any man down to his size.

"Truly," Alasdair went on, "there is enough dust in here to build a string of islands and you continue to bloat it full of useless objects. For what purpose?" He clasped his hands in front of him with a familiar expression. A legitimate answer was not only appreciated but fully expected as he continued to watch me sweat the reply.

"Why are you here?" I opted for rebellion.

My father's shoulders rose and dropped with annoyance. He glanced over at Chase, who nodded, reasons for which I anticipated with dread.

"It has come to my attention that Chase has extended recent attempts to bring you into the company and your steady refusal is nothing I have not heard before. In order to alter the chance of recidivist denial, gaining the same drawn-out response and lecture about our traditional familial ways, I have settled on fresh negotiation."

"I will not—"

"You *will* listen first." The dominance in my father's voice silenced me, leaving me simmering in inadequacy.

Alasdair continued on as if no protest broke his thought process. "Subtleties were never my style. Passive-aggressiveness pains me, you are aware of this, and yet you insist on cowering behind lesser Magics." He sneered down at Donovan's still limp body on the floor at my feet. "In coups, no less, to destroy the empire I have built since before the inquisition. So once more, son of my blood, I gift you an offer." I held a breath in wait, ready with a dismissal as per normal. "This ritual stone will be returned to you. I have no concern for the soul invading the vessel of that woman you insist on following from body to body." I nearly lost it for my father further trivializing Nya's takeover. "Alternatively, since my attempt to quell your lover's existence has not hastened your adherence to my wishes for you to activate your position in the company, you will be given your wife's soul to do with as you wish."

The breath I held fell from my lips in astonishment.

"Father!" Chase's protest died as our father's gaze hammered the objection.

Looking back to him, I could hardly focus on what my father was proposing.

"You cannot have both," Alasdair proceeded. "The ritual stone and your return to Sophie, taking along with you this little puke, is one option." He motioned to Donovan who was still unconscious. "That or your wife's soul. Of course, if you choose...." My father paused, searching for something.

"Cora-Lynn." I knew my father was goading me into speaking her name aloud to try and sweeten my drive to choose her.

"Yes, Cora-Lynn." Alasdair ghosted a pretentious smile. "If you choose Cora-Lynn's soul with the belief Sophie can be saved another way, then this is your choice. However, Cora-Lynn will not be simply handed over. Choosing her includes your enlistment." Chase was shaking his head at this. "Join the company as you were born to and desist from these childish games to destroy our people's only foundation."

"When it comes to joining you and the heinous acts of cruelty you subject our people to, my answer will always be a resounding no." I had no reason to think on the proposal. Others have been offered and this one was as easily refused.

Blood quaked within me wanting nothing but to lash out and murder the two heads of the company here and now, to crumble the Sovereignty for good. Success in that venture was impossible. Maybe with Donovan awake he could keep Chase busy long enough for me to inflict some damage, but my father was a great Magic. Stronger than most others and around long enough to learn a treasure trove of creative avenues to make me suffer if the battle was fought and lost, including killing Donovan.

"You have left me no choice then. Cora-Lynn's soul will be destroyed."

The smile on Chase's lips was grotesque.

"Excuse me?"

Alasdair took a step towards me. "Punishment for Cora-Lynn's crimes has passed well beyond her sentence. You have mired this process long enough. With no further use, her soul will be discarded, and any remaining lineage will be informed of her disposal."

Seething, I would have called my father's bluff, yet knew this was not one. Alasdair did not bluff. Familiar enough with the ruthlessness of the man to know my father's follow-through would be accomplished without lingering concern, simply another deal on the daily agenda. One presented precisely to pit me as the one deciding to destroy my wife's soul and not the manipulative actions of my father.

Oxygen barrelled through my flared nostrils. "Yet another example of the cruelty you wield and pass off as someone else's doing. Cora-Lynn deserves to live on, without me if she must. You have no reason to end her. Searching the world will not bring her to me. No Soul Magic was established before her capture, and neither am I her Overseer. You gain more by letting her live than by ending her."

Alasdair's lips tugged down at their edges, but this was not a frown. Hilarity coloured his cheeks, yet the man did not smile. "If you accepted your role long ago, then maybe your negotiation skills would be more...compelling." This time he did smile. "Join or Cora-Lynn dies."

Why did it need to be this way? If I was truly Sophie's Overseer, then how could I be forced to do what was against her best interests by joining the Sovereignty? If Fate existed, it was a grave atrocity that I knew nothing of what was expected of me.

Seconds ticked by as my thoughts whirled.

"If I join you," I began with subdued panic in my near whisper, "Donovan is to be left as he is, unharmed, with the ritual stone." It was a condition I was not ignorant enough to believe would automatically be obliged.

"I see no reason to do otherwise," Alasdair said as Chase grumbled. "The life of that girl and her mate have no bearing on my success or undoing, especially with you leaving their Coven. Let us get on with it. Schedules wait for no man. We must swear you in."

Realization that the countless years of fighting my station came to an end did nothing to elevate my father's mood with any discernible variance of the norm. That was how Alasdair operated, acting as if once a hard deal was bargained, he knew all along he would win his share. The crushing defeat left me numb from the ragged turmoil of abandoning Donovan and consequently Sophie.

They were my world again and again and I could no longer watch over them while within my father's walls without posing them a greater potential danger.

Handing over the ritual stone, Alasdair made his way to the exit to the stairs leading to the store above as Chase followed. Alasdair kept moving as Chase paused in wait for me.

Bending to a still unconscious Donovan, I slipped the ritual stone and the old picture into his jean pocket. Looking at the man below me as if in nostalgic contemplation, I felt for my own pocket for the gold key that brought us here—grateful for our location on the opposite side of my brother's line of sight—and slipped the one needed off of the ring and into Donovan's pocket with the stone and picture.

Before Chase started in with impatient demands, I left one of my Charges defenceless, strewn in the stacks of his life's memorabilia and turned my back, knowing what came next would be the most difficult of all tasks, more difficult than Donovan finding his way back to Sophie.

Once sworn into the Sovereignty, that bond would mean my life and, somehow, I needed to leave that intact and find a way to ensure Cora-Lynn was released as promised and save Sophie from Nya in the field before she reunited with her ancient love and took Sophie away from them for good. At this point, all else paled in significance. With my focus frayed into a thousand noted filaments of dread and shame, I followed my family to play a role I abhorred and resisted since birth.

22

HEAVY HITTERS

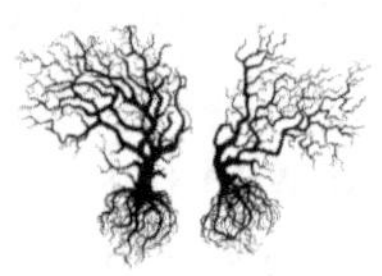

Donovan

Before opening my eyes, I swore I'd spent the night at the bottom of a bottle of Jack that was now swimming in stinging streaks across the surface of my eyes straight through to my brain stem. Whatever dug into my back didn't help.

I tried to sit up. My brain sloshed. I nearly yakked my stomach onto the floor.

Pressing the heels of my palms into my eyes didn't help. I couldn't open them, and it took too long to evoke some power to ease the pain before I slumped down and didn't get up again.

Blinking through the bright light around me, my blurred vision cleared after a couple of tries. Nothing was familiar. Boxes and random shit towered over me. Where was I?

Wait. Vincent's storage place.

It all came flooding back.

The ritual stone.

The vision.

Elysande.

A gasp left my lips as I thought of her and Betyn performing the Soul Magic that got Sophie and me into this mess, the love and pure devotion heartbreaking and overwhelming as their lives ended too quickly, yet at their own hands for the sake of love. The ritual stone was a key element in creating the power needed to ensure their souls found each other when they recycled.

Knowing where it all started gave me renewed drive, though muddied in doubt as I was half the man Betyn was.

"Vincent?"

The stacks prevented me from seeing everywhere, so I searched for a minute or two calling his name as I did. The objects were in my pocket. No one else could have put them there, but why leave me?

A narrow, steep staircase beckoned to me as potential freedom. Vincent said this place was beneath a business he owned. Maybe he was up there.

As I reached the staircase landing, I moved slowly, checking around the corner in small increments in case it wasn't safe.

I turned right and found a door to a small office. I turned the knob, finding it unlocked. I opened it and a blonde woman grasped her chest and screeched as I came through the door.

Okay. Not Vincent, but if she was dangerous, she would have attacked already.

I didn't apologize before taking another two steps and bursting through the next door in search of Vincent.

Stopped short, I realized I wasn't in another office, but was standing in a store. To my left, customers perused and mussed clothing stands and shelves, and to my right, floor to ceiling windows with double glass doors allowed a visual of the furniture goods inside. Looking from one side to another, I knew exactly where I was.

"Betyn?" The small voice called from behind me. The blonde woman in the office now stood inside the store, next to a younger woman who came around from behind the cash register to gape at me in utter confusion. "Bent u Betyn?"

Not surprised she was speaking in Dutch instead of English,

since apparently, I was in freaking Amsterdam, I thankfully knew the language. Since I just learned the name Betyn myself, I was even more surprised at her using it.

In Dutch I responded, "In éénleven, ja," letting her know that in one life, yes, I was Betyn. At my admission, the younger one glowed and didn't strain to hide her excitement as the older blonde scanned our surroundings as if paranoid at who may be listening in and called me into the back office.

Following her, since this person knew something about anything, the older blonde ordered the younger woman to return to work and closed the office door behind her. An angered pout lingered on the girl's face even out the glass window of the door.

In the small space, the older blonde sat at her desk and straightened a folder on its top as if she strived for order her head couldn't quite grasp.

"Where's Vincent," I asked in Dutch. She may have spoken English for all I knew but this worked all the same.

Sitting back into her chair, it dipped with her weight, her blue eyes warring with her to find the words. "He left."

"Left? To go where?"

Her small mouth opened but at first her words failed as she fought to understand what was happening. "I was working on inventory reports. I had not seen the boss in a few months and was expecting to—"

"Boss?"

"Yes," the blonde looked up at me as I refused to sit. "Mr. Llewellyn. Vincent, he has owned this place for a very long time."

It was the place Vincent talked about, the clothing and furniture store the parents of Sophie's past identity owned. Vincent kept it open all these years.

"Alright. You saw Vincent. Did he tell you I was here?"

She shrugged. "Not in so many words. He said Betyn needed me. I didn't know who that was, yet understood it was important and was going through papers to try and find a reference to the name when you came in. I have not known you by that name, but I have seen pictures, and knew of your story."

I nodded wondering why Vincent would share this with her and who the woman was to Vincent other than a shopkeeper.

She went on. "I'm surprised Vincent risked speaking Telepathically at all with his father with him."

Shit. "His father?"

"Yes. And his brother."

"Chase?"

She shrugged and nodded as if I should know who it was without the explanation. For all I knew the guy was one of a dozen. He sure as hell didn't tell me everything. Even less than he's evidently told this woman.

What the fuck is happening? "How long ago did he leave?"

She checked her wristwatch. "An hour ago, maybe a bit more?"

Obviously sometime after I hit the floor, we had a few visitors. Or did Vincent leave with them voluntarily? Did he call them to him?

Raking my fingers through my hair, I didn't know what to think. Leaning on the wall behind me, I shoved my hands into my pockets and jumped at a sudden encroaching vision. I pulled my hand out of my pocket, recognizing the energy well enough to know the ritual stone was inside my jeans. I didn't need it knocking me unconscious again.

Grabbing some tissue from the woman's desk, I used it to cover the ritual stone, isolating it from my touch. I also found the gold key Vincent used to send us here, plus the picture of Sophie and me as our past selves, her happiness radiating from the paper so profusely I was drawn in while fighting to look away.

Maybe Vincent wasn't a coward. His father and brother could have taken the stone, but Vincent left it in my pocket. To keep it away from them? Or did they not want it?

Looking at the key, I didn't realize the blonde stood up and was looking into my other hand at the picture. "You..." her voice barely a whisper. "You are truly him." All reservation left her worn features. "Mr. Llewellyn wanted me to help you, but why are you here?"

Now that definitely didn't sound as though Vincent was abandoning me in some fancy double-cross with the Sovereignty. What was he doing?

"I go by Donovan now. I'm not sure what this man's name was." I motioned to the picture, head lilted to the side, saddened that I didn't know or maybe that I didn't see myself as one and the same person. "I know your language, but I'm not from here in this life. Vincent brought me to get something to help Sophie. To help her." I slid my thumb to indicate Sophie in the picture.

The woman stepped back. "Still? You still...After all this time, you still find one another?"

I nodded, feeling the weight she spoke with. Clearly this woman thought this was a tragedy and not the romantic story as Elysande and Betyn intended it to be. It surprised me she knew as much as she did. Maybe she was a Magic?

"Why don't you end it?" she asked.

Valid question, but not one I cared to entertain. An end to the Soul Magic may have been easier yet letting go of Sophie was not happening. "Please, where did Vincent go?"

She paused, regretting her question. "I'm sorry. I don't know."

Defeat overruled as I looked through the office door then through the large storefront windows as it rained outside. Next to the door was an old picture, enlarged. I couldn't see details, but it was the storefront as it appeared after it was built. No doubt Sophie was in that picture, maybe even Vincent and me.

Where the fuck was the bastard?

"Can you not use it?" she asked. Confused, I pulled myself away from the picture and back to her. "The key?"

Lifting my hand with the old key nested in my palm, I tried to think of what Vincent said before he used the key that brought us here. The full incantation was spoken too quickly to stick in my brain.

"Mr. Llewellyn possesses many keys. This one is his direct line to this establishment. Only with the right words can he travel here and only with the right words can you travel back."

"Back to the estate?"

She shrugged. "To wherever you were before you came here. The key will return you to the place from which you came."

"What's the incantation?"

"There isn't one for returning. Not a formal recitation. You need to ask it properly and it will transport you where you need to go."

No doubt my expression came off as rude as hell as the woman was serious and she recoiled at my non-verbal response. Not purposefully meaning to insult or ridicule her, a personality trait I was certain she never painted on whatever idea of my past selves she envisioned, I tried to soften my expression, to find my inner "good guy". Ridiculous I was about to sweet talk an inanimate object. Then again, most magical items contained some type of trick. This one needed to be asked nicely. I possessed manners when I needed to.

I stuck the picture into the pocket without the ritual stone. "I just ask it to take me back?"

"Yes. It can only go back to the place you came from. Useful if that place is a safe place."

I sighed in resignation, happy to be returning, and anxious it meant seeing Nya again.

"Donovan..." She paused as if uncomfortable with calling me that name when she knew me by someone else in Vincent's stories. "Mr. Llewellyn wouldn't let you down. After all this time as your friend, he could never. I know him well enough to have faith in his loyalty."

Sweet as candy, but I didn't buy that this woman knew anything about the secrets the man kept from those he was supposedly loyal to. Instead of arguing or evoking a smile even I knew was impossible to come off as genuine, I focused on getting out of this festering memory of a place.

I closed my eyes against my skepticism. All right, key. Please—

"Sorry. You need to speak it aloud."

Of course I did. She could be saying that to learn where I was headed, but I didn't have another choice.

I readied myself again, held the key, and spoke in German as Vincent did to travel here. "Key, please bring me back—" Before I could conclude with "the Ballard Estate" the office around me wavered slightly and disappeared, the walls of the estate's upstairs hallway appearing. As with walking casually through a portal, I felt no lasting impact in the scenery change.

Gravity disappeared. I slammed into something hard. The bones and cartilage in my shoulder screamed. My body slid across wood flooring, my skull cranking into the wall stopping me. Footsteps scrambled as I fought to see through the pain.

"Save the body contact for the bastards who deserve it," a woman argued.

I blinked to see Bronya as she pressed Lincoln into the adjacent wall before she allowed him to shove her away.

"Give it up," Lincoln returned. "He's saving his body contact for someone else."

Bronya volleyed with a collection of mumbled threats, but I was beyond caring and demanded to know what was going on.

Apparently, upon the shimmer of my entrance, Lincoln attacked as he and Bronya guarded the upstairs hallway while the aforementioned "bastards"—the group of surrounding Tainted outside—forged their attack.

"The wards are holding up for now," Bronya explained with that doe-eyed look I hated, "but everyone is headed to the field. We're just giving them a chance to leave."

That explained the empty hallway.

"Where's the portal?"

"Attic." Lincoln chinned in its direction, and I set off to bolt through the door. "Wait!" I stopped. "Nya's outside. The wards aren't strong enough. She's powerful and boosting them until we can all get through the portal."

I hightailed it downstairs and to the front door, though I didn't particularly want to see Nya. However, if Nya was in danger, so was Sophie.

Out in the snow stood Nya in Sophie's flesh, wielding a streaming power that prickled my skin far more than the cold. Dozens of Magics stood outside the ward's limits, slamming their powers against it like cannon shots that exploded without the destruction they anticipated. Not even Nya could single-handedly hold back so many forever.

"Nya!" I yelled above the barrages of power beating at the wards.

Without the lips I would fight to kiss again, Nya spoke to me. *"Minutes remain. The battle is to be fought elsewhere. Leave now. Sophie's fate will not end at these mongrel's hands."*

Walking away felt the same as running away from Sophie and leaving her to her potential death. Too many enemies. If they got beyond the wards, Sophie would die alone at the hands of the enemy, and I would have left her with no one but Nya to accompany her in death.

Stalling on the estate steps, I didn't move. Angry and scared shit-less, my thoughts raced with indecision. Nya turned to me with blank features, leaving a hand outstretched at her targets and reached towards me with the other, and then I was flying backwards into the house and skidding into furniture like a bowling ball. To punctuate her point, Nya telekinetically slammed the door between us. I didn't have to check it to know she locked it as well.

Barely recovered from Lincoln's hit and now this, I gathered myself, having no clue if either hit affected Nya in any way, though it didn't seem so. I ran back upstairs, bypassing Lincoln and Bronya heading to see what the crash was, and rushed up into the attic, yelling at them to follow me.

Chaos wasn't exactly the term I would use to describe those in the attic, as many were either pumped for action or quietly fearing their deaths in wide-eyed stares and jittery movements. I thought they would all be gone by now. Members of my Sect tried to slow me down with questions, but I had my own and needed to find the Elders.

Finding Ranlyn and Veata, Kim and Hall with them, Kim's shoulders dropped in relief when she spotted me then yelled at me for taking off.

I ignored her. "Ranlyn, Nya says time's up. We gotta go, now."

"This is it, you know," Kim started again. "The big fight and you're just showing up now? Where's Vincent?"

"He ditched me in Amsterdam and left with Chase and his dad." None of them expected that. "I've got the ritual stone."

"Wait. With Chase! He left with Chase?" Kim panicked.

"Alasdair?" Ranlyn questioned.

"Yes!" I yelled impatiently. "I don't know why and don't care right now. Are we set? Nya can't hold on any longer, and we have a herd of angry beasts outside ready to tear the house down."

"The house would never allow that," Olive piped up, though I never saw her approach the group.

I huffed in anger trying not to let myself drown in it. "Are. We. Set?"

"Donovan." Fox spoke my name with sharp enunciation as he came up behind me. If anyone had seen me on this thin of an edge, it was Fox. And maybe because it was the first time seeing him since getting back from the compound, an inch of tension in my shoulders let go.

"Everyone knows what's expected of them, kid." Fox was far too calm. "Do you know what you're doing?"

Without saying so, it was as if Fox knew what I would do on the field and wanted to ensure it was truly what I wanted. When I nodded, again a wordless exchange told me Fox understood why I was doing what I planned and why I hadn't asked the Elders for their permission to proceed. Nothing could stop me.

"I'll let them know to begin," Fox said to Ranlyn.

"What are you up to?" Kim's tone was softer and full of worry.

"I need to get Sophie back." She didn't need to know anything else.

Reaching into my pocket, I removed the picture of Sophie and myself from those two short years in Amsterdam and handed it to Olive. "Here. Add it to the Ballard Grimoire." No matter what happened to the estate, I knew Olive wouldn't leave the Ballard Grimoire behind.

Olive gasped, reached for her chest, and tears sprung to life. Kim searched over her shoulder and shared much the same reaction.

"In case we don't find each other again," I added, praying that wouldn't be the case. Though, this communicated a clear sense to them that I expected neither of us to survive this fight.

"Donovan...." Kim began but I couldn't handle her saying anything more. This time it wasn't her habit of annoying me, I just couldn't deal with her sympathies. Not now.

"Where are we dropping in?"

"Under tree cover," Veata answered, the only one who'd given me a straight answer. "Heavy hitters in the front, second string comprised of mostly every other, Seedlings and Fox in last. Pick your place."

Nodding in appreciation of her directness, I enjoyed the fact no one tried telling me where to stand. This wasn't a dance recital, and I wouldn't be complacent with following whatever order was given no matter who gave it.

Since I considered myself a part of the "heavy hitters", I turned to catch up with the first few and stepped through the portal.

23

AN OBSERVATORY ROLE

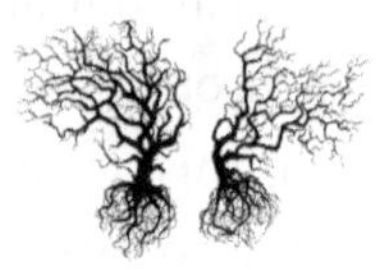

Sophie

Dreams I could handle. Since the ones starring Caine trapped in his worst nightmare stalking me through a rain-filled park and then those of Aunt Lacey's murder and all the bloodshed that followed, all other nightmares were weak. But this was nothing like a dream.

I was awake when Nya allowed me to be awake. Aware of my surroundings as Nya controlled my eyes, sweeping rooms and landscapes where my feet took me without my permission. Being awake didn't mean I was in control.

Only when Nya chose to do so did I dwell in the nothingness. My thoughts still swirled in an endless loop without a sense of time. Feelings ran wild without the physical results of worry and fear. After some time, my general emotion was numbness.

When Nya disengaged me from experiencing things as she did, it was as if I were shoved down deep into myself, staring up at the light, too far away to look through the portholes that were my eyes. My world now consisted of the dull, green light of my soul all around me as I floated around inside my vessel without limbs to connect to. It reminded me of being inside of Kim when I read her soul at Ranlyn's after she and Miklos went through the veil together and pieces of their souls were mixed inside their vessels. Now, I had less access to my power. Maybe Nya made sure of it.

Unless our power was being used, I was held back. I realized that when Nya engaged her power, it automatically propelled me to the surface, and I could see again. I was still beyond the control of my own energies, an arm's length and a finger's touch from anything more than experiencing sensations as Nya did all the wielding.

Was this how it was for Nya all this time?

Nya fought against my involvement. She found it easy to force me away from being present for anything she didn't want me around for, which was probably most things.

With two souls inside one vessel, you would think loneliness was far from an issue. If only. I had never felt so lonely in my entire life. Inundated with so much to feel without the ability to soothe myself, an over-abundance of desperation to scream and no lips to scream with, losses of time and place as though I was suffering from dementia was how I spent most of my time and couldn't even tell how much that time was.

If Chase knew anything about how I felt, I would not have put it past him to use this soul implantation as part of his prisoner's torture methods. This was a thousand times worse than Tobias's cells. Even with what happened to me at the compound, what Donovan forced me to go through, I'd opt to relive that over this suspense.

Now that I experienced both, feeling too much and being able to do something about it, even if it was simply holding onto myself, was better than feeling something and not being able to do anything at all.

When permitted to observe life through my own eyes, I noticed the people I cared about avoided making eye contact. The ones who didn't look away made a point to sneer with such disgust it was almost scary. Granted, they weren't directing this hate at me personally, but for some reason it still hurt.

I knew Nya shared in my pain. Every moment passed with her thoughts entrenched in memories of Gareth. Of times they were together from the day they met until the regrets of their passing. Nya's brain played these images like a favourite record on repeat as if her soul knew nothing else.

I understood the obsession. I had felt it for a short time with Caine and hated myself for not doing something more to avoid sleeping with Donovan that day. Soul Magic may have done its job, but Caine didn't deserve to be treated like that, and I wished I could go back to feeling those flutters in my stomach at seeing him outside of my dreams before he hated me. We found healthy ground to stand on since, but it wasn't the same. I ruined it.

Except for when Nya took over those first few minutes, Donovan hasn't looked at me. As with outside of the compound cell, he couldn't face me. Now I was someone else and he still couldn't find it within him to look me right in the eyes and say anything with any amount of importance.

I didn't miss his attention, though I did miss how things were before he showed his true colours at the compound. After Brock, I told myself I wouldn't be that person again. That I wouldn't fall for the guy whose greatest agenda was to capture me and then manipulate me into sticking around while he was busy dicking it to other chicks.

We were trapped in this Soul Magic cycle, and I wondered if in any other lifetime he did something similar to other versions of me. Was the connection strong enough to detect his betrayals back then?

He promised to save me or protect me every chance he could, and yet, here he was somewhere else most of the time avoiding what his actions helped happen. Nya's takeover was my fault, but I wouldn't have been so weak if I didn't have to endure him forcing me through so much pain.

It was too much to ask for Nya to cut the crotches out of his jeans or kick in his flat screen, but Kim would do it for me without me asking. If she wasn't too busy eye-fucking Caveman behind Frog's back. Maybe her loyalty was as strong as Donovan's. Since I wasn't fucking her, it wasn't my business.

Maybe Frog was a backup option for me. Or Ranlyn. Or maybe even Vincent. At this point, I almost didn't care. I wanted Donovan to hurt the same as I did, so maybe it meant all of them with a side of Caine to drive home the point that Donovan was not the only one who could inflict invisible damage on the other. I was capable, and I sure as fuck wasn't his.

I let similar thoughts keep me company when nothing else felt right. So much anger. So many resentments. So often with nothing to do but feed it until I was on the brink of losing it.

Ooh. That tingle. A tell-tale indication that Nya was bringing me back into an observatory role. When I was drawn to the surface as if from the bottom of a well, the light around me was so bright that if I could, I would have blinked away at my tear-stung eyes.

"What's happening?" I questioned her, knowing Nya could hear my every thought, especially when so close to the surface.

"What do you see?" Nya asked in place of answering.

All around me were flares of light in sprigs of darkness and faint colour. Other Magics hurled attacks that were somehow stopped and fell short of their target. Surveying Nya's view, the scene became clear of where we were and who the target was. That fact terrifyingly obvious.

With my power accelerated through Nya, I was astonished at the light show of souls ahead of me. Lined up, Tainted soul after Tainted soul lashing out at the estate's wards. With the hum of power through our vessel and the stance Nya adopted, the wards were only withstanding the onslaught due to the addition of power. There was no explanation behind this—Nya didn't feel the need to clarify herself in anything—confusing me of why the Magic would bother.

"Why save the estate? You don't care about it or my family. Why not let it burn?"

"Doing so would not advance my purpose nor does needless death

excite me. Those within the estate will fight a battle I cannot singu-larly succeed in. At present, they are useful."

"Cold-hearted bitch," was all I thought, not calling Nya names, simply categorizing her into a box she understood. Plus, no filter existed in here. I thought it, she heard it. No hiding knee-jerk opinions under niceties even if I wanted to.

Regardless of its intention, the comment was ignored. It wasn't clear to me why I expected anything different from an ancient vessel-hopper, but for some reason I did. All of my family members and Coveners within the estate were nothing but distractions. Foot soldiers before the Cavalry raced in to collect the triumphant win, galloping over the sacrificed bodies of naive Infantry fighting for a cause they've only been briefed on, while the full spectrum of the plan was built and executed behind the scenes resulting in death. My family was cannon fodder and nothing more. Any relation to Evaristus should be seen as a weakness, if properly considered, regardless of the fact he spent centuries trying to kill us off.

Times like this made me wish I never asked any questions. Curiosity gained me an answer, yet I couldn't do anything with the answer but dwell on it while Nya still controlled our vessel, shoved the people I cared about in front of the enemy to be hacked and burned, while I watched in horror as if binging a true crime marathon.

"Nya!" A voice called from behind us.

Even without the control of my eyes to check it out, I knew this voice. Excitement flared through me until I reminded myself they were no one to be excited about.

Donovan wanted Nya to leave with the others, but she argued she was saving them and lied about my safety as she assumed he gave a shit about it.

He didn't leave right away, and she finally looked at him in a way I could also see. He was frazzled, his scowl too familiar, but it was shadowed with more than I could read before Nya knocked Donovan back into the house with a shoving blow and slamming the door, locking him away from returning to the front steps.

The door left my sightline as Nya turned back to the targets in front of her, leaving me in a gasping shock, having no clue if Donovan was conscious to tell the others it was time to leave. If he was knocked out, Nya's efforts will have been wasted.

I tried cursing at Nya and screaming for her to do more for those inside, to save the rest, to curse her and Gareth for their weak-ass attempts at a future together. And as in the beginning when I tried fighting for control of my body, a familiar sense of being lowered into a cold well tingled as Nya began to disengage me from reality to sink me back into nothingness.

The view of the enemy beating the wards with fists, weapons, and magic disappeared into distant tunnels and then portholes of the world. I screamed louder and louder, blaming Nya for every foul thing that's resulted from her presence in my life, including the death of Aunt Lacey. Anything that might create a dent was hurled at her as I fell further away from myself, sobbing tearlessly as the prospect of being free felt less and less like a reality.

24

———

CHANGE IN LEADERSHIP

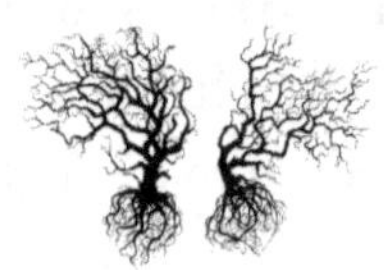

Stopping Donovan from going for the portal just to get chewed out was pointless, so I didn't bother even though I had an important question I didn't know if the others considered: How was Donovan going to use the ritual stone when Vincent was MIA and he couldn't Extract Nya from Sophie's body? No one would have this answer, not even Donovan, so I knew Donovan rushing from the attic portal through to the battlefield was Donovan being overly cocky or driven to suicide, which amounted to the same.

I was going to lose them both.

Looking to Hall at my side in the Ballard attic as we waited in line with the others in front of the portal, he may not have been able to read my mind due to the privacy spell, but something in his eyes said he still knew what I was thinking. This revelation forced my gaze away as he stood too close and I shifted my body to create illusionary space, something he would no doubt comment on since he found it impossible to keep his thoughts to himself.

I gave him a questioning look for him to say whatever bothered him already instead of him insisting on the staring bit.

"You are capable of more than assisting Fox and the Seedlings."

I rolled my eyes and watched the line behind me consisting of ramped-up and terrified Coveners. The fact my hands vibrated with anxiety didn't change my responsibilities. "I won't leave my Sect."

"Of course you will."

I glared at him.

"You'll be frontline when the Creation is cracked open, if only to ensure Sophie survives. Not to mention Caine and probably Donovan even if you hate him half the time."

My chest tightened in warring emotion, mostly aggravation and the thought of any of them dying, and cursed Hall for hovering over me. Without wanting to show him he was getting under my skin, I gritted my teeth and kept my eyes straight as those in the frontlines disappeared through the portal.

Hall grabbed my arm in a vice of fingers and pulled me towards the front of the line.

"Hey!" I dug my heels in trying to stop him.

"Consider me your personal bodyguard."

"Wait!" I yelled gathering the attentions of those around me.

Hall paused his advance.

"I already told them—"

"That you would die protecting them if need be. I know. This way you'll protect them and live to lead on." Finding this reason enough, he kept on going.

Fighting him didn't work. I couldn't stop him no matter the yanking I did—his grasp on me unyielding even if it didn't hurt—but I couldn't leave the Coveners to think I abandoned them.

"Stop!" I yelled again and Hall froze in place. Literally. His long, purposeful strides suspended mid-step as my attempt to slow things down ended up locking him a spell. "Oh, for fuck's sake."

Even though Hall wasn't going anywhere while trapped in my spell, his grip was stuck on me. Slipping from his grasp was impossible and I knew if I attempted to pry him off, the same as with Joelly outside of the Creation, he would be free of the spell and would only drag me to the frontline faster before I could stop him again.

"Gwen!" I yelled down the line and waited until someone found her.

Gwen's eyes widened when they took in Hall's statuesque pose, and I spoke quickly before some helpful Covener came along to release him.

"Just because he says he can, it doesn't mean Hall can keep you alive," Gwen argued. Being a Prophetess didn't come into play here, it was common sense.

"I know, but the jackass is right. I'd sneak away and help Sophie or Caine or maybe even Donovan. Please, let them think I know what I'm doing and for them to stay with Fox. Remember, if anything happens, the Sect is in your hands, so stay with them."

Gwen nodded in acceptance of the responsibility, but panic glinted in her eyes. She couldn't manage a word before leaving to speak with the Coveners regarding the change in leadership.

Re-establishing Hall's freedom was not going to be fun. I took a breath and grabbed onto his wrist of the hand firmly attached to my arm. The spell broke. Hall stuttered a half-step forward before catching himself and jarring my shoulder in the process.

While I swore in pain, Hall hesitated and then looked back at me as if he fought to compose his anger first.

When he finally faced me, he stepped in close, inches away without removing his grip on my arm. I met his heavy glare in challenge. Clearly, not only did Hall know what happened but his ears were still in operation, and he heard every word, which even if he was right, he shouldn't have dragged me away like that and I wasn't about to pretend his behaviour was okay.

Without saying anything he let his grip fall. I screeched and was looking at the floor, my ponytail hanging in front of my face as Hall carried me fireman-style towards the portal.

"Hey! I can walk!" I struggled with where to put my hands to keep myself from bobbing around. It didn't help they first landed on his ass. Tight muscles beneath worn jeans clenched as he walked, adding to my distraction until I shifted them to his back, and again, found more muscles. It took effort to remind myself where exactly Hall was carrying me to, and that the portal could lead to my death.

"You heard me," I struggled to talk as blood rushed to my head. "I said I'd go. Let me down."

"Calm yourself, kitten." Hall punctuated his directive with a firm smack to my ass. "Almost there."

"What the fuck, dude?"

Anticipating that the spank would cause me to struggle harder, Hall held onto my legs now with both hands, preventing me from bucking off his shoulder as he laughed in a low grumble, greatly satisfied with himself.

The portal line congested in the front, and even with people moving smoothly, it was too slow for Hall. Pushing myself up as much as I could, hands planted on the muscular roping of Hall's back, I caught sight of Andy as he watched in question and fear. He probably thought Hall was kidnapping me.

I pressed my fingers to my lips and threw him a kiss with what I hoped was a big enough smile to convince the kid everything was okay. I needed him to know I wasn't being hauled off by an actual Viking in any immediate danger sort of way like he may have seen in movies or TV shows. Or I was in danger, but not by this particular Viking. Whatever. Hopefully it worked.

Before Hall got to the front of the portal line, a rush of energy burst into the attic. I gripped onto the Viking with everything in me as power from him and everyone around us swelled and people dropped into defensive positions in anticipation of a strike.

Hall flipped me off his shoulder to his front and curled over me to shield me from whatever was happening.

I squeezed my eyes shut against the Viking's chest as my power vibrated within my skin, energy gaining such ferocity it had me swallowing it back before it threatened to bust out of control, helpless in his arms without any attempt to even face what joined us in the attic.

Not the best show of heroics, but there was no time to act before my skin prickled with goosebumps and Hall was saying something I couldn't hear.

25

___

DRINK IT DRY

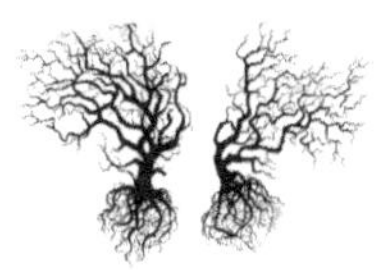

Donovan

Milling about the field on surveillance, the enemy was cocky. Watching from the darkness within the pines, I ground my molars and peered through the leaves at the bastards laughing as if a war wasn't about to break out. Granted, these particular bastards didn't know I was hiding in the trees, waiting for the opportunity to get this shit-show on the go.

Rosemary took up my flank as soon as I arrived. I didn't complain and she didn't attempt any idealistic promises or try to talk me into a safer position in the line of soldiers. She was an absentee mother, but she wasn't stupid.

If only the others would hurry up coming through the portal.

A steady stream of them spilled through and into the field, though not quickly enough, testing my already dental-floss-thin patience.

An exhale of wind thrust at my back brought with it a rush of voices, which were quickly shut down, even though their mouths were all still moving.

Magics from the attic stood behind me as if they had all been shit out of the portal simultaneously, Nya standing impassively in front of them. She must have shoved them all through to the field and then spelled them to remove their voices before they gave up our position.

I looked back at where the enemy stood well ahead of our location. They hadn't caught anything happening besides their own conversation.

Everyone was concerned with their voices not working, but I focused on Nya who approached Olive.

"If you survive," Nya spoke with Sophie's voice to Olive unhindered by the silencing spell, "the place you call home may not exist to retreat to."

Seeing what I did with Nya outside of the estate, I assumed the Tainted Magics surrounding it broke through the wards or Nya didn't care enough to hold them back.

Olive's lips fell slack at Nya's crassness as she clutched the Ballard Family Grimoire.

Hall let Kim down from his arms. She overheard what Nya said to Olive and went to Nya who was on her way out of the cover of trees without worry of exposure from the enemy.

Kim grabbed Nya's elbow to stop her and said something Nya's spell silenced.

At Kim's touch, Nya spun, and with a quick twist, broke Kim's arm, removing herself from Kim's hold. Kim's mouth opened wide in a soundless scream as she dropped to her knees. Hall pitched himself forward like a bear, his claws hitting nothing but air as Nya was suddenly many feet ahead of the group having disappeared and reappeared so fast I didn't see her walk a step as she continued on a calm stroll.

Healing Kim's arm was no emergency—many could heal her. The hurt on Kim's face at what Nya did while in Sophie's body was far more damaging.

The silencing spell quit working. Everyone was hushed. If they wouldn't keep their traps shut, someone else would silence them all, but they were in a battle situation and shouldn't need to be told to shut the fuck up.

Enraged and full of adrenaline from the break and Veata healing her, Kim snapped into her role. Her stance straightened as she turned to Olive, telling her to gather the others she and Lewis introduced her to earlier. I had no clue who Kim was talking about or what her plan was, though Hall stood aside with a subdued smile as if he was proud as hell.

Whatever Kim planned, it didn't include her hanging back in Fox's group.

Following Nya to the forest edge as far as I could before being seen, I watched her walk right into the open. David and Ross, two assholes I recognized as a pair of brothers, lackeys from Tobias's flock, were both indifferent to Nya's arrival.

Damn. She was expected. At some point she must have made a deal with them. Did they know she was Nya? Or did they think she was Sophie and that she turned her back on her Coven? No way they could believe that.

I struggled to keep my anger in check.

The brothers didn't rush for others or look in our direction. Nya must not have disclosed our location. Nor for or against us, it was another reminder of Nya having her own agenda.

In my position, it seemed David and Ross were simply Nya's welcoming committee. Others were called into the clearing from the trees across the way, ones I recognized.

Tobias was expected. Hinapouri and Miklos were not. Nor did I expect to see Caine's Aunt Bernadine saunter into the field as if she faced battle every weekend and had become bored with the concept.

An army of Magics waiting in the wings to kick ass once the others and I made our presence in the field known would be no surprise, though Tobias's flock wouldn't be the only ones. The majority of the Mother Coven equipped with their own battle plans and backup waited as well, anticipating the waves of evil to take their chance to bring us down somewhere off in the trees, they too probably hidden under some type of cover spell.

Though I had to remember some of those Magics waiting to kill me were actually members of my own Sect. Not everyone wanted the Creation opened and we were chancing everything on this mission.

The Coveners at my back were a mixture of skilled Magics and Seedlings with control issues. Thankfully, the enemy didn't have Fox. If all went well, Fox would get into position and he and the lesser—or specified—skilled Coveners would take care of us so I could focus on getting Sophie back. Checking again, I added Sophie's mom, her twin aunts, and Andy amongst those Fox would be taking care of. Whatever forced them all to flee the attic, it meant dropping everyone into the snow-filled forest. Those who didn't plan on fighting were without their winter gear and were shivering, Andy included.

The look on the kid's face was a quiet terror as he stuck to Fox's side. Lu's was pure panic. Neither could suss out what happened and wanted to be anywhere else but a cold forest.

Fuck. I totally forgot about Andy when I left, proving more about myself than I was willing to look at right now, though I was happy to see him, Fox, and the others in that group race to a more advantageous position within the trees to provide access to the whole field.

If we couldn't end Evaristus, the least I could do was rip Nya from Sophie's body and retreat to safety. I would be happy with that.

To me, Evaristus, Loring, Caine, and the survivors were all inconsequential if Sophie remained a prisoner within herself. She would want to fight for everyone but herself, but she had to be in control of her body in order to do anything for anyone else.

I saw Hinapouri pass Tobias the discus. My father walked into the center of the field. After some anticipatory tension, the discus began to emit a dull light.

The power within the discus was activated.

Tobias's head dropped back as he was reciting something, too far away to overhear, though his reverent tone carried as if it were creeping from my dreaded childhood memories.

I wanted him dead so badly my hands shook even more. I could end him bloody right now, but then I would forfeit my opportunity at rescuing Sophie, and even that revenge wasn't worth her life.

Separating his hands, head still back, and babbling on, I watched as sand sprinkled from Tobias's fingers as he brought them to his sides. The discus was now nothing but tiny particles. As they fell in a shimmer that glinted off the moon, these particles began to swirl above the snow at Tobias's feet then wisped though the air before hitting a barrier where the invisible wall of the Creation stood. The discus particles adhered to the Creation wall, those particles spreading, multiplying far beyond what comprised of the discus, and began eating away at that wall. That's how it would create a door.

Something slapped down onto my shoulder before I moved a step. Ranlyn's hand. His eyes remained on the field. "Hold for the most opportune moment."

Right behind him stood Veata, Kim, Hall, and Kim's small collection of Magics, one looking too young and terrified. Kim tried to assuage her worries with whispered encouragement and a strong arm around her meek shoulders, then suddenly the young girl was running off. I guess the girl didn't have the stones to be in the thick of it and that was Kim giving her the okay to bow out.

A waver of movement drew my attention to our left across the field to a pair of bodies semi-hidden in the trees. They were shadowed until the creeping couple grew an aura that radiated around them, and since seeing auras or souls was never in my repertoire, I was fully confused.

"To distinguish your enemies," Rosemary, still at my side, reminded me of the spell.

"The other Coven Magics are in wait for their opportune moment as well," Ranlyn added.

"Just keep them off me." Time to worry about them was long gone.

Noise filled the field, a gnawing emanating from the Creation wall as it was eaten away like hungry tiny scarab beetles were chewing their way in.

The wall was thick, but the discus was made for this very destruction and regardless of how long it took, the veil between the Creation plane and this one would fail.

As the wall thinned and the others and I grew antsy, I kept my eyes pinned on Nya. Her expression changed while stepping towards the Creation as if her body moved involuntarily at the thought of Gareth on the opposite side waiting to greet her after countless years of separation.

Tingling down my spine had me rolling my shoulders without the stir stopping. Hearing a slight rustling, I noticed the others around me did the same. Fox. In position within the trees somewhere he was already amplifying our powers, using the Magics with him to strengthen his own in order to protect us all.

Good. He was in place and ready to go. At least I knew that was one Magic I could trust to do their job.

"Hold." Hall reiterated Ranlyn's directive seeing everyone further amped by Fox's boost. Hall was crawling in his skin with anticipation, but he held steady forcing me to wait for the strike command along with him and everyone else.

Cursing, I couldn't handle it anymore. The infinitesimal thread of patience I possessed obliterated. The Creation was being slowly eaten away. Evar could pop out with Gareth right behind him and both could be too far from my grasp and gone before I got free of the trees. Orders were shackling, causing me to hide like a cowering rabbit.

No fucking thank you.

Stretching to full height, I was on the move. An equally damning curse came from behind me, but Hall was following, bringing at least a dozen others with him including the Elders, the Tactical Team members, plus Kim and her helpers.

"Be smart," Hall hissed at me. "They can't see us under my cover spell. Keep your speed casual and don't use your power or it'll cancel the spell shielding us. I, for one, plan on surviving this. This isn't just about you and Sophie."

"Then you shouldn't've followed me."

Pulling the tissue-wrapped stone from my pocket, I held it in my hand as I stopped no more than twenty-five feet from Nya still hidden beneath Hall's spell.

I attempted to reach Sophie Telepathically, pulling back when I sensed the barrier Nya constructed to keep Sophie bogged down, not wanting to tip the wrong person off or cancel out the cover spell yet.

Fox's power increased around me, bolstering my confidence in getting the job done.

I took a second to steel myself and then removed the tissue from around the ritual stone. The vision of Elysande and Betyn struck as I knew it would, so powerfully it nearly crumpled me at the knees, but I was ready for it and fought to regain control with the help of all the extra power being filtered to me from Fox. I struggled to remain conscious as the vision bolted through my body. Instead of passing out as I did in Vincent's storage room, I braced myself and then let go as if giving it permission as Betyn did in the vision with Elysande.

Instead of fighting its power, I absorbed it.

The injection of power once soaked up into the stone from the Soul Magic Elysande used so many years ago was now transferred to me. I felt every cool pulse of it through my veins as I drank it in and allowed it to flow from inside the stone to fill me up. The embrace of such power energized every nerve in my body as if I siphoned it straight from Elysande herself.

Never had I known this kind of power, this strength. How Elysande obtained it in the first place was a wonder. It must have been truly awe-inspiring to be Betyn in that time and to orbit her existence. How completely amazing. This was what Sophie deserved to feel, deserved to be. She hid this ability somewhere deep inside her, it waiting to be tapped, without Nya's help. This was all her own, and she needed to continue on living so she could rediscover it.

I found a way to hold this power within myself and let it settle. It was as if it knew me or was at least accepting me, knowing it was not where it belonged. A part of me thanked it for trusting me with using it this way. I couldn't help but be grateful.

Now, to stop Nya.

To my right, the Creation layers of the wall began to crumble like gingerbread until specks of sunlight from the other side reached into the dark field. Still under the guise of Hall's spell as the power I took from the stone filtered straight into me without leaking into the space around me, I watched as my father pointed to a few of his flock, ordered them to venture into the Creation to retrieve their people and be sure any opposing survivors found it difficult to breathe free air.

Others in Tobias's flock spread along the length of the wall, readying themselves for whatever came out of the Creation as the veil thinned even more, leaving a large enough access point for the few men to sneak through to the other side.

All of the flock were equipped with the aura of light to distinguish friend from foe as more exited the trees. Helpful, though identifying my enemies was easy. Especially since they were usually the ones bent on killing me.

The tactic did in fact help when Magics from my own Mother Coven joined the scene and stood amongst our enemies too comfortably. Without the aura, I may have allowed Aaron—a Mother Coven member who fought on our side in the last fight—a pass that could have gotten me killed. Now that I knew differently, any chance I got, once ensuring Sophie's safety, would be spent slaughtering those traitors standing against their own.

More sunlight shone from of the crumbling veil to illuminate the battlefield. Catching a glimpse of someone inside the Creation on their way out, back-lit, too bright to see their face, but it was plain on Tobias's and few other's expressions that they could.

Clearly it wasn't Caine or Nya would have been happier.

Stone still in hand, I hadn't moved an inch when the visions rolled through me again. Over and over these pictures of Sophie and I creating our Soul Magic zinged my brain. All I wanted to do was sink within the vision to watch her face in the privacy of the trees and luxuriate in her magic as it gifted me with her life after life, but I couldn't stay there no matter how much I craved to lose myself.

Ripping myself away from the vision wasn't easy. I refocused on Nya and boiled with the allure of murder while pulling in the power the stone created, capturing it within myself even more.

Another body came through the broken veil. One of the men Tobias sent through, but on his heels was a member of Evaristus's devotees with a bastard smile across his lips as he breathed true oxygen. No one moved, all factions waiting for the opportunity to strike while a few others stepped through onto the field. All the devotees walked out to meet their cohorts, glad-handing, and celebrating their release.

A flash in Nya's eyes exposed her excitement, tipping me off. Gareth must have been close. Survivors punched through, surprising the devotees who trundled through without a care, too busy celebrating to watch their tails.

With no way around it, the "opportune moment" arrived, instigating me and the others to break our cover. War cries pierced the relative silence, all bodies bracing for the fight, hunching down into protective stances, and hurling their quickest hit of power at the line of opposing Magics who jack-in-the-boxed out of thin air mere feet away from them.

Energy fluctuated in the field as the violence from all sides flared. Devotees and those of Tobias's flock who exited the Creation were our closest targets. Thinking this was a simple rescue mission, the devotees spun expecting to find backup following behind them from inside the Creation, instead they faced a group of innocent survivors boxing in all the devotees, quickly ending the lives of a few who didn't possess the reflexes to make a stand.

Built up energy from the stone now thrummed through me with intoxicating power. With the only weapon I needed poised, I closed the distance between myself and an auburn-haired man in a whirl of

Ghosted movement, knowing that my body became invisible for a mere second before I landed on my target's back, breaking the man's spine beneath my feet, and feeling only the huff of oxygen expelled from his chest. Not only had this man not seen his enemy, but I gave him no opportunity to return the fight.

Down one kill, I realized how useful the power from the stone was and made no dramatics about seeking another target.

Next to the auburn-haired man lying broken was another Magic with their aura lit who watched his comrade go down and expelled a burst of energy straight for me in defense of the corpse. In our closeness, this would normally be a guaranteed hit. With the ritual stone's power in my tool belt, I whirled into invisibility. The energy blast passed through the empty spot my form should have been before I reappeared in time to grab the man by his collar, this time striking my palm into the guy's face and effectively snapping his neck backwards with a crunch, leaving only a sagging body in my grasp that I promptly tossed aside.

Hall fought close by, Kim staying back with lips moving in whispered incantations. I couldn't see the resulting effects, but assumed she protected herself or was helping Hall, the guy doing everything he could so Kim didn't face more danger than necessary.

One thing I noticed was that killing those two men did nothing to the reservoir of power the stone created inside of me. However, it did take the edge off containing it as it swelled dangerously inside my body. With action came a sense of alleviating the pressure, relief without leaving me empty. Psychosomatic? Maybe, but I appreciated this action far more than sitting around.

Scanning the battlefield, I sought out the only one I wanted to see. Surprisingly, Nya only fought when she was forced to, dispatching those in her way of trying to get to her long-lost love still trapped inside the Creation. Giving her assistance, since she still inhabited a body I was invested in, I felt a surge of power that burned within my chest before bursting from my hands, sending a shot of energy into the body of a few aura-lit Magics inconveniencing Nya.

Normally, this would have only sent the bodies flying, but with the extra dose within my arsenal, these enemies broke apart as if I had shot a steel rod from a cannon, spraying Nya in blood.

I felt Hall's stare on me as he followed close behind, watching my back to ensure I did what I came to do. I knew this piggybacking was unconnected to some aforementioned plan. Not because Hall told me, but because I read it straight from Hall's big brain. The immortal's mental defences were stellar, being mid-battle did nothing to cause the sudden drop in fortification. Everyone's mind was open to me. Curses, spells, battle plans, simple motions of attack, fear of dying, over-confidence in survival, prayers to otherworldly Gods, all were up for grabs, and I plucked whatever I found useful to me.

Knowing I needed to get my hands on Nya without killing Sophie, I dialled down the amount of power to be expelled and hit Nya with the same attack as I used on the others. Since I wasn't on full tilt, this resulted in a hit more akin to a gunshot than a cannon, and Nya keeled over in a surprised gasp.

The beating sun of the Creation speared through the gaps in the veil at all angles, illuminating the pain in Nya's features. In my rage, it took focus to remind myself those pained features were on temporary loan and that I couldn't do anything to permanently damage them.

Recoiling from the harm I inflicted, Nya searched for the source. Before she could retaliate, I hit her again. This time I added a pinch more power and watched Nya crumble in pain. With her face twisted in such agony, it was easier to remind myself that Sophie was a prisoner only a few layers below skin deep. The jolt to her cushy possession threatened as I swore I thought I saw Sophie on the edge of sneaking to the front seat while Nya struggled to collect herself, those golden eyes blinking back to Sophie's deep brown as the gold fought to shine again.

A half-second revealed this to be wishful thinking as Nya managed to push Sophie back again, but it was enough to know my tactic could change that.

It didn't pass beneath my notice that Nya's pain was her own. I felt nothing Nya did. No pain, no frustration, no nothing. My only hope was that when Sophie regained the reins that she felt me again.

Come on. I needed to delve deeper within Nya to access Sophie's prison, to hopefully find her and will her to the surface.

I reached into the vessel with my borrowed power in search of her, discovering nothing but the thick wall of Nya's barrier hiding Sophie away. Willing to do anything to save her, I was only spurred on in challenge. Sophie was stronger than anyone I knew. She could handle what needed to be done to free her. I wouldn't expose her to a single strike more than she could endure, nonetheless I knew how tenuous the thin threshold between life and death was and would inflict a hair lower than her limit to ensure she survived.

Not about to back down now, I hit Nya again before she could fully recover, splaying her out on the ground ragdoll-style with a genuine expression of shock. Twisting my hand with tense fingers, I telekinetically snapped her right femur with a crunch heard over the battle waging around us in sprigs of light and screams. Nya wailed with the strength of an ancient, the pressure of her voice putting weight on my chest ten feet away. This weight threatened my lungs that fought in desperate panic to suck in air as Nya clawed at her broken thighbone.

It's just Nya. It's not Sophie. It's not Sophie.

I continued telling myself this. The bitch existed centuries beyond her expiration date; now I would remind her of what the pain of being alive felt like. What it meant to be as human as the rest of us, stuck in the blood and piss of this fucked up place I kept coming back to.

The agony on Sophie's face was all Nya this time. An anger as strong as Nya's pain followed, twisting in the shadows and Creation light, playing along Sophie's face. I could have sworn I caught a glimpse of the true face of the vessel-hopper inside Sophie's body.

Granting myself more time before Evar escaped, I did one better and simultaneously broke both of Nya's wrists the same way I busted her leg so she could no longer soothe the pain of her broken body. Inflicting more damage would tamper her healing process by preoccupying it with too many points of need. This forced all her focus onto her borrowed mortality and distracted her from my true intentions as I took sick pleasure in torturing her.

Reaching beyond Nya's consumed defenses, the barrier keeping Sophie at bay was now weakened, gifting me the ability to send power within Sophie's vessel in search of Sophie. Not something I could do every day, my determination became the driving force, unwilling to assist another soul fighting on the field while Sophie remained a prisoner. By only a sixth sense of guidance, within the vessel I felt Nya writhe in her weakened state, paralyzing pain giving elbow room for Sophie to gain strength. As if waking from sleep, confused in a dark room, Sophie's curiosity awakened.

A hit of adrenaline spiked my heart rate. An exhale of relief dropped from my lungs. She was alive. Olive said Sophie was still in there, but a part of me didn't believe her until I saw the evidence for myself. Using this fragment of achievement as the catalyst, I concentrated on the stone now vibrating with such energy my hand grew numb, drawing on its power while it fought to break out and play within the shifting Magics, to dance among the energy engulfing the field.

Allowing that power to escape couldn't happen. I needed it too much. If anything could save Sophie, the power-imbued stone could do it.

Suddenly the stone began to pulsate differently, my hand no longer numb, my body more aware. Funnelling within me, I felt as if I found a hidden doorway and accessed the stone's essence. Not only *reading* it as my natural power would but grabbing a hold of it and ripping it free for myself.

Once upon a time, Aunt Lacey told Sophie I needed more power. This had to be it. My reservoir to drink from, and I'd drink it dry if need be.

I closed my eyes for what seemed like a single heavy blink against flashes of Betyn and Elysande performing the Soul Magic ritual, the vision stealing my focus. When I opened my eyes, Nya was getting to her feet in the process of healing her broken bones with the help of another.

Caine.

Caine helped Nya to her feet, reaching a hand towards her in gentlemanly assistance. As Nya's eyes caught Caine's, I knew they belonged to Gareth. The flash of gut-wrenching relief in Nya's eyes said everything.

26

TO THE POINT OF CHAOS

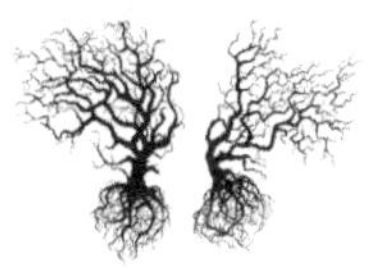

Donovan

Acutely aware of the surrounding activity, the rest of the Creation survivors were free, their thoughts still open to me. Frenetic cries screamed of freedom and retribution against those who tormented them inside. All attacking who they could, except the Blind survivors who were directed off of the field to Fox's grouping by Kim while Hall still pulled protection duty on my co-Sect Leader.

Ness lingered in conflicted anger, torn between leaving Caine, getting him away from Sophie, and protecting herself and her brother.

"It's Nya. She's taken over," I relayed telepathically to Ness as Gareth and a fully healed Nya embraced, oblivious to the dangers around them. *"You can help."* With Ness's skills, I had sudden plans for her.

A quick plan was cooked up as the others battled. A Necromancer in Kim's group was now equipped with enough dead within his control to cause a dent in our enemies numbers. Many perished with nothing better to do anyway. Enemy or ally, that detail didn't matter as the Necro drafted every one of them to our side as reanimated pawns.

"*Now!*" I demanded of Ness looking away from the battling dead.

Her eyes narrowed in concentration as her brother stood not a hairsbreadth away assisting.

Their first attempt failed as the kid was nearly killed by one of the traitors within the Mother Coven until Kim shifted some resources to give them more space to work without interruption.

No doubt Fox's troops would be helping as well, even if only to boost Ness and Felix's Illusion abilities.

Before Nya and Gareth could complete their greeting and split into happily ever after, Ness dropped them into a world of her choosing, leaving them both searching for the other as if they disappeared before each other's eyes.

Knowing the illusion wouldn't last long—especially since Gareth was well aware of Ness's tricks—I focused all of my power on Nya.

Grasping at her chest and stumbling back, Nya called out for Gareth. She couldn't see or hear him as Gareth called her name in the franticness of Caine's voice. Taking advantage of the window Ness created, I busted through Nya's defences, immediately finding what I was looking for.

This time, Sophie was hyper-aware of the situation, wading right below the surface. Pushing that door open wider, I hoped Sophie could opportunistically regain control and keep it long enough to overthrow Nya with a little struggle of wills.

Sophie blinked, chasing away the gold of Nya's influence, her dark eyes hers again for longer than a fraction of a second for the first time since the compound escape.

"Hold on, Sophie!" I yelled above the battle noises. "Hold on as long as you can!" Telepathically was more effective, but I felt compelled to scream.

Sophie nodded but was sucking down air as if her hold was already slipping. Grabbing her head as if a battle were being waged within her skull, Sophie dropped to her knees with a cry that made me ache to hold her.

Too soon after Ness and Felix stole the world from their view, Gareth clued in to what was happening and roared in anger with a pulse of power. The illusion dropped. Hall jumped at Gareth, slamming an uppercut to his jaw. The hands-on approach knocked Gareth off kilter, split his chin open, and had him crashing to the ground, giving Ness a chance to snap up another illusion.

As per the plan to prevent the world from living Evar's potential hell on earth if he escaped the Creation, we needed to gift him a soul to create a killable target. One no immortality could cure.

No one saw him yet and I found it more and more difficult to witness Sophie in such pain as she continued to grit a wail between clenched teeth and clawed at her head while thrashing on the ground.

Fuck it.

I couldn't stomach any more of Sophie's suffering. We could find another way.

More light poured onto the field as the Creation wall continued to crumble. The power within Diluculo vibrated the ground with such intensity it filled every Magic in the field to the brim. With this uncomfortable gorging of energy and the ritual stone's power, I was overloaded and didn't intend on keeping it to myself. Sophie needed it, and I needed to hurry, terrified the power would escape me before I could use it to save her.

Dropping next to Sophie, I laid my hands on her shoulders. Her head snapped back with a raucous gasp from her lips before her neck fell limp, her head lolled to the side and backward as her mouth hung open.

Overwhelming defeat slammed into me. I held onto her thin shoulders to stop her from collapsing to the ground and attempted to transfuse what power I possessed straight into her. I didn't know what it would do, but all I could hope for was its help.

Streaming into her head, the ritual stone's memories soared along into her with the emotion of the event, the strength it took to create the Soul Magic, the commitment needed to brand the stone and lock our futures filtered through and blinded me from my surroundings. Cocooned in nothing but her, flashes of our past hit so strongly that it took everything I possessed not to let her go as they overwhelmed me.

Mixed in with the ritual was an amalgamation of memories I never saw before: *Arguing. A verbal altercation with a man. Grating loneliness. Loring's face. Being dragged away. Fire. Giving in to the flames. Looking to a man at my side and reciting the words needed before the flames won. Looking down at the bodies of a short, pale-haired woman and dark-haired man being burned alive, a gathering of spectators surrounding them, floating above yet somehow not immune to the pyre.*

Pain ripped within me as the culmination of the vision left me in a snap.

My arms were so wrecked I couldn't hold Sophie up any longer. She slumped, unconscious, to the ground. I fell beside her in half-melted snow. A huff of my breath hung in the air. I hadn't noticed the cold before. Now, it was biting.

Calling her name without an answer, I rolled onto my side and called for her again, trying to shake her awake, but she didn't move or open her eyes.

How would I tell if what I did worked? What was all that other shit I saw?

Completely sapped of energy, I felt empty. The stone was no longer in my hand and the magic it gifted me was run-down or maybe used up.

Hall bared his teeth with blood dripping from his face as he pinned Gareth to the ground. Ness still worked her magic and Hall was probably using his own power to keep Gareth complacent as Kim hovered and danced on the balls of her feet at his side while trying to keep an eye on everything around her.

Wait. Wasn't Kim next to Ness?

Bolting upright and onto my feet, I realized the figure beside

Ness wasn't Kim. This woman was completely different. At first, I didn't believe I was looking at the woman from the visions I saw while holding Sophie. Seeing one of the Transmutators in the form of panther ran through her ghostly, disembodied form solidified this.

Nya.

The visions I saw were of Nya and Gareth's final moments in their original bodies and now Nya was doing something to Ness to cause her magic to falter. I figured what I did must have expelled her from Sophie's vessel and now Nya was searching for a new one, doing her best to hop inside Ness, but it wasn't working.

"Nya!" I gained her confused attention. "Grab her!" I yelled at Kim nearby.

"Who?" she yelled back, then ran and grabbed Ness's arm thinking I meant her.

"Back off!" Ness protested and shook her off, Kim looking back at me trying to guess at what I wanted with her.

Shit. Kim couldn't see Nya.

I didn't know what the hell was going on, so I reluctantly left Sophie and sprinted the fifteen-foot gap, gunning it straight for Nya who was now desperately trying to possess Ness's vessel. Ness staggered, her hands out to catch herself as if she might faint. Thinking I was charging for her, plus Kim's confusing tussle, Ness dropped the illusion, Gareth free to see who was messing with him. Hall growled and leaned into Gareth, who was using all of Caine's strength to try and buck Hall off of him.

Never having the ability to see the dead before, I didn't know the rules but didn't stop my sprint. Thankfully, when I contacted Nya, I felt something tangible in my hands as I tackled her to the ground. Somehow, the buzz of the power from the stone rang through me again while I perched on top of Nya's spirit or soul, pinning her to the slushy ground by her throat.

Wriggling beneath me, Nya didn't attempt to strike magically. Actually, by the look of it, in this form she didn't possess the ability to. She could barely muster the strength to struggle, accomplishing nothing but a seething glare and weak thrashing. Looking back at Gareth, I found Hall and Kim standing above him as Kim employed her trusty spell to freeze him in place.

In her mind, I read that she hated that it was her go-to spell, but was glad it gave them enough time for Hall to perform a Binding, the two magical solutions hopefully enough to keep him down.

I was grateful for Gareth's immobilization, though it meant someone must stand guard since physical contact may break the spell. Easy on a normal day, not so much when a battle waged around us.

Wayward bodies and discharges of magic hit everywhere, and we were on babysitting duty to a statue and a ghost.

"What are you doing?" Kim called to me.

"I have Nya. I need to keep her from jumping bodies until—"

A ripping sound slashed through the air. Chunks of the crumbling Creation rained down. We could see straight into Diluculo, the intense heat Evaristus preferred already having melted much of the snow around the opening. A blue sky hung high in Diluculo, showing snaking cracks, and threatening its integrity throughout the entire Creation.

Maintaining a firm hold on Nya, I ignored the ancient in my grasp as my sights fixed on what was strolling out of the Creation.

Evaristus.

Of course, he wasn't alone. Lackeys were present including a limping Loring, all of the sneering Tainted refusing to be destroyed along with the Creation and seeing their own window of opportunity breaking off in slabs around them as pieces of their sky gave way like failing roof tiles.

Fuck. The enemies in the field were keeping their heavy-hitters busy. Too busy. I needed all possible help to centralized on our biggest threat in order for this plan to work. Letting Evaristus escape into the general population would severely cripple our world and we couldn't have the world's first taste of true magic be of Evar's evil. The Blind would be slaughtered before they realized it wasn't a wannabe street act.

"Evar's coming! Signal the team!"

Kim instructed Ness and Felix to watch over Gareth, reiterating they keep their hands off of Caine or they would break the spell. When Ness nodded in understanding, Hall and Kim took off to check on Sophie. Kim shook her again, still unable to wake her. She then yelled at someone I couldn't see.

Gregor from the Tactical Team popped up next to me. We saw Evar was a few steps away from freedom. Talking into a comm set in his collar, Gregor relayed the importance of getting their asses to the entrance then swung his dark eyes down at me. "You may wanna move before you end up trampled?"

"Sorry, chief. I've got an ancient ghost pinned under my ass. I need you guys to keep Evar busy until I can insert her into him, or nobody will be killing him today."

Clearly Gregor couldn't see Nya and didn't have the information to put it all together, but it didn't matter. Priority one was always to kill Evaristus, so Gregor agreed while I tried to figure out how to pull off the plan without Vincent since he was the one responsible for the crucial element of soul insertion duty.

Kim dragged Sophie beneath her arms farther off to the side of the field as the Creation continued to rip and groan. I didn't know when it happened, but now the majority of the Magics around me were all playing for my team and encircled the Creation, doing everything possible to close ranks to prevent the enemy from breaking through to access anywhere close to their Master. Some moved robotic-like, the Necro sticking the reanimated dead in the frontlines to distract the enemy from those still alive. After their first death, the dead didn't blink at getting sliced down a second and third time. If they could walk, slither, or bite, the Necro kept them on the job and primed to strike.

At Kim's side, Hall's eyes locked on the image of Evaristus now within spitting distance.

This was it.

Leftover devotees in Evaristus's personal camp took their first steps towards unfiltered air while the Creation trembled. A particular devotee stepped onto the slush-covered ground and blanketed the ring of Magics trying to attack their Master with a coat of searing flames. They were so hot I flushed with sweat but retained the where-withal and quick reflexes to erect a snug shield around myself in protection.

Burning up my arm sent me growling and flailing to douse the flames eating at my shirt as they licked around the shield's edges. I held onto the shield, the flames still biting into my skin as the onslaught of fire caused others to scream, drop, and roll. Others used water or different gifts to smother them and save themselves and their friends.

Hall sprinted for Kim. He found her singed and dirty.

Sophie wasn't as lucky.

Before I could yell for someone to help her, not wanting to let Nya's spirit go but ready to drag Nya over to Sophie if left with no other choice, someone was already batting at the flames eating at her right side. To my surprise, the person doing so was Tobias. No hero move, my father worried for himself as he then heaved her lifeless body over his shoulder.

Piece of shit opportunist.

Rage surged through me at the thought of Tobias's hands on Sophie. I didn't know how he managed to flank us, but there was no way in hell I was letting that psychopath steal her away from me again. With my fingers still digging into the soft flesh of Nya's ghostly throat, I rushed to my feet ready to drag her along with me until Kim and Hall saw what Tobias was doing and went after him.

In the middle of the action, as the Necro let the dead burn and roam the field as another source of weaponry to scare away their enemy, Gareth still lay frozen. Felix covered his head, seated like a scared child behind his sister as Ness sat in concentration with her eyes closed, no doubt doing her best to set an illusion for the evil bastards exiting the Creation since she, Felix, and Gareth were square in the middle of their walking path.

This was the first time I noticed the blood. Large quantities smeared on the hands of Magics, splattered on their clothes, staining the snow and pooling around the dead left unusable for reanimation by the Necro. They may use magic to kill each other, but this was still war, and death equalled blood.

I had to do more. Sitting here babysitting was a waste of my goddamned time. Making sure Nya didn't disappear or find another vessel besides the one I needed to inject her into was important, but in the meantime if everyone else suffered for it, it wouldn't be worth it.

Evar stayed back with Loring until his devotees or Puppets effectively laid their lives on the line before sticking his neck out. Maybe Ness was blinding him, I couldn't tell. Now that their first line of defence was preoccupied, Evar and Loring took a few steps closer to the exit, primarily due to the Creation falling down around them. It became obvious they knew they couldn't cower within its safety much longer.

Out of the bodies of those attempting to rip each other apart, Rosemary stopped, looking battle-worn yet resilient as she ran for me.

"What are you doing?" she yelled over the Creation crackling loudly and making the ground quake again.

I tried to relay that I held Nya's spirit, but I didn't manage my mother's full attention or understanding. With no time to explain, I moved on. "We need to pin Evar down so I can end the bastard for good."

Rosemary nodded without question.

I snuck a peek towards where I last saw Sophie. She was on the ground and Kim and Hall were busy with Tobias and my brother, Brandon.

"Help Sophie. Keeping her alive keeps me alive. I can do this!" Whether I died as she did was questionable, but make no mistake, if Sophie truly did die, I wouldn't be long behind her, connected or not.

Sophie may have not been Rosemary's priority, but I could see the hint of a maternal streak down deep within her. Plus, it gave her permission to leave my side to potentially take Tobias down, which benefited us all.

Sprinting off in Sophie's direction, I knew Rosemary would help and cut down a devotee fighting Ismail on her way without stuttering a step. Lincoln was near and hit his opponent so hard their chest exploded in a shower of blood. His battle cry rang above others as his anger for Anne-Marie's death shone in a kaleidoscope of revenge in his eyes.

"Keep them busy!" I telepathically sent Lincoln's way. Not that the man was having a problem with focus.

Lincoln ended his next opponent before turning to me, jutting his chin in the direction of the Creation. I understood his inference to go after Evar, delighted to fulfill the objective.

The moment Evar and Loring took their leap from their comfort zone, Loring erected a protective barrier around himself and his Master. Lincoln sent a blast of energy his way. It lit up brightly, the shield easily parrying the hit. Jessabelle and Ismail joined Lincoln, as did Arden, Gregor, and Bronya using a mix of purely strength-related hits with a barrage of incantations, lobbing them at their target. The field lit up, similar to a TV viewing of a war caught on night-vision cameras, hits flaring in the night until they contacted their target and extinguished.

The ploy kept Evaristus and Loring bogged down. Stealing a look down the line, Sophie was still unconscious, and the others were still fighting, leaving me wishing I was doing something about either.

A targeted hail of magic lit up the field, showered down from the sky, hit Lincoln dead on, and splayed out the others.

Fuck! Caine's flying cousin, Jet, was still a goddamn Puppet.

Diving from her vantage point, Jet took on her nickname and jetted around the field, raining down more hits onto her own people Evar controlled her. Magics ran while trying to keep their eyes on the opponent in front as well as above, many losing that battle.

Removing one hand from Nya's throat as I scrambled out of harm's way was a quick reaction that saved my ass. Nya bucked beneath me trying to take advantage of Jet's distraction. She scraped her nails into my flesh until I shifted my weight over her and squeezed her throat. Nya gurgled and flailed. She was dead, yet not immune to damage.

Jet swooped after targets and rained more magic down onto their heads. Fighting her was a lost cause. We end her as a threat when we end her Puppeteer.

Recalibrating my attention on Evaristus, I remembered an effective spell used on Sophie by Miklos. Evar may be ancient and soulless but not even he was beyond pain.

After it happened to us, I looked into the spell and memorized it. Now, I recalled the words, directed it towards Sophie's ancestor, and watched as the ancient bellowed in agony and clawed for his feet without finding the source of his pain. Evar scraped but couldn't loosen what he couldn't see, he trying to lift his leg while his feet remained rooted to the ground with invisible spikes.

Success.

Confused by his Master's outcry, Loring dipped to Evar's side to help, but moving him caused another bellow in pain and Evar shoved Loring away from him, knocking the already imbalanced man over into pools of melted snow and blood with a splash. As dignified as he could, Loring regained his footing and stood with much struggle.

Jet dove straight from the sky for her Master as if a silent call was sent for her help. The Puppeteer's first course of action must have been for her to squirrel him away from the reach of their enemies. With Evar going nowhere, Jet dropped altitude and plucked Loring up off the battlefield as easily as if she were picking flowers before flying off with Evar's second-in-command heading for the trees with no one, save me, the wiser.

Again, I was left watching as the action played out around me. This battle needed to end, and I knew I could pull it off. With Evar screaming like a howler monkey, it was clear his pain was fuelling his rage. Enough force and Evar could use that rage to break the spell and rip himself free. Even powered by the ancient energy of the ritual stone, Evar himself was ancient.

Assessing that brewing power within me from the stone, my shoulders relaxed in relief at its presence. Assuming I had a limited reservoir to siphon from, this power now filtered through me with familiarity. All mine to command.

Resolve came with clarity as I flushed from head to toe and my grip tightened on Nya's throat. Pulling myself to my feet, I dragged Nya along with me while ignoring her gurgled protests. She was much lighter in this state than in her corporeal life, making it easier to accomplish. My gaze slid to Nya's. Her eyes rolled then locked on mine; fear within them sparked a sick satisfaction in me for knowing she could sense what came next.

After everything Sophie went through, from the first time releasing Nya's power, to the guilt using it caused Sophie for putting me through pain, to taking over Sophie from the very beginning when she never asked to be a vessel, I never felt so righteous in dolling out just desserts. This woman was nothing but desperate, and if I could, I would tie her and her husband to the pyre they first died on and trap them within their bodies to recreate every millisecond of agony they should have felt from the beginning.

Unwilling to take a chance on a wild pitch, my leg muscles squeezed sending spikes of pain through my shins and drove me towards Evar who was still clawing at his feet, while he pushed devotees away from trying to help and worsening his pain. When I got closer, revenge reigned as I ran up on Evar, telekinetically threw his devotees away in a push of power, and grabbed Evar by the collar.

With the great force of ritual stone magic, I ripped Evar's feet from the ground. His roar was heard above the sound of the quaking Creation whose integrity could no longer withstand its own weight. Not a whimper left Evar's gaping lips as I held him above the ground before slamming the Puppeteer onto his back, then secured him with another set of those invisible spikes through both shoulders. This addition of consuming pain distracted

Evaristus as the stone's power ripped through my veins and pulsed in my temples.

I revelled in Nya's fear one last time as her shrieking plea went ignored. I took my chance, feeling the magic within me, and slammed Nya's ghostly meddling form straight into the soulless cavern in Evaristus's chest.

Evar sucked in an instantaneous breath. I stood and hovered over the ancient in wait of whatever may come next, taking the chance to cast energy out and send devotees desperate to protect their Master sprawling.

Power saturated the field settling heavily in the air, the stone's power now revving to the point of chaos inside of me. My chest heaved as I locked my eyes on Evar still pinned on his back as spasms shuddered his body at the invasion of Nya's soul inside of him.

Evar's legs kicked as if involuntary, he nearly taking me down at the shins.

"He won't stay down!" Hall was at my shoulder.

A glance in Sophie's direction showed her still unconscious. Kim scanned for potential enemies as Ranlyn was walking away. It occurred to me that my father and brother may be dead. Telltale signs splattered Hall's jacket and hands.

No time to ask.

I explained why Evar wasn't going anywhere.

Hall grinned, impressed. "You going to rip him apart, or am I?"

We dodged a hit of magic and Hall opted for protection detail to let me focus on Evaristus.

Using the magic of our past, I grabbed hold of Evar's head and braced my foot against one bloodied shoulder. His screams were either at the soul injected into his body or at what I was about to do, but I ensured he saw my face before I tore his head clean off of his body.

Accessing more power to finish the job, Evar's skull turned black, and then the head of one of the most powerful Magics of all time turned to ash and collapsed into the slush beneath him.

Hall was still at my side, breathing hard, covered in more blood, and appearing as the epitome of a true terrifying Viking. His war-hungry gaze slid my way in question of what I wanted him to do.

"Rip him a part."

Hall nodded, grabbed Evar's arm, braced his foot against the Puppeteer's torso, and yanked so hard Evar's limb tore off in one heave. Snatching the arm from him, I turned the flesh to ash, feeling it settle beneath my fingernails before becoming nothing. Understanding the gist, Hall peeled off a leg like it was his chicken dinner while I tore off Evar's other arm and turned both limbs to ash, letting them go as they caught the wind and continued to disintegrate.

In less than a minute, Evar was reduced to nothing, taking the vessel-hopping bitch along with him.

Evaristus was gone.

Nya was gone.

All the planning, the paranoia behind every suspicious side-eye, needless deaths, cryptic premonitions—not to mention all of Sophie's family members he killed over the years—was over. The bastard behind all of that was finally dead.

A note of "too good to be true" played in the back of my mind, but this time—in regard to Evar and Nya—it *was* over.

"We gotta move!"

Judging by Hall's tone, he shouted this more than once while I stood sunk in thought. An extra second longer passed before I understood the big guy's alarm.

The Creation.

Its walls were Swiss cheese and melting. The hum of magic the Creation emanated within the field was sporadically surging. Guaranteed not a soul knew what ramifications they would suffer if they were in the area when the Creation finally imploded, and Hall wasn't taking the chance of standing around while I was daydreaming.

I sprinted for Sophie. She was still unconscious, beautiful as if merely sleeping.

"She won't wake up!" Kim yelled over the still-battling Magics.

The fight was diminishing as more and more of the dead were added to the Necromancer's army. Puppets were no longer led by a Puppeteer, and devotees had lost their Master.

I grabbed Sophie's arm and lurched her into a seated position. Another heave and she was draped over my shoulder. Kim yelled after me as I ran for the trees hoping they would be enough protection from whatever came next.

Then I realized what Kim said.

Fuck. I forgot about Caine.

Gareth was still inside of him. Could I pull him out the same as I did with Nya?

Ness and Felix hovered around Caine's body, Ness doing her best to keep anyone from touching Caine as other Coveners now helped her. What would I do with Gareth's soul to prevent him from becoming a stowaway in Caine's vessel again? I couldn't leave Caine lying in the middle of the blast radius of the Creation if it went nuclear. Sophie wouldn't believe it wasn't on purpose, and I had to admit that it was a dick move if I did.

Whatever the game plan, we needed to act quickly. Tremors beneath my feet nearly knocked me and Sophie to the ground. The rumbling sounded like an avalanche headed our way. No choice left but to give it a shot.

Placing Sophie back down at my feet I sent a message to Ness. *"Move it before the Creation kills you and your brother."* Her head whipped up looking for the sender and found me. Before she could argue, I stopped her, promising her that I would try and move Caine, then reiterated her imminent danger and ordered her to move to the safety of the trees. Clearly torn between leaving Caine and risking her brother's life, I sent the message to Felix as well, and now Felix was pulling his sister for the trees.

Having no clue if it would work, I took a stab at it, and felt for the stone's power. The sensation built inside of me, ready for the delicate task of telekinetically moving Caine's body without breaking the spell keeping him and Gareth immobile. A buffer zone around the body was a bubble to prevent physical contact.

Once Caine's body was four feet off the ground, I felt minutely confident the tactic would work.

A struggle gained my attention. Hinapouri was in battle with Veata as no doubt Ranlyn was busy somewhere with Miklos.

A flash of red sailed through the air. Feathers from the end of the Maori warrior's Taiaha headed straight for Caine.

Was she trying to kill Caine or Gareth? Hell, probably both.

I tried shifting Caine and lost my hold. Caine's body crashed hard into the melted snow in a roll of limbs.

A relentless Veata immediately preoccupied Hinapouri, but the spear the ex-Elder threw accomplished its intended damage, and now Gareth was no longer frozen in Kim's spell.

Fuck me.

One thing at a time.

Sophie needed safety. I couldn't concentrate properly on anything else unless she was. I shouldered her body again and sprung for the trees. Ness surprised me in meeting me partway, but before I could make the hand-off, I was blindsided.

When I could look up from the ground to react, I saw Caine coming for us. Gareth was in control again and didn't care if he killed us all. Believing Caine would come after me wasn't a stretch, but he would never attack Sophie or Ness. Gareth being desperate to save his wife would kill anyone and everyone, causing Nya minimal damage if needed, as I managed with Sophie. Though Gareth must not have known Nya was long gone.

I cringed as I tried to stand. An easily healed broken rib took a few stabbing breaths to mend. "I already took Nya out!"

This didn't stop Gareth who scrambled to run for who he thought was his wife.

I raced to beat Gareth to Sophie's body.

Before either of us could reach her, a blast went off.

Blinding light lit up the entire field in brilliant white, tossing bodies like confetti before sucking them back into a vacuous roar. Overexposed to so much light, my eyesight dipped into blackness and left only the edges of a view. A halved sliver of the world around me lasted long enough to see the tops of trees beneath me as my body plummeted from the sky down on top of them.

The ground felt really far away until the sense of being suspended at the top of a rollercoaster before the first drop stole my heart and shoved it into my sinuses. I was now plunging into the wreckage of uprooted trees.

Blackness held me awkwardly as every limb ached. My insides felt shaken and stirred. My brain pounding after a 'J.D. straight from the bottle' kind of night.

I couldn't see. Were my eyes open?

Why was everything so quiet?

Panic took over. Am I dead? Was this how it was before Sophie and I recycled? Was this some kind of purgatory? Endless nothingness, blind and deaf to everything but my own nagging thoughts.

Damn. A fitting Hell, really. No one could torture me more than myself. To be left with the horrors of my mind, memories of my life in constant re-run forever until maniacal insanity takes over and distorts anything I could have ever remembered. A righteous punishment for my wasted years of whoring around, the stealing, the booze, opportunities not lost but rejected and pissed on. No wonder I didn't have Sophie beside me.

Suddenly, the most terrifying thought hit me. What if I was dead, and this time, I wasn't allowed to find Sophie again? That would be it. The worst punishment anyone could dole out. Going through this life or any other without her to share it with was tortuous. I was never the type for empty fairy tales and happy endings. I just wanted her.

The blackness and sensory deprivation wouldn't let up. Less than a minute or two in this purgatory and I was already going bat-shit crazy. Acting strong be damned, I couldn't even handle my father's cycle of childhood humiliation. In comparison, this nothingness ranked much more terrifying. At least with Tobias I could see the blades ripping me open and the concrete walls of my prisons. Seeing nothing and expecting no more than nothingness left me scrambling to grasp onto anything.

Everything I couldn't feel lit up and tasered every nerve as if fifty thousand volts crashed through me. A wrenching howl in agony thrummed my ear drums. The howl being my own shouldn't have surprised me, but its abrupt presence did. My eyesight started clearing.

Vincent leaned over me with a hand on my chest, brows creased. "Are you alright?"

I couldn't speak. Did Vincent bring me back? Did I die or was I just injured? Asking would have been nice but as soon as the question was offered, Vincent moved to someone else, apparently taking my consciousness as affirmation I would pull through.

Beneath me was a bed of destroyed trees, their roots exposed, trunks splintered. I squinted through the dark, seeing the battlefield was ground zero of the Creation blast and casualties were twisted among the wreckage, some moving, many not.

A few familiar faces were covered in mud and blood from healed wounds. If I didn't know better, I'd think a tornado ripped through and the Magics milling around where devastated home-owners peering over the remains of their houses now in matchsticks.

Where the Creation used to stand now stood a figure, one I focused on without realizing what I saw until it hit me.

Gualichu? The demon who escaped the portal in Caine's aunt and uncle's barn and took over the body of a teenaged Magic? What was the kid's name? It took me a second to remember him as Graham.

What the fuck was it doing here?

Someone ran into me, grappling me. I tried pushing them off until I heard them sob my name.

Kim? Goddammit.

She crushed me to her, squeezing my neck, then pulling back when I hissed at a vision of a tense conversation between her and

Hall, him telling her something important with a husky voice before the vision was pulled away.

"Is Sophie okay?" I looked for her, not seeing the others.

"Unconscious, but alive. Are *you* okay?"

Trying not to look shocked by Kim's concern, I mumbled, "Yeah," and scanned the field. More questions came to mind, but before I could relay what happened, I followed Vincent who was walking away from Sophie's unconscious body lying in the torn-up earth over to Caine less than fifteen feet away in much the same condition.

Going to Sophie and kneeling at her side, I found her the same way Kim said she was and as the last time I saw her. Unconscious as if sleeping; still breathing.

Tearing myself away from Sophie wasn't easy, but Kim promised to stay with her. Sophie was safe and I would be close if she wasn't.

Vincent held Gareth by the throat. Not Caine whose body still lay inert on the earth but Gareth, the spirit above Caine's body, fruitlessly struggling in Vincent's Extracting grasp.

"What now?" I asked as I came up beside Vincent.

Turning to me, Vincent's brow creased in question. "You can see him?"

I nodded as I looked over Gareth, remembering now that I was related to him through Aunt Lacey. We didn't look alike, the genetic connection far too old, but he was technically my ancestor. I wondered if Aunt Lacey was somehow around and able to see what was happening and how much drama her son caused.

Above average in the height department, dark hair, medium build, this was definitely the burning man from the vision I had when I pushed Nya from Sophie's body.

Gareth was too weak to properly fight while outside his vessel, the same as Nya.

"Donovan, can you end him?"

I remembered that Vincent Extracting Gareth's soul would simply release the ancient of the vessel as Vincent would with other souls. Unaware of how Nya and Gareth managed to inhabit Sophie and Caine in the first place, we didn't need Gareth waltzing into Caine again or finding another vessel, one where he wouldn't sit back any longer, especially with Nya dead.

"You haven't the power to end me," Gareth spat as he struggled in Vincent's hold.

I laughed. No one else could hear Gareth, not even Vincent who couldn't see Gareth either, though I'm sure Vincent could read Gareth's mind.

A slow walk took me within a foot from Gareth. Right up to the moment before I wrapped my fingers around Gareth's throat with the layer of ritual stone magic flowing through me, feeling skin beneath my palm, squeezing in a way Vincent's hold had not been able to, Gareth was confident I didn't possess the ability to truly kill him. Now, fear widened his eyes, and he realized how wrong he was about the damage I could do.

In a last-ditch effort to free himself, Gareth swung at me. I grabbed hold of his arm and held it at his side, watching defeat sag every part of him.

"I will find my Nya in the afterlife." Gareth's words were choked, but I heard enough to understand what he was saying.

"That may be true. However, I toasted her soul in the body of an evil son-of-a-bitch ancient. Chances are, he'll drag her down with him to wherever your 'afterlife' awaits. And you sure as hell won't see your mother there." Worry clouded Gareth's features. "Have fun with the search."

With that said, I drew more power forward, surprised when the stone's energy kicked into play with little effort.

Gareth, the vessel-hopping soul who complicated everything in the name of finding his wife, discoloured and blackened in my grasp before breaking down. Gareth screamed until there was nothing left of him to make noise. Wherever he went—if he could find Nya or Aunt Lacey again, or if I truly destroyed a soul—I didn't know, but I did destroy any possibility of Gareth and Nya meddling in our lives again. That gratification was intoxicating.

Feeling the stone's power subside and settle within me didn't diminish the satisfaction of taking back control of our lives by ending theirs. It occurred to me my happiness bordered on psychotic or sociopathic or whatever, but I didn't give a shit. Nya, Gareth, and Evaristus were all dead and I refused to feel guilty about killing them.

27

OFFER OF SAFETY

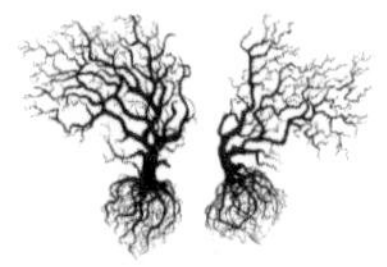

Donovan

In search of survivors, we stumbled upon Jet. If Kim hadn't intervened, Hall would have killed her, but without Evaristus, Jet was no longer a Puppet. Not that she was helpful with information as she was kept in the dark about Evar's schemes and was clueless as to where Loring ended up once she was forced to whisk him off the battlefield. If he was out there, Loring was still a threat. Without his Master, who knew when and where he might strike.

A worry for another day.

Jet just remembered waking up in the middle of a warzone with bits and pieces of the last few months here and there. She was weak and needed time to heal. Magic helped, but her injuries were greater than the physical.

Sophie and Caine were still unconscious. No one knew why. Once healed, they still didn't wake up. The only theory that made sense was that something happened to them when Nya and Gareth took them over or the removal caused some form of shock, preventing them from regaining consciousness.

When Kim asked me why I was still awake even though Sophie wasn't, I shrugged without letting my anger and despair of the possibility it meant our connection was also destroyed. I'm sure everyone else figured that was the reason for me still being awake as well, but they didn't talk about it in front of me.

Smart. I couldn't handle that conversation right now.

We needed to leave. Before we could, Vincent said he had to head off in a different direction. "I have a deal with my contact inside the Sovereignty. By a stroke of luck, he was assigned as my watchman last night, but I must return before my absence is detected, if it has yet to be already."

I gave him a hard stare.

He met my glare. "My apology for my swift absence in Amsterdam will come later and with full explanation. For now, my presence within my family's establishment is not of my choosing. I have business to attend to before I can extricate myself from my position. However it may appear in the coming days, I am *no* traitor to the cause nor am I in league with my brother, my father, or any other within the Sovereignty. I want that to be plain and understood."

"Quite convenient for you, isn't it? Leaving when the rest of us have to go in hiding and you can sit comfortably in time for family breakfast."

Kim called my name as if it could stop me.

Vincent took a step towards me. "I assure you, my role within the Sovereignty is one of a prisoner and not a respected family member. Without the time needed to break neither your childish insistence nor the need to change your mind, I leave you with the location and codes of a place of sanctuary. The Team is aware of its existence but does not possess the ability to find or access it. Lead everyone there."

Before I could side-step, Vincent palmed my forehead. The instant contact was a searing agony through my brain that sent me to the ground before my knees could lock to hold me up. When I could finally open my eyes, Vincent was gone, and Rosemary was helping me to my feet.

"We need to go." Damn. My ears still rang.

People were in post-war mode, most having retreated or were helping others heal, but Mother Coven members who were against us or other enemies have now had time to potentially regroup to come back at us.

"I can't go with you," Rosemary told me as if she wanted to make sure I knew. "My coven did what they could to save their grand Master and felt content for the kills they added to their roster, but they will reconvene and expect my presence. I must face them, and I can't have the knowledge of where you're going without potentially bringing another war to your doorstep."

With a nod from me, she stepped back as if she wanted to hug me or say something more sentimental. She didn't and neither did I. Her eyes were glassy as she turned away from me and walked off. I didn't know when I might see her again or if I truly wanted to, but I had a feeling we would reconnect at some point in the future.

Under normal circumstances, any bodies of the dead, ally or enemy, would be buried, cremated, or taken to be mourned by their families. In this case, we didn't have time. Survivors were healed and gathered, and we needed to leave before enough of the enemy's survivors made a last desperate attempt.

I called Hall over. Since Vincent didn't explain the details of what we were walking into with this safe haven, I wanted Hall to be our first line of defence with the Tactical Team on his heels. Hall was a relatively new face for me, but he was pals with Vincent and seemed tight with Kim for some reason. If that flash of vision from her was any indication, the reason was pretty plain.

Hall agreed without complaints of taking orders from me, insisting he also have Kim accompany him. She wanted to stay with Sophie. When she resisted, I promised to bring Sophie with me, since she needed to be carried anyway. Kim rolled her eyes but stood by Hall.

I couldn't lose brain cells on those two and started gathering people together to do the spell Vincent branded on my brain to transport a few Coveners at a time to safety.

I stepped to Kim and Hall and put a hand on each of their arms, instructing them to do the same with each other. Hall wrapped his arm around Kim's shoulders, holding tight instead. She didn't look entirely comfortable yet didn't push him away.

Ready to go, I recited the spell, and Kim and Hall disappeared.

Wherever they went, they were on their own until I sent through the Tactical Team members seconds later, then Ranlyn and Veata, before working through the rest of the Coveners. Everyone was gone from the field within a minute or two, facing a few resistant people who wanted answers I couldn't give them about where I was sending them. They either trusted me or they trusted they could distinguish, run, and escape the enemy who could be anyone in the Mother Coven.

Until some kind of talks occurred with all governing peoples of power, we were in danger and would have to pray that one day others would forgive and forget.

I doubted that would happen, but we needed to go, and I couldn't get myself and Sophie to safety before getting the others there first. Listening to some whine wasn't in my job description and I made it clear I had no problem leaving them behind unless they left immediately.

Most took my offer of safety.

Ness and Felix went through with Jet as she clutched a grateful and emotional Andy. They passed through with an unconscious Caine. Relief hit when he disappeared with his group. I was afraid I may experience issues trying to transport him and Sophie while they were unconscious.

Where were my father and brother? Did they die? How about Hinapouri and Miklos? How many of our own didn't make it? I didn't look at all their faces to do a running tally on who still breathed and who we would be leaving behind. That could be done when we reached safety.

When Fox finally stepped up with a few remaining Magics who helped him on the field, I noticed he slouched as if he was drained from the effort he put into boosting those in battle. I hugged him tightly, happy as fuck he survived, registering the fact he couldn't hold me as tightly or pat me on the back as hard as he usually did. No words were exchanged. We both needed some rest before things got sappy.

Only Sophie and I were left. Kneeling down to her side, I looked her over. Her clothing was doused in blood and soaking wet from the snow, her hair loose in a tangled mess, completely dishevelled from head to toe. Wherever we were going, it was hopefully someplace safe. Too many times did I feel as if I put her in danger, our entwined souls bringing a risk she shouldn't have to pay for.

Not like this.

Mumbled voices in the distance reminded me of the danger we were still in. A quick second and a recited incantation later and we were...Where were we?

Marble floors squeaked beneath rubber soles as voices rang beneath high ceilings. Chaos had me hovering over Sophie protectively. Hall called my name in a growl right before Sophie and me were flipped onto our stomachs without a hand touching us. A knee in my back kept me there. In this position I saw Hall in much the same way with a guard on each limb, the faces of a few of them damaged as Hall must have given them a good fight before they took him down.

A search to my side showed me a guard restraining Sophie by wrenching her limp arm behind her back as if she may awake any second and attack him.

"She's unconscious!" I struggled to buck off those who pinned me down.

A jolt of electrocution flowed through me, contorting my body, and forcing black spots to blot out the room around me. Blood flooded my taste buds, the side of my tongue throbbed. When the electrocution stopped, I spat blood and a chunk of flesh. My shoulders warmed uncomfortably as I raged inside, and before I realized it, the tattoos Fox inked enacted, sending that same jolt back through the guards keeping me down, throwing them off of me and onto the marble. The hit freed me. I was on my feet, but it only alarmed more guards. I braced for conflict.

"Stop!" The deep voice resonated to the ceiling and every Covener and guard froze in place. Not from any spell but from the tone of command that voice called for. "Move," this voice ordered again as he made his way around the crowd.

I stepped protectively closer to Sophie as the guard moved from her to deal with me and was now standing at attention as a good little soldier does.

The crowd of guards separated around the owner of the voice, a man at least five inches shorter than me, broad shouldered, and barrel chested. He looked like an army commander or admiral and carried himself with the same amount of clout.

No wonder everyone listened.

The man peered around at the survivors, most still on the floor freezing, soaked in blood, and adrenalized by battle. "I don't know how you got here but you *will* leave in the manner in which you arrived, and it *will* be done immediately."

Explaining that Vincent told me how to get here wouldn't work with this type of man. He would assume the name drop was part of some elaborate scheme and would only listen to Vincent himself.

The answer came to me. "Of all the wars I am meant to fight..." I began and paused as Vincent had implanted the phrase and how to recite it into my brain. A bushy salt and peppered eyebrow crooked in my direction, intrigued as I continued what I started. "...this fight comes with the greatest of sacrifices."

The man took a few steps towards me. "The sacrifice of reputation..."

"...the sacrifice of my place within my family..."

"...the sacrifice in comfort by all known before..."

"...and my happiness henceforth."

I went to continue when the man waved for me to stop. "I believe you. Explain what happened."

A relaxing breath loosened the tension in my shoulders as I left Sophie under Kim's care and moved to the side of the room waving over Ranlyn. He brought Veata with him while the guards settled around the Coveners without getting too hands-on, yet keeping them in place while we went to speak with the Admiral—as I had come to think of him since we hadn't been introduced.

The guards hummed with power, the threat of what they may do with it louder, while Ranlyn and I explained the Creation falling, the deaths of our enemies, and the reason behind our need for sanctuary. The Admiral rubbed a finger along his chin and paced a step or two and back in thought before coming to some conclusion.

Giving a nod, the Admiral stepped towards the group and spoke above their worried voices.

"I am Arthur Edson, the Warden of this institution. This place is not a hotel nor is it equipped to operate as one. Its function is that of a courthouse, prison, and maybe a rehabilitation center. Since our operations have yet to commence and Mr. Llewellyn has provided our location, then all present may use our facilities for temporary accommodations. Food rations are comprised of the necessary elements to sustain a prisoner. No suggestions and no alternatives will be considered. The cells..." he stopped, "...rooms...are not meant for comfort."

"They'll do," I said helping the Admiral to his point.

The Admiral paused and continued after he gave me a familiar look I evoked from my father. A 'no need for the peanut gallery' stare I was proud to evoke anytime I earned it.

"Do you trust it?" Hall murmured at my side, talking low. The Admiral went on with basic house cleaning information.

"Don't have a choice."

"No, we don't. Thankfully Gualichu was there to gluttonously feed on the Creation excess. We would all be dead if he hadn't."

So that's why the demon showed up. If you fed off the destructive force of Magics and their world, a Creation collapsing would certainly be a buffet Gualichu couldn't miss. The demon must have realized Blind humans weren't enough for his appetite.

Another problem to deal with later.

After a moment Hall said, "Your brother and father are alive."

Without looking to him, I nodded, unsure of how I would have felt if Hall said the opposite. I didn't want them alive, but a part of me wanted a hand in their deaths. Or at least to be present to witness it.

"Veata ended Hinapouri. Miklos lives. The child's grandmother was killed. Not that it mattered to the Necromancer. She was more useful dead than alive."

Again, nothing really hit me. Hinapouri's death was a victory, one less ex-Elder to chase down. Miklos himself was as much of a threat as Loring and he still roamed the world. Now that Andy had his mother back, he could deal with losing both of his grandparents. I wouldn't assume this would be so easy for Jet.

Edson went on to explain the cell system. Motioning to the west wall of exposed brick, he explained these were our accommodations. Before stupid questions could be raised, he went on to say that every brick in the wall was spelled. The brick itself was a "room" and would one day house a prisoner. Maximum storage space for a maximum number of inmates, a full-size cell awaiting on the other side. This also ensures no interaction between inmates saving guards from collusion and riots.

Only a few communal areas were in the whole Prison Creation. The lobby where we dropped in, a courtroom, and a boardroom. Other than that, there was a supply room and a wing of offices which would one day house a panel of lawyers and a judge or two for everyday proceedings.

Normally, once an inmate was implanted into the cell system, they could not exit unless an officer of their court or another with authorization removed them. With the circumstances as they were, all would be free to leave their rooms as they wished. Meals would be given in the cafeteria and eaten in communal areas and not the cells.

Some didn't think kindly of the idea of staying in cells no matter what they were called. Edson's authoritative demeanour didn't soothe their apprehension. Under no circumstances was he there to hand-hold and sleeping in the common areas was deemed inappropriate and wasn't permitted.

After everything, I didn't wait for Edson to finish. He could keep hammering the message, but I got the gist. We would be tolerated only as long as required, then booted to the curb the second that toler-ance ran dry. Instead of enduring the lecture, I went to Sophie still laying on the ground, scooped her up, and walked over to the console Edson explained was used to implant a prisoner into a cell. Bypassing Sophie's family members and anyone else who cared about her, I punched the info into the console and entered one of the cells. Guards were preoccupied listening to Edson and didn't either see me or expected Edson to stop me.

No one did.

If anyone wanted to follow me into a cell, they could. They knew where I was, and I couldn't lock the door.

Once Edson finished with the orientation rundown, the rest would pummel me with a million questions. I didn't have it in me to pretend to care about any of them. The Elders were around, so was Kim. They could do their jobs and leave me alone.

I didn't need a tour of the cell to know what amenities it included. Four windowless walls, a toilet, a shower, a bed, and a small slab of concrete from the wall meant to be a table or a desk. Nothing more would be expected. One cell was probably the same as any other I had been holed up in.

I laid Sophie on the single-sized bed, took her wet shoes and socks off, and covered her with the white blanket provided. When I moved a few strands of hair off of her face, no vision flickered. It was safe to say that while within the cells no one's magic worked. Considering my power blinded me, this happened to be not such a bad thing. Instead of worrying, I enjoyed the casual contact.

I didn't know when Sophie would wake up. A twinge of dread hit me when I realized I didn't know what to say if she did. Sorry? The apology didn't fit. Plus, what would I be apologizing for? She would expect specifics and half-assing it would only piss her off more.

I sat next to the bed on the cold floor and held her hand, weaving my fingers with hers and watched her face for signs of life. Later would call for the answers I needed. Who else died? The list was likely larger than Hall provided. Who lived that we will only have to track down later and kill? How can we mend the division among the Covens from inside a prison? Could Vincent sneak away from the Sovereignty and be of any help? He created this place, and we couldn't stay here forever.

What if Sophie didn't wake up and our connection was still broken? That was the big question for me.

If she hated me, she wouldn't want to be connected to me. Not in this life and especially not in others. I wouldn't see her again as Betyn and Elysande planned. After all these years of love and magic bringing us together, this would be it. My heart broke at the thought of it, bringing tears to my eyes. I didn't want to lose her, and I didn't want to be the cause of my future selves never getting the chance to have her in their lives.

I've fucked everything up.

If Sophie didn't open her eyes, and I didn't find a way to fix what we had, none of those answers would matter, and I would end this life for the both of us.

———

Sign-up and stay current on book cover reveals, sales, giveaways, and more with S.J.'s newsletter! http://www.sjcairns.com/newsletter-sign-up

———

Read on for a teaser of the never before released DETERMINED, SOUL SEER CHRONICLES, BOOK 7 coming September 2023.

DETERMINED TEASER

Determined, Soul Seer Chronicles, Book 7

I hate him. Every ounce of me wants to rip apart our connection like an old love letter and burn the pieces. Why can't everyone see Donovan for what he is? A liar, forcing me to do what he wants.

Missions with the Tactical Team retain my sanity while I ignore others' distracted libidos and insistence on fixing our broken Soul Magic. No matter if it means it continues to poison us, I can't forgive. Give me a target and let me loose.

If only.

In typical Loring fashion, he causes a scene, one the world cannot ignore. We can't let him enlighten the Blind of his Tainted ways or Magics of all kinds will be seen as evil and hunted into extinction.

All I want is to kill Loring, pluck Vincent far away from his father, and live my life free of anyone else's influence.

What's so wrong with that?

ABOUT THE AUTHOR

S.J. Cairns creates paranormal romance fantasy from her hometown in Southern Ontario, Canada. When S.J. is not plugging away at her laptop on her comfy couch, you can find her chasing around her three-year-old daughter alongside her husband of over twenty years or working in true chaos at local homeless shelters and an anti-human trafficking safe house.

Website: www.sjcairns.com
Facebook: www.facebook.com/SJCairnsauthor
Twitter: www.twitter.com/SamiJoCairns
Email: samijocairns@gmail.com